WITHOUT LEAVE

BY DEBORAH FLEMING

PRESS

The Black Mountain Press
109 Roberts Street,
Asheville, NC 28801

By the same author:

Migrations

Morning, Winter Solstice

Yeats's Influence on Robinson Jeffers

"A man who does not exist": The Irish Peasant in the Work of W. B. Yeats and J. M. Synge

Learning the Trade: W. B. Yeats and Contemporary Poetry

W. B. Yeats and Postcolonialism

For that friend without whose story this narrative could not have been written.

Without Leave

a novel

by **Deborah Fleming**

ISBN: 9780970016560

The Black Mountain Press
109 Roberts Street, Asheville, NC 28801
First Printing, December 2013
10 9 8 7 6 5 4 3 2 1
Library of Congress Control Number: 2013943604

Printed in the United States of America
Cover Design and Painting: Jarrett Leone

PUBLISHER'S NOTE

This is a work of fiction. Names, characters, places, and incidents are
either the product of the author's imagination or are used fictitiously.

Acknowledgements

Thanks to the following people for their invaluable help: Allison Armstrong; Perry Corbin; Frederick Devore; Robert Iden; Michelle Jordan; Jerry Kosanovic; Edward Lense; Petty Officer Thomas Miller of Great Lakes Naval Training Center; Kari Repuyan; Karen Stine; Dr. Pablo Stewart formerly of the Haight-Ashbury Free Clinic; Peter Summerville and Marianne Thompson of the Treasure Island Development Authority; Paul Vigeant and the docents of the USS Hornet; Pat Walker formerly of the Fort Collins Chamber of Commerce.

Special thanks to my readers and critics Clarke Owens and Jeri Studebaker.

Very special thanks to that friend who shared his sometimes painful memories that I might understand what happened during those years.

ONE

Before he could see it he could smell it—Patchouli and Sandalwood incense cloaking the sweetish aroma of marijuana and mingling with odors of cypress and holly trees—and before he could smell it he could feel it—young people not hiding as he and his friends did in hotel rooms to smoke pot or drop mescaline, but openly celebrating what was usually unseen. It was May 21, 1967. David Shields, Seaman on the *USS Loyola* aircraft carrier returned from Westpac and docked at Hunter's Point Naval Shipyard, lengthened his stride up Haight Street, consciously abandoning the marching rhythm he sometimes involuntarily fell into and imposing a different beat as if he were climbing, with every step leaving behind his youth in southern Ohio, his family, the Navy. In the plate glass window of the café on the corner of Masonic he caught sight of his shaved face and prominent jaw, his black hair cut short around his large forehead. The bulging muscles of his upper arms filled out the sleeves of his green and brown plaid shirt.

The sun was bright, the sky blue and cloudless. He knew the air was not really clear, though. It was made of particles, as Newton theorized, and filled with subtle pastel refractions of purple, blue, pink, and yellow. Waves of light shifted with breezes, shadows, sounds. His eyes normally filtered them out, but they were always there—just beyond conscious reach, until now.

Voices resonated around him like music. A pale man with voluminous, curly blond hair encircling his head talked to a shorter, paunchier guy in a black Lenin cap. Near them on the pavement, two men and two women wrapped in long striped blankets sat in the lotus position, their eyes hidden by dark, round glasses that concealed the herbal boost behind their meditations. A motorcycle revved loudly and sped west around slowly-moving cars, and David saw the winged insignia on the back of the rider's jacket and read the word "NOW" spray-painted on a wall across the street.

Through a shop window he saw T shirts, wooden carvings of elephants and tigers, Buddhist prayer wheels, and bronze statues of four-armed Vishnu. Slightly shabby Victorian houses lined both sides of the street; Christmasberry and juniper grew in little islands of grass erupting from the pavement; ragged weeds occupied the bits of soil around tree trunks. He passed a barefooted woman in a long denim skirt—her straight brown hair reaching past her shoulder blades—talking to a white man with a narrow face wearing frayed jeans and paisley-print shirt and a black man in camouflage khakis. A shorter, round-faced man with political buttons covering his vest played a flute. Although the musician hit some sharp notes, David tossed a quarter into his beaked cap, which lay turned up on the pavement.

On the first warm day of spring three years ago back at Ohio State, walking down Thirteenth Avenue in Columbus, he heard "Mr. Tambourine Man" from the open window of an old frame house. The dew on the grass sparkled like silver, and he felt excited and happy, as if something wonderful awaited him, although he spent most of his days alone and confused. That moment now felt far in the past, but here he sensed the same energy, and all at once he wanted to dance.

Crossing Ashbury he stepped through the door of a shop where they sold psychedelic posters. He was drawn to one that had a background of bright blue above a level, rocky plain from which volcanoes spewed purple and orange lava. Above them in the center of the sky a multi-colored, twelve-pointed star exploded into smaller sunbursts that radiated outward and sent globes of red and gold spinning into the void. If he let his eyes go out of focus the colors vibrated, reminding him of news footage of an Army truck in Vietnam launched into the air by a bomb, flying above the jungle canopy as it trailed a rope of fire out of a great blossom of yellow flame that expanded almost in slow motion. He considered buying the poster and shipping it home but then decided to save his money.

He turned and headed up the street, walking in sunlight. Two barefooted girls with bright eyes looking not much older than fourteen ran up to him laughing, and he placed a handful of loose pocket change into their outstretched palms. For a moment the smell of frying hamburgers and onions mixed with the scent of cinnamon from the bakery. Four cycles cruised down the street in the opposite direction, engines revving above the other street noise.

A seaman apprentice he knew came up here on liberty two days before and jawboned with the men in the working party who were taking a break from chipping paint off the bulkhead. "Man, are they filthy," he told his buddies, tossing his cigarette butt into the briny bilge water.

"Yeah," another volunteered. "Throw um all in the Army. Not the Navy."

The men laughed out loud except David and his friend Tim, a gunner's mate.

"I heard that stuff they take, that LSD, is manufactured in Russia."

Tim rolled his eyes, picked up his hammer, and started banging at the metal. He came from the south side of Chicago and didn't want trouble with these white guys who talked out their buttholes and didn't know shit.

At Clayton, David saw people hanging around outside the door of the Free Clinic. A girl with rosy skin smiled broadly at a fellow in a wide-brimmed, flat-topped leather hat; in a harness on her back, a baby waved its tiny arms and kicked its stubby, bare legs. David walked under the green-striped awning of Be-Jay's Children's Shop and past the glass windows of Pacific Drugs. In the next block, the marquee of a theater read "Peace," and farther on the tree canopy of the park rose above the grid of trolley wires. He glanced up Shrader at the white houses on the steep hill. Finally he crossed busy Stanyan and followed the paved footpath into the park and through an underpass where stalactites of concrete thrust from the arching roof.

Walking out of the tunnel he saw the spreading branches of a palm tree and the gray under-fronds pointing downward against scaled bark. Birdsong mingled with the sound of voices. He followed the curving pavement toward a slope surrounded by tall trees and covered with people sitting or lying in the grass. Seeing a trash barrel filled to overflowing, David took his city map out of his pocket and shoved it down inside.

Three men wearing bandanas sat crossed-legged in the grass.

"Did you hear thirty people got busted Tuesday night after that street dance?" one said.

"Yeah. Ten got jail sentences, I heard. For dancing."

"Somebody cut the valves off the tires of their stupid paddy wagon."

"I was there," a third one said. "They broke some chick's jaw."

"They busted a band on Masonic for disturbing the peace."

David could hear the birdlike sounds of a flute as he watched three barefooted girls in long dresses skipping below the hill. He felt older than most of these kids, having turned twenty-one the previous February. On a level place he slipped his knapsack from his shoulders and sat propped up on his hands in the grass under a large old Monterey pine. A few yards away people listened to a guitarist who was competent but new at music; he played the same chords—A, D, and E—over and over again. A girl sang, and someone began to shake a tambourine.

At home the weather would already be warm and humid, while here the temperature never rose higher than seventy degrees, and he didn't feel the fatigue of the languid Midwestern climate. Nor would a California gull fly down in front of him like the one he now watched investigating something on the grass and depositing its runny shit.

Earlier that afternoon David and Tim caught the downtown bus outside the gate of Hunter's Point and rode to Fisherman's Wharf. Avoiding the most crowded streets, they wandered into and out of little shops. In one of them David picked out a small ceramic vase painted bright blue, sage green, and rust red.

"For your girlfriend?" Tim asked.

"My mother," David replied, reaching for his wallet. "You know I don't have a girlfriend."

"Never too late, my man."

"Right. In the bowels of a ship."

The sales clerk wrapped the vase in several layers of tissue paper and placed it inside a little cardboard box that she wrapped in red and gold paper, folding the edges into triangles and taping them on the sides. Then she put the wrapped box into a shipping carton, sealed the edges, and wrote the address as David told her.

He folded his wallet and shoved it into his pocket. When they walked outside David caught sight of paper cups and debris floating in the water near the pier and felt his stomach contract and his throat close when he thought about returning to the base. Around two o'clock they walked to a bar they knew on Stockton, chose a dark booth, and ordered Budweisers.

"What you looking at?" Tim asked. His eyes were luminous, his curly hair cropped close to the scalp above high cheekbones. Tim had been acting more and more distracted lately, and his question surprised David, who gestured at the fishing nets and old-fashioned ship's wheels that decorated the walls.

Tim shook his head. "I hate the Navy."

"When I signed up they let me believe I'd have my electronics certificate after one hitch," David said. "Then they tell me if I want the whole training I have to re-up for two more years."

"Damn fools can't do anything but kick people around," Tim answered. "One day they're all loose and friendly and the next they have a wild hair up their ass and order everything by the book. Call us candy-asses." They both knew that what bothered them most was not the officers' moods or the broken promises.

"And what's it all for?" David asked.

"So nobody can say they lost their lousy-ass war," Tim answered.

"And here we are," he continued after a pause, "in this big city where we could hide and they'd never find us."

"Yes, they would."

"Look around you. All kinds of people talking all kinds of languages. They aren't going to turn us in, are they? Most of them probably illegal anyway."

"You'd always be looking over your shoulder," David cautioned.

"Not if you know how to blend in."

"How serious are you, Tim? It's a big decision. There's a war on."

"I know. We've seen it, haven't we?"

Tim rolled his eyes.

"You've already done more than two years," David reasoned. "You don't want brig time. And even if they never catch you, you'd have to be on the run, being somebody you aren't."

They both knew men who'd disappeared after a liberty. Most of them came back in a few weeks and either did some brig time or extra work detail. They said they lost their nerve about deserting or they just needed to stay out awhile, or the Navy chasers caught up with them. Then there were the ones who never came back.

The Chinese waiter collected their glasses, or maybe he was Korean—a small, older man who looked fifty but was probably in his forties, from one of those immigrant families where someone obtained a visa and then brought over relatives who lived crammed into an apartment in Chinatown where everyone— even the children—worked and saved every penny and then bought a house or business or sent a son to college. The next generation spoke perfect English and moved to Richmond, and their kids bought houses in Pacific Heights.

"Want anything else?" he asked.

"No," Tim said, and the waiter placed the bill on the table.

"Thanks very much," he said, bowing slightly and turning away.

Tim and David stood, laid some bills on the table, and walked outside into the bright sunlight. Shrieking seagulls hovered above the shimmering water of the bay.

"Gotta meet somebody," Tim said quickly.

"Okay," David answered, surprised and a little disappointed. "See you back at the iron dungeon."

"Right," Tim replied. "Goddamned Navy. See you bro." He held his right hand palm up in the air.

"You know I feel like an asshole doing that," David said.

Tim grabbed and hugged him tightly, then abruptly turned on his heel. For a moment David felt like running after him, and as he watched Tim disappear into the crowd David's stomach tightened. Walking back toward the wharf, David saw a tour boat set off with engines chugging and two trawlers head toward the magenta bridge. Western gulls perched on the masts while others soared overhead, and four brown pelicans flew in line right above the boats. Looking out over the water always made David feel free for a moment, though he knew the Navy would reel him back in the next day.

After about half an hour he decided he'd wasted enough time and walked to a stop for the Haight Street bus. He might have been making a mistake, but when the bus pulled up to the curb, he stepped onto it, pushed the quarter through the slot, found a seat in the back, and watched the city rush past: glass-fronted shops, open-air restaurants with tall ferns in large clay pots near the pavement, Victorian houses decorated with scrolls like layer cakes, shimmering water beyond palm leaves and oleander. The driver called out Masonic; David was thrown forward as the brakes screeched and the bus slowed and trembled to a stop. The doors were flung open. Feeling a slight thrill in his stomach, he stepped down to the pavement and faced the dark windows of the corner café.

David brought his right wrist from the grass to see the angle of four o'clock on the round face of his watch. Hunger gripped his stomach, but eating would spoil the lightness he felt. Glancing up, he saw a woman about twenty feet away take a paper sack from her shoulder bag and scatter crumbs on the ground. She was taller than most women and very thin with narrow hips, and he could tell in spite of loosely fitting blue jeans that her legs were slender like a dancer's. Her low-cut, buff-colored shirt had full sleeves and blue embroidery on the front. She wore her light brown hair in a long braid. He wouldn't have said she was beautiful but imagined she must have a nice body under those faded jeans, which tapered to frayed cuffs above her sandals. Sparrows alighted first at the free feast, followed by two jays, then a mallard angled its noisy way in. She swung her arm, throwing more crumbs, and David half expected her to take off into the air.

He unzipped his knapsack, took his recorder out, fitted the mouthpiece, and began to improvise. A few people gathered near him, their faces in his peripheral vision like white blooms on a green hedge. When he finished they clapped and sat waiting for him to play something else, but he opened the instrument case, and they rose slowly and ambled away in different directions, one saying "Nice, man." The woman who'd been feeding the birds stayed. Even from yards away he felt energy circulating around her. She stepped closer, and he could see her turquoise pendant earrings, clear blue eyes, and high cheekbones. Sunlight turned her hair golden.

"Sounds good," she said. "Why don't you want to play more?"

"I'm a little tired," he said.

"Where you from?"

"Long Beach."

"You moved up here?"

"I drifted here," he answered.

"Good place to drift to," she said. "My name's Diane."

"David."

"Diane Cavanaugh. You know, you play better than most street musicians," she continued, sitting down on the grass beside him and clasping her hands at her ankles.

"Are you in the military?" she persisted. "Out for a last fling before you get shipped off to Vietnam?"

"What makes you think that?"

"Your hair. I don't blame anyone who's in the military," she went on. "The ones at fault are the ones at the top."

"I'm not en route to Vietnam," he answered, thinking, I just got back from there.

She pulled a pack of Tareytons from her bag and offered it to him. He waved his hand and she drew one out and lit it, then scraped the spent match back and forth on the ground. The smell of tobacco smoke mingled with the scent of pine as they watched two jays squabble over something in the grass.

"We have room, if you need a place to stay. Got a sleeping bag?"

"Not with me."

"We have a mattress."

"I can afford a place," he said.

"Okay. I think I'll get going," she said, standing up and running her hand along her buttocks.

"I'll walk with you a ways."

David stood, picked up his knapsack by the strap, and slung it over his shoulder. Usually he towered over women, but he cleared her by only a few inches. They set off toward Stanyan, and he found he didn't need to slow down for her. She covered so much ground with each stride that she seemed to float, carrying her shoulders back.

"You really do play well, you know," she said, breaking the silence just as David was beginning to feel awkward. "Where'd you learn?"

"High school. Played clarinet and oboe in band. A college teacher turned me on to the recorder."

"My mother taught me piano when I was a kid, but I didn't stay with it. I play guitar a little."

"Been here long?" David asked, raising his voice above the roar of cars accelerating. "Or are you a native?"

"Since April. Got a ride with some kids driving out."

"From where?" he asked.

"Fort Collins, Colorado."

"Going to be here long?"

"Who knows?" she shrugged.

They stopped for the light. A chopper tooled slowly around the curve, the driver in a denim jacket and no helmet, a girl behind him wearing a fringed shirt and standing barefooted on metal sidebars. She raised one arm and shouted something as the driver revved up and roared deafeningly past. Diane took a long drag from her cigarette, dropped it on the pavement, and crushed it under her sandal. They crossed Stanyan, and as they reached the other side she turned and said, "Sure you don't want to stay over one night?"

She had broken through his barrier of solitude, and now, looking into her blue eyes, he found he wanted company after all.

"If you think it'll be okay with the people you live with."

"Great. Come on then."

They walked across the grass of the Panhandle where people were trying to start a fire with sticks and paper.

Crossing Oak, the street that bordered the Panhandle, she headed for a blue-gray Victorian where steep concrete steps led to a small covered porch with a pillared railing. A large bay window with stained glass insets at the top, partially obscured by a rose-colored curtain, took up the rest of the side facing the street. Below the window, the wooden door of a one-car garage stood closed, and sparse grass thrust through cracks in the pavement. David followed Diane up the concrete steps, across the wooden porch, and through the tattered screen door into the dark interior. His footsteps echoed on the bare wooden floor of a short, dark hallway.

Walking through an archway into the front room, David saw his reflection in an old mirror encased in an ornate wooden frame hanging above the mantel of a fireplace long ago converted to gas. It reminded him of the one in his parents' house. His hazel eyes staring from the glass looked startled, and his ruddy skin contrasted with his black hair. A brass statue of Shiva sat on the mantel, and in front of it a slender young man with big eyes peering out of wire-rimmed glasses lounged on an old upholstered chair, one leg crooked over the arm, his other bare foot on the faded red Oriental rug that partially covered the floor. His bony elbows protruded from the sleeves of a brown T-shirt, and a mass of curly pale hair surrounded his head. He looked up from a newspaper printed with large orange letters on the front page.

"Hi," David said, slipping the knapsack from his shoulders.

"What's happening?" the bug-eyed boy answered, nodding his head. Blond curls fell across his pale forehead and around his ears, and the light brown color of his wispy beard made it look even thinner than it was.

In front of a scuffed coffee table to the right near the wall, a battered rocking chair stood empty. On the table a black stereo set appeared to be the only new item. To the left of the coffee table a door led to another room, and beside it David saw a poster with an orange circle on a light blue background. The room smelled like concrete and mold accented by the acrid pungency from the brass Shiva.

Hearing a grumble to his left, David turned toward a man slouched in an overstuffed sofa and wondered why he hadn't noticed such a large guy sooner. The man eyed David up and down from under his dark, bushy brows as he smoothed his beard with the thumb and middle finger of his left hand.

"What have you brought us this time, Diane?" the man asked, the skin wrinkling on his forehead and around his mouth as he pulled a pack of Camels from the pocket of his black T shirt.

"He's a musician, Daryl," she answered. "He just needs a place for tonight."

"What's your name?" Daryl asked, drawing a cigarette with the middle and ring fingers of his right hand.

"David."

"David what?"

"Just David."

"Make yourself at home, Just David," Daryl said as he slipped the pack into his shirt pocket and lit the cigarette with a lighter.

"This is Terry," Diane said, gesturing toward the chair. The boy nodded.

"C'mon," Diane said.

Feeling embarrassed, David shouldered his knapsack and followed her out of the front room to the hallway and climbed a staircase to a landing. The bathroom door stood ajar, and David could see brown beer bottles and papers on the floor and towels on hooks. A square window at the back stood open.

Diane turned the glass knob on a door to reveal a small room where a mattress covered with a tattered quilt lay on the floor. In one corner an old chest—its chipped, white paint now discolored to pale coral—stood against the wall near a wooden crate filled with records. The closet door rested ajar on broken hinges. Branches of a spindly knobcone pine pressed against the window.

"We put a lot of people up here. Set your stuff anywhere. We're probably going to eat soon."

"Are you sure it's okay with your friends?"

"It's okay. Terry lives here. Daryl just hangs around."

A woman appeared at the half-open door. She was shorter than Diane and not as thin, but shapely in a long green dress. Her hair was brushed back from her face and held at the sides by large, old-fashioned looking combs.

"Heard somebody was crashing with us," she said.

"Rennie, this is David."

"Hi," Rennie said, smiling at him so widely that her dark brown eyes nearly disappeared, eclipsed by fair, round cheeks. "Good thing I brought some stuff from the Four Winds."

She turned away and he could see her thick, ginger-colored hair, glossy as satin, reaching below her shoulder blades.

"Rennie works on and off at a health-food café in North Beach," Diane explained. "She's sort of going with Terry. Penner is his last name. He's here making a film."

"About what?"

"The Haight."

"He looks young to make movies."

"He's a student," she explained. "Or was. At Antioch."

"In Ohio?"

"Yeah, Yellow Springs. That's where I went."

"You knew him there?"

"I did, so I came here when I got to town. Rennie's from Hayward. She was going to SF State but she quit. They've been here since last year."

"Yes, I know Antioch's in Yellow Springs. I come from Ohio."

"You do? Where?"

"Logan. Southeast of Columbus."

"No shit? I'm from New Albany. I know where Logan is."

"So we meet in San Francisco," he said. "Actually, I went to high school in Logan, but I'm really from outside it."

"You're from nowhere," she said, laughing. "I thought you didn't sound like somebody from Long Beach."

"And I thought you were from Colorado," David answered. "And what about Mr. Big?"

"He's Terry's friend. Used to major in chemistry at Berkeley. Comes from Saint Louis, I think." She stepped toward the door. "Want to stay here or come down?"

"I'll stay." He felt too shy to make conversation with people he'd just met who might be inconvenienced by Diane's invitation.

As she stepped out of the room and closed the door behind her, David noticed that Diane moved like a dancer, the motion coming from her ankles, and she carried her arms slightly away from her body like a bird alighting on a branch and folding its wings around itself. Somehow he felt he could trust her although he couldn't have said why.

David set his knapsack down and stretched his six-foot frame the length of the mattress. He'd been walking most of the day.

He was running through the *Loyola's* passageways and over endless coamings, glimpsing the gray steel bulkhead girders like giant ribs, ducking the red joists and slanting gray pipes with "sea water" painted on them in white, leaping over the enormous black links of the anchor chain, trying to find the ladder; he had to report a fire in a locker before it spread to the hangar deck where fighter jets and skids full of bombs stood ready to be loaded onto the elevators. The passageways kept branching off so he couldn't get anywhere, and the few sailors on the deck looked like wooden cutouts so far away he could barely see them. He tried to shout but couldn't force the words from his paralyzed throat. Against the wall a row of fire extinguishers laid on the floor where they weren't supposed to be, so he grabbed one and ran toward the flames, but found himself for some reason alone in the engine room looking at the rows of dials and levers. How did he get so far below? Suddenly the alarm sounded for General Quarters; someone must have reported the fire, and he ran along the ribbed aluminum floor toward the forty-foot ladder, hoping the hatch would be left open until he could get there. He couldn't hear anything except the turbine engines; usually he'd hear men shouting and shoes on iron rungs. He found the ladder and pulled himself up through the hatch but there was only another ladder, reaching far above him. He climbed iron step after step, his hands on the chains, never finding the deck.

Then he woke up and remembered instantly he was in a room in a house on Oak Street in San Francisco. Diane was looking down at him.

"Do you want to eat with us?" she asked.

He wanted to wrap his arms around her hips, grab her buttocks, and press his face into her crotch, but he nodded, stood up, and followed her downstairs.

"So many pseudo-people in the Haight now," Terry was saying. "The real thing's gone."

As David stepped through the doorway, Rennie smiled broadly. Terry looked up and said, "Lo." Daryl was gone.

Diane led David through the living room and into the kitchen where she gave him a chipped, yellow china plate. He was supposed to help himself from pots of brown rice and stir-fried vegetables on the old stove. There was bread too, but no butter. From the ancient, grease-spattered radio on the counter, the KMPX DJ's voice announced concerts for that weekend.

"Rennie made the bread," Diane explained. "We don't eat like this every day."

"Then I guess I'm in luck," David said. "I should have brought something." Hunger gnawed at his stomach.

"Don't worry about that. People show up to eat with us all the time."

Feeling like a free-loader, David carried his plate back to the other room. Rennie stood up from the rocking chair, perched on the other end of the couch from Terry, and drew the folds of her green skirt around her. Diane sat down on the floor and crossed her legs.

"Have a seat," Terry said. "Di says you're from Ohio."

The caning was broken in several places; David hoped the chair would hold him.

"Yes."

"I go to school there—when I go to school at all." He grinned at Rennie and stuffed a large chunk of brown bread into his mouth.

"Diane told me," David said. "Antioch. Are you from Ohio then?"

"New York," Terry answered. "Long Island."

David wondered why Terry's speech had no trace of eastern pronunciation. His green eyes behind spectacles appeared huge beside his arching, knife-blade nose.

"Who'd you interview today?" Diane asked.

"Some weird cat who wears these white Hindu robes and teaches

17

prisoners at San Quentin," he answered, swallowing a mouthful of rice. "Dude got all emotional talking about man's inhumanity to man. Has this great place on Ashbury. Indian rugs and art on the walls, beads hanging in the doorways. Found out about him from that doc at the clinic I talked to last week.

"This other fellow was with him," Terry continued. "Older guy, must have been at least twenty-five. He didn't have a 2S, so I asked him how he'd stayed out of the service, and he said when he went for his exam he told the Army psychologist he wasn't going to do anything whether they drafted him or not. Shrink said he'd sign a mental disability deferment for him; shrink didn't care, he'd been drafted and was just serving his time. He'd worked in a loony bin and knew what to write. Dude was out and on the street in nothing flat. Been seeing the country ever since—Montana, Idaho, Utah—in his old man's pickup."

The front screen door creaked open and banged shut, and after a few seconds Daryl's form loomed in the archway. He wore the kind of black leather boots that bikers preferred, and his legs in tight, soiled denim jeans looked slightly bowed.

"Hey, man," Terry said. "You bring something?"

"You'll find out."

"Want anything to eat?" Diane asked, looking up at him. Rennie stared at the floor.

"Nope," Daryl answered. His well-muscled arms and the massive chest beneath the black T-shirt made him look more like an ex-linebacker than a chemist. The man ate regularly somewhere.

Daryl took a film tube from his pocket and proceeded to fill and roll a cigarette paper.

"Ever tried this stuff, Straight Man?" he asked David.

"Yes," David answered.

Rennie stood up and in what seemed to David like one fluid motion drew the rose-colored Indian-print drape across the window, lit a stick of incense on the mantle next to Shiva, and put a record on the stereo. "The Sunshine of Your

Love" emanated from the speakers.

"In honor of our guest from Ohio," Daryl said, taking a lengthy drag and passing the joint to Terry.

"Gold, man," David heard Terry say. They sat in silence a long time, passing the joint and listening to music. The first time David smoked pot he went with some Navy recruits to one of the cheap hotels in Waukegan's waterfront district to celebrate graduation from boot camp. The whole sleazy room vibrated like a brightly-colored painting and when they went outside the few scraggy, leafless bushes looked like a cartoon in Technicolor. Now everyone around him seemed to stand out in relief like figures in the Viewmaster he'd had as a child.

After awhile Daryl got up and left, and Rennie and Terry climbed the stairs.

"I'm going too," Diane said. David realized as he followed her that he hadn't looked at the time since four o'clock. Watching her small, round behind, he wondered whether she might sleep with him, but on the landing she opened one of the other doors, stepped inside, and closed it. Inside his temporary room David slipped off his shirt and jeans but kept his undershirt and shorts on, pulled back the quilt, and stretched out on the mattress again.

Lying on the old, thin, coverless pillow, he floated in the mist of a shallow sleep when the door opened with a sound like inhalation and Diane stepped inside. She had unbraided and brushed her wavy hair; it fell around her face as she knelt beside the mattress and ran her hand along his shoulders and neck, then began kissing him as her hands explored his legs and inside his shorts. He unbuttoned her shirt and ran his hands over the smooth skin of her neck, prominent clavicle, and small breasts. He arched his back off the mattress in order to allow her to pull his shirt over his head. Her hands found their way inside his shorts again as she drew them towards his feet. Straddling his pelvis with her long, slender legs, she eased herself around him, throwing her head back and closing her eyes. He reached again for her breasts, sensing the restless ocean behind her skin. He felt as if he were penetrating far into her, as if he could feel her pelvic bones as she moved her hips up and down, forward and backward. He tried to control himself for her but had to surrender as his whole body shuddered.

� ✕ ✕   ✕ ✕ ✕   ✕ ✕ ✕

He woke up on the mattress and reached for her, but his palm touched the cold sheet. After they made love they lay talking for a long time, he remembering his year at Ohio State, she telling him about two years at Antioch and the couple she stayed with in Fort Collins on her way west. She had overcome his reticence; lying together with her, he felt there was almost nothing he couldn't say, and even admitted to her that he'd been in the Navy and spent six months in the Gulf, leaving out the fact that he was still enlisted. In a few hours he told her more about himself than he'd ever told anyone else except Tim.

Light streamed from the window. Wishing it would be after eight and at the same time anxious that it was, he checked his watch. The short hand pointed to nine, the long one to twenty-five after the hour. He was late—technically UA—but he could go back and take the reprimand and extra work detail. They couldn't classify him as a deserter until after thirty days. He could hear the Division Commander calling him a goddamned lazy slacker, though he usually threw himself into his work because hard physical labor helped him forget how much he hated being there. Almost half his hitch was up; to leave now would be foolish. But to be part of all that for two more years? The memory of building bombs disgusted him to the point of nausea. And the thought of going back to the same work—washing down the walls and floors of the weapons storage area, passing crates from the high line, banging the paint off hulls and bilges and repainting them—depressed him. And all for something he couldn't believe in any more.

When he first transferred to Alameda he went drinking often with his friends in the Mission District, Fisherman's Wharf, and North Beach; after a few months, he stopped taking liberties because he couldn't stand having to ask the Navy for anything, even permission to leave for a few hours. After they got back from Tonkin, Tim persuaded him to take the time off—he'd go crazy if he never left the iron dungeon, and David was already acting depressed. The usual rumors circulated that the ship was going to be deployed again to the Gulf sometime that summer, and if it did he wouldn't get to spend any more time in San Francisco for maybe seven months. But whenever he took Tim's advice he found it harder and harder to go back to the base.

Remembering Tim's words that no one could find you if you knew how to blend in, he stretched his long arms outward.

TWO

"Do you know you're ineligible for the game this weekend?" Mr. Barrow asked, leaning over the desk. David looked up from his book and forced himself to focus on his history teacher's flushed face. The scene he'd been reading, where the hero faced an Arab wielding a knife, still played before his eyes. The January wind gusted against the pane.

"Why?"

"Athletes are required to have a passing grade for every class each week or they are ineligible for the game. We have had no tests this week, so the only grade is for recitation. You have not participated in recitation at all this week."

David looked into Mr. Barrow's small, pale eyes, but on the periphery of his vision he could see other kids turning their heads. David was a senior on the varsity basketball team and the highest scorer in five years at Logan; without him they'd have little chance of beating Grove City this Friday.

"Then I'll have to miss the game," David said.

"I expect you will," Mr. Barrow answered and continued slowly up the row, hands clasped behind his back.

David scanned the lines of print to find his place again, but he couldn't concentrate any more. Barrow didn't like him because he didn't participate in class—which consisted of the teacher shouting questions and the kids shouting back in unison the answers memorized from the textbook. The class always went that way except when Barrow told the students how he'd served in the Air Force during World War II and declared, "We'd be fighting them here if we weren't fighting them there," never specifying who "they" were. He resented the ingrate Cubans and blamed Kennedy for the Bay of Pigs, saying he should have bombed the entire island to rubble. After last November, Barrow pretty much shut up about JFK except to claim that Cubans had to be behind the assassination; he hadn't looked shocked or sad the way everyone else did the day the principal announced over the intercom the news from Dallas.

"I knew a man who wouldn't serve in the military," Barrow informed the class once, "and I asked him 'What would you do if somebody broke into your house with your wife and kids in it?' He said 'I'd kill anybody who did that.' I told him, 'It's the same thing'." Throwing his right arm forward and downward, he continued, "And you know, he couldn't *see* that."

Barrow also objected to the TV ads where a young guitarist sang that "college is America's best friend"; the teacher claimed it was America's worst enemy since colleges and universities were hotbeds of free thought, and half the professors were Commie kooks and conscientious objectors anyway. The Civil Rights movement was communist inspired, too. Negroes worked alongside whites in every factory in the country: there wasn't any racial discrimination. Barrow speculated this Martin Luther King was communist and not a real minister.

At dinner the evening of his encounter with Mr. Barrow, David's mother Ruth sighed as she set bowls of green beans and thick chili on the table.

"I cooked a half package of hamburger. Forty cents a pound," she complained. "Bill, shouldn't we should buy a steer and put it up in the freezer the way we used to when the kids were at home?"

William Shields spooned thick red chili onto his plate. His stomach was beginning to sag and his black hair was graying.

As Ruth sat down she ran her hand along the tablecloth. "My whites aren't turning out right even when I scrub them," she said, examining the red knuckles of her right hand.

Raising his glass David drank the cold, mineral-hard well water.

"I won't be playing this weekend," he declared, setting the tumbler down.

Without lifting his head, David's father peered at him disapprovingly the same way he did when David first asked to take music lessons.

"What have you done this time?"

"Barrow says he'll declare me ineligible because I don't participate in class."

"Mr. Barrow," Ruth corrected him.

"And why haven't you done that?" his father asked.

David made no answer.

"It seems to me a boy who wanted to play would make sure he stayed eligible."

"David, I don't understand why you have to test people all the time," his mother said, sighing. "That isn't the way we raised you."

"Why do you say I test people when I haven't done anything?"

"Don't talk that way. You test people till they get exasperated. You know you do. Now this is what *you* get," she said, pointing her right forefinger at her husband, "for never spending any time with your son."

His parents had been born in Logan, graduated from the high school there, and married one year later after William got a job as a machinist in a factory in Lancaster. Their five children graduated from the same high school. David's two older brothers worked in factories in Columbus and Lancaster; one sister taught elementary school. All were married and had children. When his mother spoke to people other than her husband, she referred to David, four years younger than his closest sibling, as her "accident." She always called him "your son" when talking to her husband.

The next morning David went to the basketball coach to tell him he would be ineligible for the game on Saturday. The coach had deep-set brown eyes in a handsome face wrinkled like a mountain crag and framed with thick brown hair.

"Mr. Barrow told me he's given back your eligibility," he said.

"Why?"

"Because I talked him into it," the coach responded. "I told him you listen even though you don't say anything, and I brought up the fact you make the honor roll every semester. Besides, the SAT results came in yesterday and you scored higher than anyone else in the class. Barrow agreed he couldn't keep a student who was that capable out of the game."

He paused.

"David, what do you get out of challenging people?"

"I don't challenge them," David answered.

"We all have rules to follow."

"I listen in class," David insisted. "You said so yourself. I read every assignment. I turn in the homework—even if it's nothing but copying answers out of the book. Some people don't even do that."

"You know that's not what I mean," the coach sighed. "Go on back to class."

During the autumn when David was ten he walked farther into the woods than he ever had before. At the bottom of a steep incline he crossed barbed wire dragged down by brambles and saw across a field an old barn with missing boards and holes in the slate roof. It must have been the place where the widowed farmer died in his house and wasn't found for days, and afterwards no one wanted to buy the place because they said it was haunted. David walked through the tall grass to the open door of the barn. In the dark interior he could see pieces of a rusted disk and an old milking machine lying on the ground. Cobwebs hung from wooden beams. Boards from old stalls lay in the aisle ways, but two stalls were still intact, with straw and dried cow dung on the floor. Far above, near the highest point of the ceiling, the old hay hook hung from its cable like a giant jaw. He heard the sound of a large bird flying from rafter to rafter high above his head, but in the dim light he couldn't make out whether it was a red-tail or a kestrel.

When David walked out of the barn the sun was already disappearing behind a ridge, and he knew it must be late. His father would be angry if he didn't get home. He ran back across the field toward the woods and snagged his corduroy jacket as he crossed the barbed wire. Running the rest of the way up the hill, he leaped over a stream and landed in black mud. Fighting his way through brush up the hillside, he climbed over an old stile and ran across the pasture. The light was on in the living room. Hoping he hadn't been missed yet, he burst across the porch and into the kitchen to face his mother standing with her hands on her hips.

"I got lost in the woods," he blurted out.

"Look at you," his mother said. "Look at your shoes." She put her hand on his shoulder and turned him. "And what have you done to your jacket?"

"What is it this time?" William asked, stomping in his stockinged feet from the living room, the newspaper dangling from two fingers. "Where have you been?"

"Snyder's farm. I didn't mean to stay out so long."

"Do you know what time it is?" Leaning over him, his father appeared enormous with his narrowed hazel eyes—the eyes people told David he inherited—and lined forehead. Still holding the newspaper, his father began to unbuckle his belt, and David imagined himself tiny as a firefly, running back into his own throat and down his ribs, which reached like a ladder into a dark void where he could be safe. Most of all he wanted to disappear. This time his father didn't even have time to pull his belt through the loops. His oldest brother Bill Jr. trod from his bedroom down the stairs into the kitchen and stepped between David and his father.

"Don't you touch him," his brother warned. He was a senior in high school and taller than William. "He didn't mean anything. He said he was on Snyder's farm, so what harm could he do? He lost track of time."

David ran out of the kitchen and up to his room, shut the door, and pulled the curtains, wondering what would happen when Bill left home.

On his first hunting trip with his brother, when David was fourteen, they picked their way quietly through the woods to the place where they would wait for the deer to pass. He wanted to please his brother and make him think he liked hunting, but what he really liked was being in the woods, especially in the sharp autumn air. Unexpectedly his brother stopped, raised his hand, and pointed straight ahead at a big buck standing just off the path. Bill raised the .284 and brought the deer into his scope. David, who had looked forward to this day so much, suddenly wanted to grab his brother's arm and shout at him not to do it, but he stood silent as the buck leaped and ran, and Bill aimed and fired. In mid-stride the buck went down on its knees and fell over.

"Got him," Bill said and started toward the spot where the buck lay. Behind him David walked more slowly.

"Big sucker," Bill said as he knelt over it. "Twelve points." David forced himself to look at the smooth mound of brown hide along the flank, outstretched neck, tapered ears, and fine muzzle. He would never love hunting the way Bill did.

When David was in high school his father worked the day shift and came home by six. While they ate he usually made one or two sardonic comments about work and sat silently as his wife articulated the details of everything she did that day. His father watched the news on television before leaving the house for his machine shop set up in an old storage shed. There he worked quietly, his face contorted in concentration, disassembling engines and repairing them with parts from other machines. The shop smelled of grease, oil, cobwebs, and concrete. Old lawn mowers, rototillers, chain saws, and lawn tractors stood sometimes for weeks before he got to them, but he could make any gasoline engine run.

One evening in late May of David's sophomore year, William looked up suddenly during dinner and said to his wife, "Ted Shepler asked me if this boy'd be interested in clearing a hillside for him. Only way to do it's with a scythe. It's grown pretty thick. Says he'll pay good."

The farmer, who was shorter than David and walked with a slight limp caused by a fifteen-foot fall from a haymow years earlier, leased the large field behind their house. David knew him because sometimes the farmer brought his power mower to Bill and stood talking with him for a long time. Shepler's face was darkly tanned even in winter and creased like eroded soil so that he seemed older than he was, and the nails of his right middle and ring fingers had been blackened in accidents. His wife was a short, somewhat plump woman with a weathered face who wore glasses with pale pink plastic frames. Even when she was dressed up she looked as if she were about to clean out the chicken coop.

Stabbing his fork into a boiled potato, David mumbled, "I'll go see him."

The next day David surveyed the slope where wild carrot, sow thistle, and stinging nettle grew about five feet high. He gripped the handle of the scythe and cut a wide arc. David swung fast at first, but then adopted a slower, more rhythmic pace, clearing a wide swath with each swing. When the blade swept near the fence line at the end, he felt surprise rather than relief. Standing back, breathing hard, sweat pouring from his forehead, he looked at the smooth green slope. Never before had he worked so hard for so long, even during basketball practice.

A red-tailed hawk soared overhead while four vultures circled, casting their shadows on the ground. Before him to the east, wooded hills rose blue on paler blue. Ted Shepler's tractor came over the crest of a hill cutting hay while swallows circled and dove around it, catching insects on the wing.

Every summer after that, he worked for Ted Shepler, mostly baling and stacking hay, cutting weeds, and loading hundred-pound sacks of grain. That kind of work made David so tired he didn't have time to feel depressed or lonely. Pumping gas paid better, but he enjoyed this more, and it gave him a good excuse to be away from home. Now that Bill Jr. was busy with his own family—he married at twenty-one and had two sons in the first two years—David didn't go hunting any more, saying he'd rather earn some money. He always felt a certain sadness in the laconic farmer and wondered whether he saw in David a little of his own son who'd been gored to death by a bull when he turned his back on it. The boy had been twenty years old and engaged; his plan was to go into farming with his dad. If Shepler did see his own son in David he never gave any hint; although he taught David to drive the tractor and baler, fork-lift and backhoe, he never asked David much about himself except how he liked playing basketball. The farmer never stopped moving all day; the only times David ever saw him standing were during those conversations with his father over old machinery.

In the first warm week of April when David was sixteen, he left the window open, wanting to feel the night breeze on his naked chest and loins as he lay on his back, left hand underneath his head, his right hand trying to wrap himself in the warm ache of desire. He imagined pressing his body against a woman although none of the girls at school inspired him, even the popular ones in band or cheerleaders who dated varsity players. Their stiff, sprayed hair and skirts too short for their chubby legs reminded him of little dolls. He'd had exactly one date last summer—another basketball player's girlfriend fixed him up with a girl from Newark and the four of them went to the State Fair; the girl hadn't been outgoing, and he found it difficult to talk to her. One of the shyer girls at his school—the only girl among four boys who worked second period in the science lab—tried to get him to talk. David couldn't imagine dating her—she didn't look bad but she wasn't popular, she was even less confident than he was, and going with her would invite teasing from the other athletes, at least the popular ones. Even if he could bring himself to ask her out, what would they do? All she ever talked about was going to college, as if her life hadn't really started yet. So he imagined the girls' cheerleading coach, a blonde only a few years out of college whom the athletes declared to have the best legs on the faculty.

A mourning dove cooed and a June bug hurled itself against the screen. Hearing his mother sigh as she struggled up the steps and down the hallway toward her husband's room, David reached for the end of the sheet and drew it across his body in case she happened to walk into his room. He wondered why she was pacing this end of the house so late. Ever since his older sister left home, his mother slept in the bedroom her daughter vacated. David listened to the faint screech of hinges and the sound of hard, square-heeled shoes on the wooden floor.

He jumped at a boom like thunder, pulled on the bottoms of his pajamas, and ran barefooted to his father's room to see his mother crouching on the floor and crying into her hands. In the dim light he saw the dresser drawer pulled out and a basket of folded underwear tipped over on the floor. David knelt beside her, his bare chest near her graying head. Never had he heard her cry so noisily before.

"Didn't know it was you," his father mumbled, laying his .22 inside the gun rack. In the lamplight, David saw a hole in the wall near the dresser and chipped plaster sprayed on the floor. He thought he saw a sheepish look on his father's face.

David lifted the laundry into the basket and laid it on top of the dresser. Taking his mother's hand he helped her up and with his arm around her shoulder walked her back to the room where she slept. William repaired the wall himself the next day, mixing plaster and scraping it with a trowel, setting his lips the same way he did when he repaired machinery. When the plaster dried he primed and painted the surface, but David could still find the faint outline of the hole. Every evening afterwards David checked the guns before he went to bed. If they were loaded, he took the shells out and laid them inside the rack.

※ ※ ※   ※ ※ ※   ※ ※ ※

A few weeks before graduation, David walked through the old orchard and out to the field where he played as a boy and which his father now leased to Ted Shepler. The dogwood blossoms had fallen and even the mayapples were finished, but the violets blazed purple in the bright green grass.

In the middle of the field, David stopped and looked back. The three-story brown shingle house standing alone looked absurd and gangling, but at the same time it wore an almost startled expression in its dark windows. The front porch roof sagged at one end, and the wooden steps to the wrap-around veranda bowed in the middle. Three reddish-brown asbestos roofing tiles and a section of steel gutter which David and his father replaced the previous summer looked new and out of place. The spacious kitchen and utility room added onto the back stuck out at right angles. Paint peeled from the dormer windows of the second-floor bedrooms.

David vowed to change his life and, if he had to, become someone else. He would kill David Shields, basketball star, first clarinetist, and honor student at Logan High. Once free of this place, he would never come back.

The following September David enrolled at Ohio State because he thought the huge campus with 50,000 students would be the opposite of his tiny high school. Finding a cheap room close to campus off Tenth Avenue in Columbus, he began with the idea of majoring in music, although he wasn't sure what he'd be able to do with it.

Teachers didn't seem to care how he performed, so he did his assignments just well enough to pass. In philosophy recitation class the graduate assistant, wearing blue jeans, a gray-purple shirt, and a brown sport jacket with dark leather elbow patches, stood in front of the room and tried to get the students to debate the question of whether it was justifiable to kill one person in order to save a million. Someone argued that was what happened in wartime—soldiers sacrificed for larger numbers of people at home—and was happening now in Southeast Asia. David wondered how the question could matter to the graduate assistant or anyone else in the room, who had no power to save a million lives, or even one.

The social life disappointed him most of all. Students swarmed everywhere, but David didn't meet many of them. Except for English and philosophy, the classes were formal lectures in large rooms where the students didn't talk to each other very much. How people got acquainted remained a mystery. The guys in physical education talked about sports and their sexual conquests the weekend before, and while he knew most of their bragging was lies, David envied them that they had relationships at all. When some guys invited him to go out with them one Saturday night, they worked their way up High Street from bar to bar, drinking Stroh's low beer, laughing louder and shoving each other harder as the hours passed. Although the beer made David feel relaxed, it did not loosen his inhibitions; he spoke only when someone asked him a question. When one of them called another a cock-sucking queer, the guy landed a fist in his companion's eye, and the rest of the men tried to hold them back from each other until the manager strode over to their table and ordered them to leave. They scattered out the door near Lane Avenue where David left them and walked back down High Street toward his rooming house, trying to clear his head in the night air. For a while the beer and loud conversation had made him forget his loneliness, but lying awake on the foreign bed he began to think more clearly. These were not the kinds of friends he expected to meet in college. What was he doing here?

One afternoon in February as he was playing the recorder in his room someone knocked on the door. He opened it to see the bearded face of one of the men who lived on the floor below him. His name was Mark, and he invited David to his room. Mark and his roommate Craig were both philosophy majors, so David asked them what they thought he was supposed to get out of the intro class where the graduate assistant's questions seemed irrelevant. They told him he wouldn't have any real courses until his second year—the first year was all Mickey Mouse designed to get rid of students who shouldn't be there. They told him to read *Notes from Underground, The Trial,* and *Invisible Man,* which he did; afterwards, he knew little more except that he wasn't the only one who felt alone. He still found it difficult to talk about himself because he couldn't find the words to explain his feelings; instead, he listened to Mark and Craig, sometimes for hours, debating some idea or complaining about the escalating war in Vietnam. Johnson promised to end it, they said, and now look—he ordered in combat troops.

In Mark and Craig David thought he'd found the kind of friends he'd expected to meet in college and nearly worked up the nerve to ask them to introduce him to some girls, until one day he realized they didn't know any and didn't want to. Still, he hung out with them so he could listen to them talk.

His luck changed in April when David took a psychology course where the students were required to participate in experiments. At the lab he had to look at a series of letters, read a sentence, and see if he could remember the letters. The first time he couldn't, but during the subsequent trials he made up words beginning with those letters in order to remember them. The experimenter, frustrated that she couldn't succeed in "building the memory inhibition," told him he could go and asked him not to discuss the experiment with anyone.

The assistant who had taken down his name, address, year in college, and age sat behind a desk watching him as he walked out of the lab.

"What is all this about anyway?" he asked.

"It's for her dissertation," the girl answered. "On learning theory." She leaned forward. "It's pretty interesting, really."

"Are you in psychology too?"

"I want to be a clinical psychologist," she answered.

Her name was Susan. They talked for a long time, and she invited him to her place off campus. For a student apartment it was spacious—three rooms and a bathroom—and she furnished it herself with things her family gave her, even pictures for the walls.

He walked from the hallway into the living room shyly, not knowing whether this was in fact a "date" or not. Susan brought him a can of Budweiser, sat beside him on the couch, and placed her palm on the back of his hand.

"Tell me about your music," she said.

Susan had clear, fair skin and thick brown hair that she combed under. Her eyes were pale and small but bright, and her breasts were full and round although she was not at all chubby. He couldn't do anything with her the first time, but she was not in a hurry. She told him about the fiancé she'd broken up with; they had dated almost three years and slept together for two. She was on the pill and had had a couple of short relationships since breaking off her engagement.

"I just got the feeling I didn't really love him anymore. I was doing what everyone else was, marrying a guy I'd been going with so I wouldn't be left out after I graduated. You meet someone your sophomore year, you get pinned your junior year, and engaged your senior year. I knew when I went home to look at gowns; I was bored. It was like my mother was more excited about the wedding than I was. And he kept telling me more and more what to do, things like what classes to take and how I spent too much time studying. He never used to do that. Or like changing the subject when I had something to tell him."

When she asked David about his other girlfriends, and he replied that he didn't have any and in fact never had, she laughed and told him he shouldn't be embarrassed to ask girls out; he was good-looking enough. She herself wouldn't go to bed with a guy who wasn't good-looking, and she certainly wasn't going to marry one.

"If I'm married to him that means I've got to go to bed with him day after day, year after year," she said, rolling her eyes, "and he'd *better* look good."

"But that's not all you care about," he answered.

"No; he'd better not try to tell me how to live my life, either."

They saw each other throughout April and May, and David gave little thought to his classes or the questions that plagued him earlier about what he was going to do. He wondered whether he loved Susan and where the relationship was going, aware that she wasn't telling him everything about herself. A few weeks before the end of the quarter Susan rolled over in bed and raised herself on her elbows. Usually after sex they lay talking.

"I've made it into graduate school," she said. "Miami. I have to finish my thesis in two weeks, and my parents are picking me up right after commencement. I have to pack all this up, and my fiancé wants to get back together. I don't think I'm going to be able to see you again." Her beautiful round breasts hung over the sheet.

After a moment David muttered, "I thought you didn't like him telling you what to do."

"I think he may have learned his lesson."

David pondered a crack in the ceiling plaster.

"If that's the way you want it," he said.

"You're not disappointed?" she asked, sitting up.

"I think I always knew I wasn't the only one," he answered.

He washed and pulled his clothes on with the bathroom door closed, something he had not done after they got to know each other. When he came out she was wearing a long, loose T-shirt, kneeling, and arranging something in a drawer, but she looked up and smiled.

"Good luck, David," she said, standing, the T-shirt falling to mid-thigh.

"You too," he said, brushing her lips with his.

He opened and closed the door behind himself quietly, walked across the living room and into the hallway, down two flights of stairs, and outside into the hot, hazy air of June. The street was like an oven after Susan's air-conditioned apartment. He headed down High Street past rectangular concrete university buildings. While seeing Susan, David had felt no need to meet other women, but now he realized he was alone as he had been before he met her.

After the quarter was over in mid-June, David pumped gas at a filling station in Logan and baled Ted Shepler's hay. William Shields died of a heart attack two weeks later. David was asleep when his mother opened the door suddenly and cried out that Daddy was dead. He had not heard her blubber so noisily since his father mistakenly shot at her. Rolling out of bed he stumbled sleepily along the hallway, seeing at that early hour the haunted house he sometimes walked through in his dreams, with moth-eaten drapes covering the windows. His father lay face up on the rumpled bed, his sightless eyes wide open. Trying to shake off the vision, David dialed the local hospital and asked them to send an ambulance, then called the gas station and explained why he could not come in that day. His mother sat crying into her hands, wearing an old gray cotton bath robe with tiny yellow flowers that made her look older than she was. He sat down and put his arm around her shoulders.

"Come on, you need to call Bill," he said. "You'll feel better after you've talked to him." But she couldn't stop crying, so David called each brother and sister.

Even after the funeral Ruth refused to move anything William owned until her daughters insisted that she let them give his possessions away. David heard them talking as they took their father's clothes out of the closet and packed them into boxes for the Goodwill store along with old copies of *Guns and Ammo* that lay neatly stacked on the floor of his closet. They also suggested that David clean out the machine shop.

Smelling like stale oil and concrete, the shop felt as if no one had been in there for a long time. His father's big tool case, covered with a thin film of dust, lay open on the heavy work table beside a ratchet and an old red rag blackened with oil and grime. David remembered the shirt that rag came from. His father had stopped working on other people's engines, so the only mowers and tillers in the shop were ones he bought cheaply to recondition. He could always make an engine run again, no matter how old. David wondered whether Ted Shepler might be able to use them. Laying his hand on the ratchet he sat down on the high stool. His father had been the last one to touch this handle. David could almost hear his father sigh as he shifted from work table to project. This dingy shed was the only place he truly belonged.

David laid the ratchet down and opened the worktable drawer. Inside lay neatly stacked, grimy Kohler and John Deere manuals and next to them one soiled, well-thumbed magazine dated January 30, 1961. It was small, about the size of the *TV Guide*, and the cover showed a picture of a girl whose clothes were half torn off. David never saw his father reading stuff like this; he'd never seen his father read anything but engine manuals or newspapers. He knew his parents hadn't slept together for years, but he thought his father too old to want to. Had William known the same unrelieved tension, anxious self-doubt, and loneliness David did? He'd always assumed his father married young because there wasn't anything else to do; maybe instead William feared being alone. David had never taken the trouble to imagine his father's feelings all the time he lived in the same house, ate dinner at the same table, and slept in a room just down the hallway. David raised his head and swallowed hard to check the tears that were rising to his eyes, but because no one was there to see, he let them fall down his cheeks. He licked the salt tears, remembering the nights when he was twelve and thirteen, stifling the sound of sobbing into his pillow and vaguely aware that if his father or brother saw him he would feel more ashamed of himself than he felt at any other time. Yet he desperately wanted his father to walk into the room and ask, "What's wrong, David? Why are you crying? I heard you from down the hall."

At four or five years old, David ran to him when he came home but

William held him back by the shoulders. "Let him hug you," his mother said, but his father replied, "I haven't even taken off my coat yet," and David burst into tears. "Don't act like a baby," his father said, and David remembered feeling even then that it didn't help to say that; it didn't lessen his agony. Later he found any excuse to be out of the house when William came home grumbling about his stupid boss, some incompetent new mechanic, or the drivers on Route 33.

Now David coughed, and he pulled his handkerchief from his pocket and wiped the tears from his face, realizing that his grandfather had also been remote and unsympathetic, so maybe his father didn't know how to be anything else. William had been a worker; he never missed a day, and he paid the bills and put a roof over the heads of five children. Had he ever had any fun? Had he taken the time to analyze his own feelings and been afraid of what he might find in the bottom of his soul—the knowledge that he spent most of his life with a woman he didn't love, who didn't love him? Or had he loved her, and something went wrong that neither of them ever talked about? Now David cried into his hands because in nineteen years he never even tried to get his father to talk to him. He was a smart person; all the teachers said so. But if he was so smart he should have been the one to figure out how to reach his father, especially after David was big enough not to fear the belt anymore. Had William finished his work? Had he known as he drew his last breath—alone in that room where he'd shot a hole in the wall—that he was dying?

David stopped crying, sat up, opened the magazine, and turned several pages. He felt angry at his mother for pushing her husband away and yet blubbering and sobbing when she found him dead; still, she must have suffered from his remoteness, too. "Let him hug you," she said. Maybe loneliness fueled her incessant talking. He felt pity for them both, impatient that not one person in his family—himself included—could find a way to reach another. There were many things he couldn't even tell his brother Bill. He carried the magazine around the back of the garage to the old oil barrel where they burned trash. There he struck a match, touched the bright feather-flame to the glossy cover, and watched the little curtain of yellow grow larger as it consumed the paper. Holding the burning magazine in his hand until the flames nearly singed his fingers, David finally let it drop to the bottom and watched until the fire died back into blackened ash shaped like pages whose thin edges glowed.

At noon, as he sat alone on the living room couch, dirty and sweaty from throwing hay bales into the mow, "July 28, 1965" flashed on the television screen and faded to the commentator's round face and thinning black hair. President Johnson announced an increase in troop levels by 165,000, doubling draft quotas. David listened, remembering he'd registered for the Selective Service when he turned eighteen, expecting to stay in college for four years when he imagined the fighting would be over, and vaguely recalling some news story about a year ago when the Vietnamese—or was it the Russians?—fired on an American ship. After his father's death David felt that if he did decide to go back to college he would have to earn the tuition himself since he knew his mother would have less money to live on than before and she made it clear she was determined to stay in that big farm house. He had not applied himself the first year as he could have and delayed registering for the fall thinking that if he took a year off to work he might figure out whether he should stay in college. In the space beneath conscious thought, he knew the decision of what to do next would be made for him and that for a long time to come his will would not be his own.

The letter came three weeks later, and David drove to the county office where they told him to go to the Selective Service headquarters in Columbus. There he took a test that was so easy he almost laughed, and afterwards a man in a short-sleeved tan uniform explained the options: he had a month to enlist if he wanted to—two years in the Army or Air Force, four in the Navy with the opportunity to go to school; he was good enough for Special Forces, and he might consider that. The good-looking Navy recruiter talked to him longest, telling him he could go in as a seaman apprentice instead of a recruit and choose the kind of training he wanted because of his high test scores and one year of college, although he seemed to have an aptitude for electronics that would certainly lead to a career. If he wanted to go back to college afterwards, the GI Bill would pay for it. David glanced around the orderly, cream-colored room where the men worked quietly in their smart-looking tan uniforms with chevrons and bars on their sleeves. Behind them on the wall, posters showed a helmeted man in an airplane on a flight deck, a man climbing a rope ladder, and one signaling to a helicopter pilot beneath expansive blue skies with billowing clouds. The caption read "ARE YOU MAN ENOUGH?"

During the next two weeks David thought about little else besides the decision he now had to make. Bill Jr. told him he needed to decide for himself, but the Navy's offer of training sounded good; on the other hand, his chances of surviving were really pretty good, too—only a fraction of the guys who went in ever saw any combat, and if he didn't like the Navy, four years was a long time. On the morning of August 22nd he drove his father's old red pickup to the Armed Services Center in Columbus, strode through the door, and told the recruiter he wanted to enlist in the Navy. The man clapped him on the shoulder and congratulated him. He explained the contract and let David read it over, reiterating what he'd said earlier, that David could go in as a seaman apprentice and not just a recruit, and that he'd be guaranteed electronics training. David took the pen and wrote his name, letting the nub flow smoothly along the line, proud he'd be able to earn the rest of his way through college, or if not he'd have a profession he could take anywhere. The recruiter took the pen and signed his name right under David's.

※ ※ ※   ※ ※ ※   ※ ※ ※

Strong wind blew across the gray waves washing up on the dark brown sand of the undulating dunes of Nunn Beach where wild oats, cattails, and mallow grass bent in the storm. Locust and pine trees found enough soil to survive at the edge of the marshes. The dark lake stretched to the horizon under the steel-gray November sky.

The old red-brick structures of the Great Lakes Naval Training Center built before the First World War reminded him of a college campus. The imposing command center stood at the end of Ross Field, its ancient clock tower visible from most of the base. Next to it, the old gray hospital building now used for offices sported a green cupola. On the opposite end from the command center the red-brick galley with large, graceful arched windows trimmed in white looked like an arboretum. He felt more grown up here than he had in college, partly because he lived so close to home then, but also because there he could sleep in, show up for class late, or do some assignment half-assed if he didn't want to bother. Here there were consequences if he didn't follow orders.

Last September, for the first time in his life, he climbed aboard an airliner in Columbus; while the plane sat on the runway before takeoff, the cabin vibrating with the engines at full throttle, his stomach tensed with anticipation and purpose. The plane landed in Chicago where he and more than a dozen other guys his age met a military transport that took them to Great Lakes. Around eleven at night he and a hundred other men turned in on bunk beds in a huge hall, and David fell asleep thinking he was about to embark on the first real adventure of his life. His dream about wandering in a big old dilapidated house full of endless corridors was broken by a spotlight flooding the hall and the drill instructor shouting through a bullhorn, "GET THE FUCK UP, YOU SHITHEADS." It was three a.m.

After the first days the men in David's company, numbering one hundred instead of the usual eighty, marched in the rain from the brick barracks at Camp Barry to the wooden ones at Camp Lawrence where the Negro sailors lived before desegregation, re-opened to house the huge number of draftees. In the fog off the lake it looked like the set of a World War II-era movie. David's feelings of loneliness and isolation were punctuated with the sense that he was walking into history.

Boot camp, which was supposed to be twelve weeks long, lasted only six, but it was long enough to make his former life seem a lengthy dream and all he'd been taught useless now that he lived in a world with its own code and ethics. It was bad news to stand out in any way, or they picked you first for special punishment. If anyone screwed up the whole company suffered, so the pressure was on, not for yourself, but for the others. Sometimes the more sadistic DIs kicked or pushed a man; all the men at some time got singled out and called candy-ass, lazy sonofabitch, or coward. David's desire to be part of tradition turned to disgust with drills, cadences, and monotony. This wasn't about fighting or protecting anyone; it was about perfectly doing tasks that made no sense. The only thing the DIs praised was getting the job right the first time and making the company look good. Just as he had at home, David wanted to be invisible, and he realized he'd missed what his life was supposed to have been. Maybe if he'd stayed in college he might have met more women than Susan and learned what it meant to be in love. Just as he was finding out, he allowed himself to be forced into a life still more isolated than anything he'd experienced earlier.

After boot camp and three months at the Naval Air Station in Memphis, David was back at Great Lakes for electronics training. At the beginning of the first week the men were told they'd get half their training and if they wanted the rest they'd have to re-up for two years beyond the four-year hitch. At first David couldn't believe it: he signed a contract, and the recruiter did, too. How could they renege on their promise when he wasn't allowed to? This wasn't the Soviet Union. He couldn't concentrate during the morning and barely paid attention during the afternoon. Weeks later, when the career counselor called each man individually from the class, he told David he was a very good candidate for completion of the training. David looked into the open, flushed face of the Lieutenant Junior Grade.

"By joining the Navy I added two years to what I had to serve," he answered. "When I signed up they told me I'd receive the whole training. Now you tell me if I triple my service time the Navy'll give me what it promised in the beginning?"

"The training is longer and more comprehensive," the man replied.

"What assurance do I have that I'll get the rest of it even if I do sign up for two more years?" David asked. "They lied once; they can lie again."

David thought he saw the man's shoulders tremble and his jaw grow rigid. The career counselor never called him out of class again, even when at the end David earned the highest score on the exam.

Gradually David got to know the other men, especially when they asked him to go with them when they went to Chicago or Waukegan. On the streets they began to stride in step almost as they did when they marched. He liked them better than most college guys, but he couldn't figure out why he was so different from the others; although he had more friends than ever before, he didn't laugh as loudly as they did at crude jokes, didn't enjoy drinking as much, and couldn't strike up conversations with women as easily as they did.

David turned away from the water of Lake Michigan and saw the clear white light of Venus shimmering in the west above the tops of trees. He crossed the beach, his shoes sinking in the wet sand, finally meeting the wooden slats of the boardwalk near the road. On the other side of the pavement he turned down a path that led up through the ravine—the only area on the base that wasn't flat—cut into the earth by Pettibone Creek. David headed up the steep slope through wet leaves, listening to the faint sound of water trickling over stones. He found the old crumbling concrete steps and climbed them two at a time.

He heard the clack of shoes, and a man emerged from the fog. Even in the weakened light David could see the two gold bars on the uniform. He pulled his shoulders back and saluted. The lieutenant, walking quickly, erect but relaxed, had not seen him until that moment, and returned the salute almost casually, without altering his pace. He carried his responsibility naturally, without the fanfare the DIs insisted on. David walked quickly across the road and down Ross Field, proud for a moment and thinking maybe he'd made the right decision after all.

After electronics training, David was assigned to a frigate in Long Beach and given a week to report for duty. It was June 1966. David took the train to Ogilvie, changed to the red line, and rode all the way to Geneva. There he found his way to Highway 38, carrying his sea bag and feeling entirely on his own for the first time. He didn't have to wait very long anywhere for a lift; he crossed Illinois the first day and slept in his Navy-issue bag under the roof of a picnic shelter at a rest stop near Cedar Rapids the first night. The next morning he washed in the restroom and was standing by the highway before seven in the morning, looking out over the vast level plain as the sun came up and feeling happier and freer than he had felt in a long time.

One young guy in Nebraska driving an old rusty black pickup with wooden racks stopped for him outside North Platte and drove him all the way to Ogallala. The guy, who said he'd just graduated from high school, wore a weathered tan cowboy hat and boots with skin-tight, faded denim jeans.

"What do you do?" he asked.

"I'm in the Navy. Going to Long Beach."

"Long trip," the guy commented. "If they draft me I'm going to join the Army, but if I don't get drafted I'm not joining. I don't like the way things are looking in Vietnam." He glanced at David.

"Good plan," David answered, and the guy seemed to relax.

Crossing Nebraska took another twenty-four hours. In Colorado on his fourth day a man with white hair driving a Lincoln sedan gave him a ride from Greeley to Golden. When David told him he was in the Navy and heading for the base in Long Beach, the old man sat straight up.

"I was in the Army," he said, "but didn't get to see any action. Wish I had. I'm glad to know some of our boys're doing their duty instead of burning their draft cards and making fools of themselves."

"I haven't heard very much about them," David lied.

"I think the government should round them up and set them to hard labor," the old man went on.

David didn't answer, thinking that the old guy just wanted him to listen. The man even went out of his way to drive him to Estes Park so David could get a glimpse of the mountains. He introduced himself as Mr. Grayson Evans and bought David lunch at a café in Estes Park where they sat outside on a wooden veranda.

When he let David out near Golden he said, "If you're ever in Colorado again, look me up." David waved as the Lincoln pulled away.

He stayed in a cheap motel outside Durango that night and set off the next morning on Route 160 south into Arizona. In Illinois, Iowa, and Nebraska all the lifts were from truck drivers except for the young guy. In Colorado and Arizona they were men in their thirties driving pickups or older men driving sedans. Before the Navy, David had never been west of Dayton or east of Parkersburg, West Virginia. While Chicago fascinated him, the west mesmerized him with its brown-purple sage, intense heat, and flat desert stretching to the horizon.

David spent the fifth night in a cheap motel in Kingman. The next morning he had coffee at the motel restaurant, hoisted his sea bag onto his shoulder, and walked to the highway. He still had two days to make Long

Beach. One lift took him over the Colorado River and the state line to Needles. A Marine en route to the air training center picked him up and drove him across the Mojave Desert. Then he got another lift to Yucca Valley where a white Mustang with whitewall tires and California plates pulled off the road, kicking up the dust. When he opened the passenger door he saw the driver was a woman wearing cheap plastic sun glasses.

"Where to?" she asked, turning the radio volume down.

"Long Beach," he answered.

"Climb in," she said, picking up her white canvas bag by the handles and throwing it over her shoulder into the back seat.

David thought she looked older than he was. She wore a sleeveless white blouse with a red scarf, red and green striped pedal-pushers, and tan loafers with no socks. Her short brown hair was fastened back with bobby pins. Her face was pale, but her arms were brown.

As she launched the car into traffic onto Route 62 she asked, "So where you been?" As the car accelerated he began to tell her about his trip, wondering why she wasn't scared to pick up a male hitch-hiker.

"And I had you figured for a college kid from back East."

"I went to Ohio State for a year," he said, bracing himself as she guided the car into the oncoming lane and accelerated past a dump truck spewing diesel smoke. He had never seen a woman drive so fast.

"And then?"

"I quit."

"Why'd you do that?" She guided the car back into the right lane and drove with her left hand on the wheel. "Were you fed up?"

"My father died and I didn't want my mother to have to support me."

"I'm sorry. I didn't mean to pry." She adjusted the rear-view mirror.

"You aren't prying," he answered, surprised at himself for revealing far more to this stranger than he ever did even to people he knew. "I thought I might work a year, but then they drafted me."

"Lousy thing, the draft. But I'm sorry—go on if you want."

"I hadn't done that well my first year. I thought the service might motivate me some."

"How long you been in?"

"Just under a year."

"And has it motivated you?"

"No," he answered.

She laughed out loud, throwing her head back.

They stopped at a roadside restaurant in Palm Springs that had green plastic tables and plastic trees in pots. When she took off her sunglasses David noticed her dark eyes above the small, pointed chin. She pushed the stiff pages of the tabletop jukebox selector.

"I'm twenty-seven if that's what you're wondering," she said. "My name's Joyce."

"David. I wasn't wondering that," he lied.

"I'm from Yuma," she continued. "Married my high school sweetheart when I was eighteen and divorced him when I was twenty. That football hero needed to grow up."

A man, woman, and two little girls with their hair in pony tails pulled out the plastic chairs and sat at a table in the middle of the floor.

Joyce fished a pack of Salems and a lighter out of her canvas bag. She drew a cigarette out, offered David the pack, and put it back into the bag when he shook his head. Then she lit her own, turned her head, and blew smoke into the air.

"Married an older man two years later. Owned a car dealership. I was a salesgirl in a department store in San Diego. Went there thinking it might be exciting." She rolled her eyes. "It wasn't."

"What happened to him?" David asked, hoping he was not the one prying this time.

"Divorced him after four years. What a jerk. I'm going to be more cautious from now on. Got that car out of it, though. Maybe he was good for something." David liked her honesty. He knew few people who'd been divorced once, let alone twice, and they never talked about it.

She ordered a BLT with a Coke, he a burger, fries, and coffee, thinking he hadn't eaten a full meal since the man in Estes Park bought him lunch.

"I was going with a Marine stationed at Pendleton," she continued. "Seemed like my type, but I was wrong. Maybe it was the uniform I liked rather than him." She smiled and sucked Coke through the straw, then stirred the melting ice. She wiped her mouth on the paper napkin and laid it, covered with lipstick, on the table.

"I'm a cocktail waitress in a bar in Irvine now," she went on.

"How do you like it?" he asked.

She laughed. "What are the alternatives? Receptionist? Salesgirl? I make more money in the cocktail lounge. It's the kind of place where married lawyers and doctors bring their girlfriends, and they tip *big*." He smelled the menthol from the cigarette smoke trailing away from the table into the artificially cooled air.

She pushed a quarter into the slot on the jukebox selector and pressed two buttons, after which Mel Carter's voice singing "Hold Me, Thrill Me, Kiss Me" mingled with the customers' talk.

Suddenly David liked her, sensing that for all her casual poise she felt alone as he did, but she was worldly-wise and responsible for herself. He picked up the check when the waitress laid it on the table in front of him.

"I didn't give you a lift in order to wheedle lunch out of you," she said. "But you can pay this time. Gotta use the rest room."

As they stood she took one of the small white paper napkins, wrote something on it with a ball-point pen, and thrust it into her canvas bag before heading across the room for the pink door with the picture of Olive Oil on it. David headed for the blue door with Popeye. He was waiting for her when she came out. She had freshened her lipstick but wore no other make-up.

When they approached Los Angeles she focused on the traffic that weaved crazily across lanes without signaling on the largest highway David had ever seen. Joyce insisted on driving him all the way to the base in Long Beach and pulled up in front of the gate. With the engine still running, she shifted the gear into park, turned toward him, and extended her small hand. After he shook it she placed in his palm the napkin she'd written on in the restaurant.

"Here's my phone number," she said. "If you want to get together, call me. Good luck."

"Thanks," he said, "and thanks for the lift," shoving the napkin into his pocket and getting out. He opened the back door, lifted his sea bag out, and slammed the door shut. She waved as she pulled the Mustang out onto the street. He watched the white car with California plates disappear into the stream of traffic.

✶ ✶ ✶   ✶ ✶ ✶   ✶ ✶ ✶

"Hello?"

"Hi, this is David. David Shields," he repeated after a pause in which he thought she might be trying to remember who he was.

"Yes, of course. I gave you a lift to Long Beach. That was weeks ago."

"I'm sorry I haven't called, but you know they keep us pretty busy here." Actually, he'd been debating with himself whether to get involved with her. "I have twenty-four hours, and I thought you might like to go out."

"Where are you?"

"A phone booth on the base."

"Why didn't you give me a little warning?"

She had him there.

"I'm sorry. You're right. I should have called earlier."

"I'll pick you up in front of the gate where I left you off."

An hour and fifteen minutes later he saw her white Mustang pull out of traffic. They drove to a Mexican restaurant in Long Beach that she described as "authentic" where the male owner in a spangled white-and-gold costume played a guitar and walked around the tables singing gaucho songs while his plump, dark-haired senora communicated orders in Spanish to the young waiters and waitresses, who were probably their children or nieces and nephews, and the cook, probably the owner's brother or sister.

Joyce recommended the enchiladas, so he ordered those and then looked at her sitting with her fingers crossed. She had brushed her hair forward around her face, and she wore black polyester slacks and a low-cut white chiffon blouse that still didn't reveal much of her chest. She used much more make-up than she had when he first saw her—foundation that made her skin look darker, pink blush, blue eye shadow, and lipstick.

"Tell me what you've been doing," she said, lighting a cigarette.

"The captain promoted me right away and chose me for his pistol team," he began. "It's a good assignment, but I'm a little concerned."

"About what?"

"There's this racial thing. Boot camp was completely integrated. I didn't think anything about it when my class in electronics was all white. Here it seems like all the guys on the upper decks are white, and all the boiler techs, firemen, and ship fitters with the dirtiest jobs on the lower decks are all Negroes or Mexicans. The captain told some of the ETs we were going to get top-secret clearances, and every one of us is white. We all got promoted to E-4."

"Congratulations," she said, switching the cigarette to her left hand and tapping it on the side of the glass ashtray. "You know, the Negro fellows may want things that way."

"Maybe, but I noticed it first when we chose up sides for a basketball game and one side was all white and the others all Negro. It was tense."

"Why don't you invite some of the Negro guys to play basketball with you?" she asked.   "I thought of that," he answered, "but I'm not sure they'd accept me."

"There were some bad riots in LA last summer, you know. Did you hear about it back East?"

"Yeah, we did," he said, amused at her description of half the country. "Anyway, enough about that. What are you doing?"

She was still working in the same cocktail lounge making, she said, pretty good money; what she didn't like was one of her regulars, a married salesman in his forties, coming on to her.

David saw her several more weekends when he managed to get a liberty; the sailors he hung out with started ribbing him about having a girlfriend. Each time she picked him up in her Mustang and brought him back to the base, and once two guys he knew hung around the gate to get a look at her. After David and Joyce had been out four times she asked him back to her place. She lived in a townhouse bought with a settlement from her second divorce, small but well furnished with a living room and kitchen downstairs and two bedrooms up. She brought him a whiskey and soda. He didn't like the way she left lipstick on every glass she used, and he wondered whether she expected to have a long-term relationship with him—who could not imagine himself falling in love with a woman seven years older than he was. But he forgot his reservations as he kissed her. They walked upstairs to the bedroom and began undressing each other, he to his shorts and she to her bra and panties. Then as he guided her to the bed she slipped out of his grasp.

"Catch me," she said, dashing out the door and down the steps. He followed her into the living room where she'd drawn the blinds and when he began to get close she ran into the kitchen and around the table.

"Come on, Joyce, what's this all about?" he said.

She laughed out loud and ran for the stairs again. He caught her hand, but she pulled away and ran into the bedroom.

"Joyce, this is infantile," he said.

"Is it?" she asked calmly. Then she walked up to him and when he put his arms around her she pushed him hard. As he regained his balance she ran behind him and started pulling his briefs down. She unfastened her bra, then pushed him, laughing, onto the bed, and ran behind the door.

"Joyce, what are you doing?" he asked, sitting up.

She jumped naked from behind the door, threw her panties at his head, and straddled his lap as she pressed her lips to his.

Seen from the naval training center they called Treasure Island, San Francisco appeared white. In the haze to the west the magenta bridge spanned the strait between the city and the hills to the north. Waves washed the huge black rocks along the edge of the island, and cold wind gusted from across the water even on hot days. Gulls lighted on the rails of the piers, pelicans dove straight in, Canada geese foraged on grassy patches, and black and white murres floated on the waves, so close to shore he could hear their chirring. A cormorant perched like a sentinel on a rock. Palm trees lined the western and eastern shorelines. Angel Island to the north erupted from the water like a floating jungle.

You couldn't escape history here: the curving façade of the Comwest Seafron building with long, vertical windows and statue of bare-breasted Pacifica reminded David that this place had been constructed for a world's fair. Behind it, across the causeway, a gray World War II-vintage torpedo hut stood on the shore of Yerba Buena. The whole thing was like a village except that all the buildings were painted the same uniform cream color. From the athletic fields close to the northern shore you could look across the water and see the Berkeley campanile.

After three months at Long Beach he had been transferred to Alameda and the carrier *Loyola*. His officer at Long Beach petitioned Navpac to keep David there, but even the captain was overruled. From the window of the military plane flying from Long Beach, he watched the land convoluting itself into the snow-capped Sierra Nevada and the dry coastal range before the aircraft dropped altitude, banked, and circled over high buildings, wooded hills, and the wide waters of the bay that shone like blue flame. At Alameda they demoted him to E-3, Seaman, the division commander saying he had to re-earn the promotion to E-4. David spent most of his time there and at Hunters' Point shipyard except when command sent him to Treasure Island for training.

Joyce hadn't seemed too disappointed when he told her about his transfer. Maybe she couldn't imagine any more than he could a long-term relationship with somebody so much younger than she was, or maybe she was trying to make it easy for him. He'd never asked her about birth control. The thought occurred to him that a few nights' extravagance could have changed his life fundamentally, whether for good or bad he didn't know. Anyway, she knew where he was going; if something happened she'd be able to find him easily enough. He missed her a little.

When he first arrived in San Francisco he navigated his way through the city, took long walks in Chinatown and the Mission district, hiked down Columbus Avenue all the way to the wharves, followed the drive along the coast at the Presidio taking in the buttery smell of eucalyptus trees, and walked along Haight near the park, imagining what his life might have been had he not joined the Navy.

With other seamen including Tim, David started going to the Fillmore and Winterland, dropping tabs they bought in the Haight before going inside. The music wasn't the ordinary commercialized rock-n-roll but had a slowed and distorted rhythm that played with the audience's sense of time. David felt as if he were finding his way across a ship's deck in heavy fog where the air was full of different colors; the wind blew through rather than around him, and sound was an ocean of color that might dissolve him into itself. He imagined a rope guiding him through the purple fog safely toward the gangplank where he could walk to a place where the air was clear, where time still passed in minutes and seconds, and his sense of who he was still seemed connected to the earlier parts of his life—even when he decided he never wanted to go back to the solid world anyway. Although he feared his mind would disassemble itself and float away, he knew the drug eventually wore off. If he forgot that, things could become disorienting and even scary: he might enter the strange places hidden away in his memory, places he didn't want to be stranded in. Sensual rhythms led him through weird hollow places, morphed into colorful liquid air, and dredged up forgotten moods until he'd forget where he was. The songs seemed to last an eternity, but they always brought him back to where he'd started. At last he was really hearing this music: feedback, drums in the echo chamber, and tambourines in the foreground in alternate beats made all time reverberate inside that auditorium. The singer held the last note a long time, her voice undulating like a wave across the surface of some vast, turbulent sea.

It was a world of water, not of land; the idea of land seemed a fantasy now as life before the Navy seemed like a story about someone else. In fair weather the sea was gray-silver or green, but during storms the water turned dark plum and smashed ominously against the hull. You couldn't tell direction without a compass, because the surface all looked the same. Sometimes a school of dolphins sliced through the waves, and once the smooth, dark back of a whale emerged and then the great body surfaced as sea water flowed off it like a waterfall before it dove, raising its magnificent fluke which plunged at last. David felt like diving over the side and swimming after the huge, beautiful creature.

The flight deck was a floating runway, the lower decks a great factory-city of forty-five hundred men; the ship was like a queen bee surrounded by her sycophants—a fighter jet, two destroyers, and a sub. The men lived above magazines full of bombs; even the galley where they ate, talked, and argued lay right above more firepower than all the Allied and Axis powers unleashed in World War II. The frigate in Long Beach had stood in dry dock the whole time David served on it, rigged up on joists, sailors swarming all over it, yard birds welding on it with their torches. The carrier stretched nine hundred feet long and two hundred-fifty feet wide, awe-inspiring when he walked to the gangplank and asked the officer of the day for permission to come aboard. Thirty A-4s in two rows rode the back of the flight deck, like wasps on the metal gutters of the old farmhouse where David grew up, and forty more were parked in the hangar deck. He was six feet tall and had to duck to go through hatches, but he felt like an insect crawling through the ship's cavernous interior.

Sixty of them slept in one compartment on thirty-inch-wide canvas mattresses lashed with ropes to aluminum frames. David slept on the lowest of three tiers, the bottom of the mattress above him hanging eighteen inches from his chest. Thirty-inch cubicles with combination locks held everything the men owned. He usually had no trouble sleeping even during rough weather because of the rocking motion of the water. Still, in a recurring nightmare he checked onto another carrier and stowed his sea bag only to find the ship deserted, its bulkhead an open shell with moonlight throwing eerie blue luminescent shadows off the metal while he ran frantically, looking for a way to cast himself into the sea. One night the heat became so intense he rolled out of his bunk and was out the hatch, up the ladders, and onto the flight deck before he was fully awake. The white A-4s parked forward shone dull gray in the moonlight.

David walked toward them. The full moon, at two o'clock to portside, rained silver from the horizon to the shadow the ship cast onto the water. The enormous black form of the tower, its radar equipment curving outward like giant wings, blocked out part of the sky. At starboard David could see Orion's belt and the Dipper standing on its handle above the water. The night was quiet, unlike the days filled with endless noise. As he watched the sky, a meteorite fell, its silver tail curving behind it and disappearing into the darkness.

A bridge across the stream they called Shit River separated the American world of the base at Subic Bay from the city of Olongapo. Sailors and Marines on their way over the bridge threw coins into the sewage where little naked boys about nine or ten with dark brown skin and eyes and supple limbs dove in after them and scrambled out again with their prizes. In San Francisco black men and Mexicans cleaned up the trash and swept the streets; in Honolulu the native Hawaiians did; here the Filipino men worked the jobs no one else wanted. Everyone seemed to work for the Navy: older men labored as janitors on the base; younger ones served as orderlies for officers; their daughters walked the city streets in the evening or kept house for Navy men who rented cheap flats while they were in port.

Sailors didn't need barmen to find women for them. With their black hair teased bouffant-style, the girls stood outside the doors and called to the men as they got out of the jeepney busses or taxis. Their forwardness put David off, but one barman who spoke very good English offered him a room for an hour and said he would send a woman around, and David said that would be okay. The rooms turned out to be lean-to sheds of bamboo thatch with canvas blinds pulled all the way down. The mattress, covered by a thin sheet, stood a few inches off the floor. David sat down on it and waited until the door opened and a slender young woman stepped inside. Without a greeting or even smiling at him she kicked off her beige loafers, untied a wrap-around white dress with designs of tiny purple flowers, and began to take off her white bra. Unfastening the hooks for her, he ran his hand down her long, straight hair, but before he could do anything else she pulled her panties off and lay down naked on the bed. He wasn't a boy anymore; he knew what to do, but he found the experience empty, like death, not life, more isolating than being alone. He paid her what she asked and watched her fold the bills and tuck them into her bra before she re-tied her dress, stepped into her loafers, and closed the door behind her.

The next afternoon David followed one of the streets of Olongapo up a hill and out of town until the road narrowed into broken stone and ruts pitted by the hooves of carabao. Brown monkeys ran across the road the way rabbits did in Ohio. Palm trees and thick foliage rose from the water's edge and covered the hills surrounding the city, swathed in mist toward the top. The water in the lagoon was glassy clear and smooth. Following a lane farther up the hill David saw a girl, dressed in loose trousers and white blouse, hoeing in a garden, her long hair tied at the back of her neck with red yarn. She did not see David watching her—the kind of girl he would never get to know without the entire family present—only a few miles from the city where her sisters or cousins sold themselves daily to American sailors.

The next evening David and his friends took a jeepney into town. It was red and had the name "Wilt Chamberlain" painted on it. The driver weaved in and out of traffic on Magsaysay to Rizal Plaza where the signs were written in English and dropped them off at a bar decorated with green neon palm trees.

Music from the jukebox blended with voices.

"Those candy asses on supply ships don't know what the Navy's all about," a man said at the next table where some guys from a destroyer were sitting.

"Shove it up your ass," a man shouted from another table.

"You aren't man enough to shove your prick in a hole."

"You shove it in your ear."

The two crews stood up.

"Hey, cut this out," a sailor from the *Loyola* said, stepping over to them.

"We're all on the same side."

"Carrier crews are pussies tied to their mother's apron strings," the first man snarled. "That's why you have to have an escort." The sailor decked him.

Someone overturned a table, spilling drinks and shattering glass on the floor, and the two crews went at each other. David and Tim headed for the back exit, but when a man called Tim a nigger, David pulled the guy off balance and landed a fist in his stomach. To David's surprise, the drunken man sank to the floor. The night had been fun, but they'd had enough; Tim and David headed for the back door and were outside in the dark, humid night of Olongapo where insects sent up a constant hum. The stink outside seemed fresh after the smoky air of the bar.

He and Tim found another place that was quieter but crowded. The only empty chairs were in the back where a corporal and PFC not much older than eighteen were drinking San Miguels.

"Those ROKs, man, they're the real fighters," the corporal said. "We had to pick some of them up at Da Nang, and after they got out the whole damn truck smelled like fish. But I'd never want to tangle with them. Those guys mean business, man. Let *them* fight the VC."

"What exactly are we doing there anyway?" the PFC asked no one in particular. "There's more of us than ARVN regulars. Rice farmers in grass hooches don't want us there. They know where the mines are, but they won't tell you."

"You take territory and the VC take it back the next week," the corporal said. "I know one thing: somebody's getting awful rich off this war."

"I was in the Mekong," the PFC continued, "there wasn't even supposed to be any VC in the area, not that you can rely on shitty Army intelligence. A patrol had us pinned down for an hour before we got any air cover. When the bombs hit, the ground shakes so bad you think your head is coming off.

"After it was all over I found my buddy laying under a tree same as if he'd been sleeping, only he'd been blown open and his intestines splattered all over the ground and the grass all around him red. There was blood three feet away from him. And his head was blown open and I could see his brains oozing out of his skull." David started to reach for the boy's shoulder, but Tim's eyes warned him not to. Infantrymen normally didn't talk like this to sailors.

"Thing of it was," the boy kept on, even when his friend elbowed him in the ribs, "his eyes were still open, staring straight ahead, and his mouth open like he was getting ready to say something."

He swallowed the rest of his beer and set the glass on the table, raising the back of his hand to his mouth, choking.

"We're going back there," he said. "That's where we're going."

The roughest water surged in the South China Sea where storms dogged them for two days. Food trays in the galley slid against the ridges on the tables and clattered in the slots. Gray downspouts from the steel-colored sky kicked up waves that blocked the destroyer from view, but the carrier's length stabilized it. Rocking on the summit of two waves at once, it shivered rather than pitched before it fell into the trough.

Once during a storm a man who'd gone up to the catwalk to watch the storm had been washed overboard. Did that poor guy know he was being swept over, or was he knocked unconscious and drowned instantly by the wave? David gripped the rail and watched water rise above the flight deck and wash over the runway like a strong river. They might think they were safe in this citadel of power, but if that ocean decided to, it could swallow them in an instant.

The sea boiled below him.

They were kept in a weapons storage area well below the magazines for conventional bombs, in a compartment that was clean and waxed with tile floors and white walls, a quiet place most of the crew didn't even know about. They were about six feet long, torpedo-shaped, and much bigger around than even thousand-pounders; some had shiny coverings like stainless steel while others had smooth white skin like the finish of appliances. They rested on racks bolted to the deck, about forty in every compartment, each one at least a hundred times more powerful than the ones they dropped on Hiroshima and Nagasaki. The men in W Division who worked down there had orders not to talk about what they did or what was stored here, especially when they docked at Yokohama and Sasebo, because Japan didn't allow nuclear weapons inside its territory.

David and eight other ETs spent almost all their time there now, cleaning and painting the walls and buffing and waxing the floor, although a rumor circulated they were going to be trained for special weapons technology. At last they figured out why they'd been transferred here, though the work was a waste of their training: they were here to fill billets; the Navy needed janitors with top-secret clearances. David lowered himself down a long ladder three or four decks below the hangar and passed through a door where a Marine sentry sat silently in a cage watching everyone who came or went to the world above. The eerie feeling wore off after a few days: David knew the bombs, which seemed almost like sleeping things, were harmless as they lay here. Politicians and Joint Chiefs claimed the military could respond to a nuclear attack within fifteen minutes, but all the men knew it took a series of regulated steps and one to three days to arm these weapons.

The Navy posters read "ARE YOU MAN ENOUGH?" but the biggest challenge the men faced was boredom. There was so little to do that work usually finished early, sometimes by eleven in the morning, and the men played cards, listened to music, read books they got from the library, or sat around telling each other stories. Except for his friends Mark and Craig, David had never heard men put their feelings into words. These sailors talked the way women did, confiding in each other about things they would never have said on the outside.

"I think she's cut me completely out of her life," an ET named Duncan said bitterly. "After saying she'd wait for me."

"How do you know?" Hammond said. "Maybe she just isn't good about writing."

"She isn't, but I know because my sister wrote me that she saw her at the new mall, and she wasn't just shopping. She was drinking Coke with some guy."

"Maybe your sister saw a girl who looked like her."

"I don't think so. They were in the same class and band together."
Duncan was a small towner from someplace in Nebraska.

"At least she's alive," Hammond said.

"What's that to me?" Duncan answered, jabbing a penknife into a block
of wood.

Hammond didn't answer for a long time.

"What's wrong, Carl?" David asked finally.

Hammond ran his hand across the top of his head and cupped it around
the back of his neck. He tilted his chair back against the wall. He was a smaller
guy with round, red cheeks.

"My girlfriend was riding with me in this van my father had," he began.
"We had just went to the movies. My dad didn't like me driving around alone
with her so we took another couple, and they were sitting in the back, making
out. It was dark, and we didn't just go straight home, we decided to go to this
place we knew. We weren't going to do anything but make out a little. What
could we do with four people in the van?

"And so we were driving," he continued, "and I looked back to see if my
buddy was getting anywhere, and when I turned I looked at Melody—that was
her name—and right then we hit this big pothole. Michigan's full of potholes,
but this one was deep, at the side where the asphalt caved in, and I hadn't seen
it because it was dark and we were on a country road."

He drew a deep breath and righted his chair. Everyone in the room was
listening now.

"The van flipped and rolled down this embankment, and everybody got
thrown around. And it was laying there on its side with all the glass smashed
out of the windows and the wheels still spinning when I climbed out."

He was silent then.

"What happened?" David asked.

"The other guy got all bruised and cut up, like I did, and the other girl broke her arm."

"And what about Melody?"

"Her head was bashed in and her neck was broken. She died right away."

He was wiping his cheeks with his palms.

"That old van didn't have seat belts. If I hadn't looked around maybe it wouldn't have happened. If we'd gone straight home…"

David put his hand on Hammond's shoulder. "Could happen to anybody, Carl. Wasn't your fault."

"I wasn't even cited. They said it was an accident. The others testified I was driving carefully and not speeding, which I wasn't. But my dad was so mad at me, he wasn't concerned about her *or* me, he was worried her family'd sue us, and he wouldn't let me drive after that and he kept on at me how much we'd have to pay if they sued.

"So one day when he was yelling at me I just walked out of the house, drove to the recruiting station, and signed up for the Navy so I could be away as long as possible."

Hammond rubbed his eyes with the backs of his hands.

"We'd just graduated," he said. "She was only eighteen."

Light blazed from between dark clouds on the horizon. David was on the 07 deck in the tower looking over the water; he'd been assigned to the electronics workshop that day and was finishing up. A Marine Seahorse hovered toward the aft end, spraying white water in a circle below it, while two escort destroyers cruised about a half mile behind. A man wearing a white hood leaned out the window as the chopper put down on the flight deck. David saw the chopper wobble, rise about ten feet off the deck, roll belly up in the air, and in the next instant fall back, nose up, over the stern into the water, sending up white spray. Three wheels had found the runway, but the fourth must have missed the edge. The man who'd been visible at the window waved his arms. Water splashed over the deck, and a piece of metal flew up and twirled in the air before falling into the sea. The siren blared and the flight crew ran shouting to the lifeline, but the chopper disappeared under the surface.

The walls of the room where G Division assembled the conventional bombs, unlike the gray walls of the rest of the ship, were painted blood red, like the insides of a gutted deer. Shifts lasted twelve hours during operations, from seven until seven, far below the flight deck and above the magazine where they stored the olive-green steel cylinders with yellow cones on the ends—three five-hundred-pounders, two seven-fifties, or one thousand-pounder to an orange skid. Each cylinder had two steel eye fittings hung on yellow, electrically controlled latching brackets underneath the wings of the planes. When the pilot released the latch, the bombs fell. An A4 carried four clusters of three two-fifties or two five-hundreds.

During operations there was a launch every hour and a half. Watching from the operations room in the tower or on the monitor in the electronics workshop, David saw the planes roll out onto the flight deck where red shirts, picking their way among lau pods, mounted the bombs, and green shirts strapped the wheels to the catapult. The Jet Blast Deflector rose through the deck, cooled with sea water to keep the thirty-foot jet-engine flame from burning it to cinders. The yellow-shirted gunner's mate signaled to the pilot, and JATO snapped the aircraft out over the bow and the wide gray water of the Gulf. Everyone all over the ship could feel it lurch forward. With only one hundred yards to get the plane going six hundred miles per hour, the engines roared one continuous blast as they shot bright red flames out the back, making the air boil. During operations they took off at twenty-five to thirty knots into the wind and flew fast enough to overtake a missile they themselves had fired. When they landed, the planes slammed onto the angled deck so hard the whole gigantic carrier shuddered with the impact. If everything went right, retaining cables caught the tail hook and the fuselage jerked back, trembling like a bronco in the chute.

Details in G Division were supposed to be a bad draw for someone usually assigned to W, but David reminded himself he was doing this for the guys on the ground, and it was more interesting than custodial work. He lowered himself through the hatch to the magazine and laid his hands on a sixty-five-pound gray metal fin. With his left hand he gripped the front of the fin and put his right against the back, aimed at the hole, and sent the fin through to the deck. He grasped another, lifted it about waist high, hoisted it through with all his strength, and bent to pick up another one.

When all the fins were up David climbed out of the magazine and took his place with two other men leaning over the cylinder strapped to the skid. With a spanner wrench he twisted off the seven-inch pointer and laid it on the floor. Then he screwed the booster charge, a shiny cylinder about the size of a large soup can, into the hollow nose inside the yellow cone. The fuses, small cylinders with propellers that looked like beanie caps with spinners, were thrown into a crate and sent with the bombs up to the flight deck where red shirts screwed them into the hole in the booster charge connected to the detonator. Set for a certain number of rotations, propellers ignited the fuse, the booster charge went off with about half the force of a hand grenade, and the bomb exploded. Bombs with small fins fell fastest, while these with the umbrellas fell more slowly and went off above the ground. When the Chief ordered the pointers left on, the men knew the bombs were meant to penetrate the ground before they exploded, probably to blow up buildings. Usually the men were not told what the operation was, but once, when the Chief asked for a thousand-pounder, he said command wanted to take out a concrete bridge. The ones they were building today were anti-personnel weapons. With their booster charges and fins they almost looked alive.

In less than an hour six men assembled three bombs; they pulled the skids forward and stepped over to the next one where three more cylinders lay waiting. When they finished twelve bombs they pulled the skids down to the elevators. With both hands David turned the nine levers they called dogs; then he and another man lowered the door to reveal the dark interior that looked like a giant oven. They rolled the heavy skids into the elevator, lifted the door, and pulled the dogs back into place as the hydraulic lift clanked against the metal casing toward the flight deck.

He watched the monitor in the electronics workshop as the planes came in one by one; they had taken fire and one of them banked in a little off center. Even as it approached the stern, he realized it was too low and leaped off the stool, his arms stretched in front of him as if he could catch it. The white Skyhawk hit the round down and exploded into red and yellow flame. The fuselage split in two and spiraled down the runway slinging aviation fuel all over the flight deck, igniting a blanket of fire that spread from the island to the stern. At least six times a day the fire alarm went off, usually for some fire that got put out right away, but this time it looked serious. Though the siren blared for GQ and men ran shouting across the deck and down the ladder, David stood mesmerized, watching the monitor as the Damage Control men in their flame-proof yellow suits dragged hoses from nowhere and ran into the inferno, foaming the deck as the fire leaped above their heads, a funnel-cloud of black smoke engulfing the deck and swirling out over the gray water. In minutes they smothered the flames and walked around like space men pulling the hoses off the flight deck. Nobody was injured, but the pilot had been incinerated when the nose of the plane hit the stern.

David was playing poker with Carothers, Henderson, and Hammond in the lounge in W.

"I don't know anything," Hammond said about a rumor that was going around, "except they were in Tonkin, and two guys were tossing flares back and forth and the ship caught fire."

"But how'd it happen?" Henderson asked. "What kind of idiot plays with flares?"

"I've been on pyrotech," David said. "It's easy to start those flares; you just pull the lanyard and the thing fires. It's magnesium—hot enough burn through metal. The flare has to be able to burn in water so if a pilot goes under you can spot him."

"When you were on pyro, you ever see anyone go down?" Hammond asked.

"No."

"I heard one of the flares caught and to hide what they did those guys threw the thing into a locker that was already full of flares," Hammond went on. "The fire burned a hole in the bulkhead and choked the whole forward half of the ship."

"It was a third of the ship," Henderson said, "and forty-five guys died. Smoke came through the ventilating system and fireballs exploded all around."

"I heard white magnesium fell like rain in the hangar deck," David said.

Brownlee strode through the door and sank onto the gray vinyl couch.

"Goddamn sons of bitches," he muttered.

"Who?" Hammond asked, looking up.

"Damn lifers. Bastard just told me a man doesn't shine the back of his shoes doesn't clean his ass." When no one responded he said, "They don't know shit."

"Why do you say that?" Hammond asked. He folded his hand. "I'm out."

"In the other life did you ever run into a real combat veteran who invited you home to help him shine his medals?" Brownlee asked.

"I never heard a lifer say that."

"I mean the ones always bragging about their combat experience. Not literally invite you home. Shit, most of them are ashamed to go home. They can't even get along with their wives."

"You know, you're right," Henderson said, throwing his cards in.

"My seventh grade math teacher was always carrying on about being a veteran and how he was going to make real men out of us," Brownlee continued. "He was the teacher they always called on when somebody needed whacked. He wielded that paddle like he was some kind of mean shit. Walked around bellowing like he was the toughest shit on earth. One day, he grabbed a kid who was a minute late for class and threw him clear across the room into the opposite wall. Kid was half his size. Well, he went and picked the kid up and shoved him back across the room into the other wall, all the time yelling about how he was going to make men out of us and how *he* was in charge of the classroom, not some snotty nosed imbecile."

"How'd he get away with that?" Hammond asked, tilting his chair back.

"Maybe the kid's parents didn't care. Principal didn't give a shit. So one day a friend of mine asked another teacher what it was this guy did in the war, and the other teacher told him the guy never left stateside; the war was over by the time he got drafted—drafted, he hadn't joined."

"Look at Ramsche," Henderson said. "When he eventually gets out—and they'll have to kick him out—would he want his buddies to know his nickname in the service was 'shithead'? I wonder what bullshit story he'll make up to tell his family?"

"Damn fuck, you guys are depressing me," Carothers said, laying his cards out. "Full house."

"Damn," Henderson said, watching Carothers scoop up the mound of change.

"What did you know about the service before you enlisted?" Brownlee asked no one in particular.

"War movies," Hammond answered.

"Recruiting posters," David said.

"All the same bullshit fairy tale, wasn't it?" Brownlee said.

"Hey, the U.S. won World War II, didn't we?" Carothers persisted.

"If you ask me, we got caught with our pants down at Pearl Harbor and Guam," David said. "MacArthur ran."

"Don't you believe in anything?" Carothers asked Brownlee, scooting his chair back from the table.

"Yeah! I believe in real sacrifice," Brownlee answered. "Real heroism is a guy shitting himself after wiping his buddy's brains off his face and still throwing his grenade at the VC heading right for him. You ever see John Wayne shit himself?"

"No," Henderson said. "I don't want to either."

"But they had to make up that stuff they show in the movies," Hammond said. "They couldn't have cameras all over the Pacific."

"They had newsreel footage," David said.

"But in those days reporters weren't allowed to write about American losses," Henderson explained. "My mother told me a lot of the stuff on the newsreels was propaganda; she knew because she worked in an office in Fort Bragg. I told her that made us no better than the Russians, and she said I sounded like a traitor. Nobody tells the real story. Not then, not now."

"So what have the movies got to do with it?" Hammond asked.

"I just know John Wayne wasn't in it," Brownlee said. "He was never in combat. He just made a bundle pretending he was. The hardest thing he ever had to do was try to make his uniform look dirty in front of some fake battle scene."

"Deal," Hammond said to Carothers, running his hand across his head.

"John Wayne and Ronald Reagan are phony butt wipes like Ramsche and my seventh grade math teacher—only richer, the bastards," Brownlee said. "And so is MacArthur. I'm glad Truman canned his ass."

"So what do you know about combat?" Carothers asked, shuffling the cards. "Another game?"

Henderson nodded.

"Nothing, but I don't pretend like I do, either," Brownlee intoned. "We're lucky here in a way. Lots of food, lots of leisure except when they're bombing the shit out of the VC, no real threat to us unless we're dumb enough to fall off the goddamned catwalk. But these lifers and those fucking actors, they don't know anything about it either. They bullshit and primp around and gas about the real Navy, the real war—most of them never been in one—and talk about when the ships were made of wood and the men were made of iron, but what the fuck do they know?"

"You really can't stand those guys, can you?" Hammond asked.

"Brownlee's right," David said. "Who would you trust your life to in combat? One of these lifers, or a drafted enlisted man? When the shit hits the fan, do you want the bullshitter you see on the recruiting posters, or would you rather have your friend to fall back on?"

"What about the guys over in the bush?" Carothers insisted. "Aren't we helping them with air support? Somebody's got to cover their asses."

"Most of the time we sit here and play poker while those guys watch their buddies die and wonder when it's going to be their turn," David said, picking up the cards he'd been dealt.

"You think you'd last in combat?" Carothers asked.

"Nobody knows how they'd do in combat," David responded. "That's one of those things you don't know till you're in it. Every guy wonders just that—would I run scared, or would I stand up for my buddies?"

"I think if we were in combat we'd handle it better than these fat, lazy-ass lifers," Brownlee insisted. "They'd be standing around waiting for the Hollywood music to start."

"You're pretty hard on them," Hammond said, bringing the front legs of his chair to the floor. "You don't know what they've been through."

"Yeah, the guys over there would be pissed off if they heard us bitching and complaining about being too safe and bored while their asses are getting shot off," Henderson asserted.

"I didn't join the fucking Navy to put my life in the hands of people like Ramsche," Brownlee said. "If something bad happens to me I want it to be for something real—not all this phony made-up bullshit. Jesus Christ! Even Shithead deserves better than that. Hell, our lives are decaying, and they couldn't even write a decent story about us."

"You don't believe in protecting the country?" Carothers asked.

"You think that if we weren't here in this godforsaken Iron Dungeon the VC would be overrunning San Francisco?" Brownlee asked.

"It's more complicated than that. If we didn't protect the Philippines, China would invade."

"Oh for god's sake will you cut that crap out?" David interrupted. "We aren't protecting the Philippines. You saw what it's like in Subic. Every poor dumbass works for the goddamned Navy—including the women. Things are better in Japan because we occupied it but never completely took over."

"The Flips are getting their share from us," Carothers insisted.

"How the hell do you figure that?" David replied. "If we weren't there, maybe those people would have real jobs, a real life."

"Pigs and pineapples is all they'd have. If we're fucking the Flips so bad, why don't they kick us out?"

"Oh, yeah, right, the Flips are going to kick Uncle Sam out of his precious military bases and live to tell the story," Brownlee said, rolling his eyes. "Right."

"They helped us in World War II," Hammond said.

"Sure they did. That was a real war, not a phony one like Vietnam," Brownlee said. "Every army and navy in the world was involved in that one, every pair of hands that could work and every spare plane and jeep they could confiscate. People joined up, and they knew what they were fighting for, or against. And the whole thing was over in four years."

"Six," David interjected.

"Okay, longer. Now here we are, this big fucking superpower, and this shit's been dragging on since 1954. Now why do you suppose that is?"

"I get the feeling you're going to tell us," Hammond said.

"Damn fucking right I am!" Brownlee shouted. "This is not about survival or self-defense. It's all political bullshit, and we, and those poor grunts getting their asses shot off over in the rice paddies, are the ones paying for it. And the pigs' asses on top of the pile, the ones making the decisions? They aren't Ramsche or any phony dumbass lifer. They're getting richer and richer the longer this stupid war drags on. So what does that make us? Heroes or stooges?"

"You really believe that?" Carothers asked.

"Tell me, I mean really tell me the truth now," David said, looking at Carothers. "Do you honestly feel what we're doing is protecting the U.S. from some kind of invasion or something? Do you really think that corrupt bunch of shit in Saigon is going to bring democracy to Southeast Asia? Then you tell me why it's taking us ten years to defeat the VC when all they've got is what they collect off our dead guys."

"They're getting it from Russia," Carothers said. "And it's taking so long because the politicians don't let the generals have free rein."

"Oh, come on, man," David answered Carothers. "You watch forty planes take off, each one of them with three thousand pounds of explosives under their wings, and come back with zero. What do you think they're doing with it all? Target practice? We're pounding the hell out of those bastards and they just go underground and come right back out when we're done. Because to them it's a war for their homeland, just like we'd feel if we really were attacked. We say we're giving them a break for Tet, but you know as well as I do we bombed their asses all during Tet. Don't tell me the generals don't have free rein. We're pounding the VC for all they're worth. We're killing them to save the egos of a bunch of politicians, and we're getting our own guys killed for nothing."

"Doesn't it make you proud?" Henderson asked.

"I'm going to Gedunk," Hammond said. "Anybody want anything?"

"Gotta go to the head," Brownlee declared, standing up and stretching.

Henderson, Hammond, Ramsche, and David watched the landings on closed-circuit television in the operations room. The planes had been out about three hours: two were back in.   An A4 banked in from the north and headed across the water toward the ship, tail hook suspended. The wheels slammed onto the deck, the cable caught, and the plane skidded to a halt just before the end, smoke rising behind it.

"Nice one," Ramsche said. "Wonder where they've been."

"Over Haiphong Harbor, probably," Hammond said.

"Where's that?"

"Where the enemy keeps his guerrillas. Do you even know who we're fighting?" Henderson asked.

"The Vietnamese. And the Red Chinese," Ramsche answered.

"Yes, but the North or South Vietnamese? And the idea is to keep the Chinese *out*," David said.

"I don't know."

"Then why are we fighting them?" David asked.

"I don't know that either," Ramsche responded. "I know I have two hundred eighty days to go. That's what I know. What I don't know is why we don't just mine their harbors and get rid of their navy."

"They don't have a navy," David said.

"Damn good thing for us," Ramsche answered.

"Another one coming in," Hammond alerted them.

The plane banked, heading for the stern. Black and white smoke trailed out the back and disappeared into the hazy gray air above the water.

"Perfect," Osborne said.

The wheels hit and the A4 headed toward the angled runway, but the men did not see the fuselage jerk with the force of the cable. Instead it kept rolling.

"He's going over," Hammond cried, jumping off his stool and bringing his fists low in front of him. "Cable came loose."

The plane skidded off the angled deck, lifted its nose slightly as the pilot tried to gain altitude, banked leeward, hung for a fraction of a second, and dove into the water. The canopy flew open and the pilot ejected like a flag unfurling in the wind. As his chute opened the fuselage hit the water and rolled, and the left wing knocked him in mid-air and carried him down. The plane sank, sending a circle of white spray outward and upward across the fore deck.

A white piece of the wing rotated in the air like a signal before dropping into the water.

Gritting his teeth and clenching his fists, David ran out the back door of the shop and down a passageway near the junior officers' state rooms where he wasn't supposed to go. Since his GQ was in Electronic Countermeasures, he always ran that way when the alarm sounded because he knew the officers wouldn't be there, and he could get to the ECM from the electronics workshop in ten seconds. Maybe the parachute or some wreckage would be floating on the water. David ran toward the ECM, hoping to be able to spot the pilot and signal to the rescuers. At the same time he had a vague feeling he might have to go into the water himself if the chopper didn't get there in time. With the ship so huge and heavy in the rough water, the wake could pull him under even though he was a good swimmer. He raced to the life line and leaned far over it, gripping the top rail with both hands, bracing himself, dreading and preparing to dive into the sea.

David strained his eyes to see where the pilot went down, looking for anything—a shadow, debris from the plane, traces of steam. His grip on the rail relaxed as he realized he would not have to vault over it. It was the closest David had ever come to knowing what a soldier felt in combat, risking his own life for another guy—profound loneliness, but the pilot must have felt more alone and hopeless, if he had time to feel anything at all.

The olive-green Marine helicopter swung around from starboard and hovered over the gray expanse, propellers churning white spray in a circle below it, engine chugging. The alarm blared.

THREE

David lay on the mattress in the house on Oak Street listening to a branch of the knobcone pine tapping the glass. He disentangled his legs from the sheet and old quilt, sat up, and fished his towel out of his knapsack. No one was in the bathroom, so he walked in and closed the door behind him. As he turned the loose knobs at the tiny sink he looked into the yellowed mirror at his prominent forehead and close-cut black hair and decided not to shave.

Through the small square window held open by a rusty latch he could see the bare yard behind the house and the backs of the houses on Page Street and hear car engines slowly accelerating. Latching the door, he stood only a few minutes under the weak rush of water from a makeshift shower in the old porcelain clawfoot bathtub. Then he rubbed his body hard with the towel and pulled on his jeans.

Back in the room where he had slept, he buttoned his shirt, laced up his boots, and strapped on his watch. David opened the door and stepped down the creaky stairs to the living room. Sunlight from the front bay window flooded the wooden floor and worn carpet. A thirties-era ceiling lamp of pink glass hung suspended by a chain from a circle of plaster leaves. The room smelled of mold, dust, marijuana, and incense. On the poster on the living room wall he distinguished an orange ship's wheel and a sphinx on a blue background. The

Roman numeral X was printed at the top and "Wheel of Fortune" at the bottom in Gothic script.

For a moment he felt tense about being UA, but when he pictured himself at Hunter's Point for muster something tightened in his stomach. Had Tim gone back or stayed out? It wasn't like him to turn and walk away without telling David where he was going, as he had done yesterday.

In the next room faded gray curtains covered two of three large windows; through the other one he could see the outer wall of the house next door and the creased trunk of the knobcone pine. A mirror in a corroded, elaborate copper frame hung above an old bricked-up fireplace on the far wall. He picked up an acoustic guitar someone had left lying on a chair and strummed an arpeggio. Hearing a chair scrape the floor in the kitchen, he replaced the guitar, embarrassed to have been messing with somebody else's stuff.

Then he heard metal banging and water running and pushed open the kitchen door to see Rennie washing the dishes from the previous night. There was no drainer, so she stacked them into a little breakable pyramid on the counter—old yellow china plates and blue mugs. Two discolored stainless-steel pots stood on their rims.

"Hi. Looking for Diane?" she smiled widely, drying her hands on a thin towel.

"Yes," he answered, wanting an excuse to be there.

"She's gone out."

"Do you know when she'll be back?"

"Could be an hour, could be all day."

"Is it okay if I hang around?"

"Sure. You can reheat the coffee in the pot," Rennie said, nodding toward the gas stove. "There's some milk in the fridge."

"Thanks."

He watched her fasten her hair back with combs; she was wearing a long blue Paisley print skirt and sandals. In the morning light she appeared attractive.

"Hang around if you want, but if you leave, don't lock the door," she said. "There's only one key and Terry has it. Sorry I can't stay."

David nodded. She left the room and after a moment he heard the front door bang against the jamb.

He glanced around the dark little kitchen at the brown and white linoleum tile buckled near the back door, the wall near the oven spattered with yellow grease stains, and the screen on the back door partially torn from its frame. Two flies crawled on the inside; he opened the door to set them free and stepped outside onto a small wooden porch. The yard was mostly bare earth with some clumps of grass. Jade, clover, and Queen Anne's lace grew in what had once been flower beds. A fence of wide wooden planks, some of them broken, surrounded the area. Two large, uncovered trash cans filled to overflowing sat beside the gate.

By this time David felt very hungry, so he turned the knob on the old stove under the battered, grease-stained pot. Wrapping the dish towel around the metal handle, he poured steaming coffee into one of the mugs on the counter, opened the door of the small refrigerator, and took out an opened quart container of milk. The refrigerator held half a loaf of bread in a paper wrapper, bowls of left-over rice and vegetables, a pot covered with a plate, and a bottle of oil; beets, potatoes, and carrots lay in an open bin at the bottom. David poured the last of the milk into the mug and shoved the empty carton into a trash can already full of boxes and paper.

Carrying the mug into the living room, he savored the bitter coffee and through the front window watched people gathering on the grass across the street. One man rolled up in an old fur coat lay sound asleep on the grass.

When David finished the coffee he carried the mug into the kitchen and set it in the sink before heading upstairs for the room where he'd slept. At the landing he hesitated before putting his hand on the doorknob of the room across the hall. A mattress lay on the floor covered with a blue and black spread, and a homemade easel stood in one corner. He smelled ink, old paper, and fine dust. Pencil drawings covered the top of a magazine table. David picked one up and examined a horned beast with a long neck, antlers, and big, expressive eyes. A large canvas leaning against the wall showed a tall, slender, bare-breasted woman whose yellow hair fanned outward around her head like rays. David wondered whether Diane used herself as the model. A silver-blue skirt draped from her hips; she held a gilt sword. Beside the painting on the table he glanced at a printed ComCo broadside and read the words "People are what people do."

He stepped over to the bureau to look at a photograph of Diane when she was a girl standing with an older woman and man. She got her high cheekbones and clear eyes from her father, her open forehead and thin lips from her mother. Her father was an architect who worked for a firm in Columbus, she told David last night. Her mother taught art in a local high school and painted portraits. Diane graduated from the University School the same year David graduated, though she was a year younger than he was, and spent the summer studying drawing and painting at Ohio State while he baled Ted Shepler's hay and wondered what the hell he was going to do with his life.

On the wall Diane had painted a sparse, rocky, desert landscape in the foreground and dark blue background like a night sky with light radiating from one side. Bare hills in the distance seemed to swallow the light, turning the sky darker. On the slope of a foothill a round clock melted, Dali-esque, along the hillside that sloped to a red stream.

From the bay window David could see more people in the Panhandle and one man walking a black Lab. The man in the fur coat was still asleep even though cars accelerated loudly along Oak.

Emboldened by the quiet of the house, David opened the door to the next room. A mattress also lay on the floor, a green spread pulled neatly over the thin pillow, near an old bureau and a small table. There was no dust in the corners. On the wall hung a pen and ink drawing of a seated woman wearing a billowing skirt and cape whose ends turned into flying birds. An old wooden bookshelf held paperback copies of *Upanishads, Siddhartha,* and something called *The Love Book* that turned out to be poems. The owner's name was written inside: Rosalind Slane. The *Bhagavad-Gita* lay open near it; an underlined passage read, "The world is imprisoned in its own activity, except when actions are performed as worship." He turned the page to read another underlined passage, "We play the part we are destined to play." Two brass statues, one of Buddha and the other a bare-breasted Hindu goddess playing a lute, rested on top of the bookcase alongside a ring binder. Clothes were folded inside a metal trunk that stood with its lid up near a corner. On a far wall a black and white poster showed an expanse of sky, beach, and surf that dwarfed the figures of a girl and boy in jeans, T-shirts, and tennis shoes, embracing as they stood on the sand.

The only other door on that hallway was locked, so David walked up the steps to the third floor loft. Three cameras and a case of film covered a wooden table, and hardbound books about cinematography, numerology, and the Tarot sat on a plywood shelf bolted to the wall. Windows looked out over the back and over Oak Street. Shirts, jackets, and sweaters hung from a clothes tree.

Leaving the door open, David walked back down to the room where he'd slept, grabbed his shaving kit, and headed down the steps and onto the porch. He strode down Oak until he found a second-hand shop. Kitchen items and tools lined the shelves, and watches and jewelry filled a glass case along the front. A tall, thin man with gray hair wearing a soiled leather apron looked up from a bicycle.

"You buying?" David asked.

"Depends on what you got to sell," the man replied and stepped behind the counter.

David opened his shaving kit. He watched the man's work-stained hands as he separated razor, file, and comb.

"Two dollars," he said.

David nodded.

As the man opened the cash register, David unbuckled his watch.

"How much for that?"

The man took it up and examined it carefully.

"Ten."

"I'll take it."

David stuffed the bills into the wallet, already fat with his Navy pay, and left the shop. He'd draw his savings out of the Wells Fargo Bank, and if he decided after all to go back to Hunter's Point he could just deposit the money again. Rolling up the sleeves of his shirt he strode down Cole to the Job Co-op where he scanned the slips of paper describing various jobs and what they paid when he saw one that read "Day Laborers Wanted."

"What kind of work is this?" he asked a young woman behind the counter.

"Lifting, I guess," she answered distractedly. "I don't really know."

"Do you have a piece of paper I can write the number down on?" he asked.

"Take that," she said.

David stuffed the paper into his pocket. He left the co-op, thinking he'd better find a permanent place to stay before he called about work. Crash pads got raided, and at the Y they asked too many questions. Avoiding some panhandlers he crossed the street and strode toward Haight where he stopped at the I/Thou Café for another mug of coffee and a wedge of poppy seed cake, finally heading back to the Panhandle, alternately feeling the warmth of sunlight and coolness of shade on his face and arms. Many more people were hanging out on the grass now. From among the faces he saw Diane walking toward him with her long, floating stride, wearing blue denim and a green shirt. Yesterday's hunch had been right: she certainly had a nice body under those jeans.

"Rennie told me you were out today," David called to her.

"Sold some drawings," she answered.

"You must be pretty good," he replied.

"Want to come someplace with me?" She acted very casual, as if she and he had not spent the night wound in each other's arms.

"I better get my stuff and find a place," he said.

"Stay with us. Why hassle yourself when you just got to town?"

"What about your friends?" he asked, embarrassed that he'd let her go on believing he was a newcomer.

"Rennie and Terry are okay."

"What about Daryl?"

"He just hangs around. What does he care what we do?"

"Well, then, I don't need my stuff," David said. "Where to?"

"Ocean Beach," she answered.

They took a bus to Grand Highway and walked barefoot along the wide beach where mothers watched their children digging in the gray sand and flying kites in the cold wind. Slanted rays of silver light streamed through the clouds onto dark waves. At the end of the strand David and Diane climbed the embankment, scrambled over a concrete wall, and straddled a ledge facing each other. They could hear seals barking far below above the sound of wind and waves pounding the rocks at the shoreline.

"When my brother and I were kids we used to visit my grandmother in Berkeley," Diane said, "and she'd bring us here."

"Does she still live there?"

"No; she died eight years ago." Diane had plaited her hair into a loose braid that hung down her back, but the shorter strands around her face bobbed crazily in the sea wind. "She always said I'd become an artist."

"And you became one like your mother."

Diane threw her head back, laughing. "Yeah, I did. Even though we argued all the time."

"You never said why you left Fort Collins."

"I had a sort of breakdown at Antioch," she said, shrugging her shoulders, "and I went to stay with these people, my mentor on a teaching co-op in West Virginia and his wife. By that time they'd moved to Fort Collins. They wanted me to stay and help with their kids, but . . ."

Her eyes followed a line of brown pelicans flying southward just above the water. David gazed at the smooth skin on her long neck.

"I kind of felt like I was getting in their way, like they sort of needed some time alone. And I got a lift with a bunch of kids who were staying at a crash pad in Fort Collins on their way out here."

"Why didn't you go back to Antioch?" he asked, feeling that she was not going to tell him the whole story. "Didn't you like it there?"

She met his eyes again. "I liked it okay. There was always something going on. But after awhile you get to thinking the co-ops were the places we were really learning, so why bother with college at all, you know?" She paused. "Didn't you like Ohio State?"

"Nobody likes Ohio State," he said.

Diane laughed. "When I was in Fort Collins Terry wrote and told me how great it was out here. I used to be roommates with his girlfriend Stacy back at Antioch. She put us in touch."

"What about Rennie?" he asked.

"She knows all about Stacy. Terry's not into commitment."

"And is Rennie?"

Diane shrugged again. "She dropped out of SF State because of some guy she fell in love with who married somebody else. She'll go back if Terry leaves. He's always talking about going somewhere else. All these questions and you haven't even told me your name."

"You know my name."

"Yes, but David what?" she asked, drawing her knees up underneath her chin.

He drew his wallet from his pocket, pulled his driver's license from the plastic sleeve, and handed it to her.

"David Shields," she read.

"Not anymore," he told her. "To your friends I'm just David, like Daryl said."

"Don't let him bug you." She handed back the driver's license, clasped her knees in her arms, and leaned forward.

"There's more to it." He flung the driver's license over the cliff where it seemed to dissolve in the air.

"Why'd you do that?" She sat up.

"It could tell people who I am."

He reached into his pocket again and drew out the ID card.

"You were right when you asked me yesterday if I was in the service."

She tilted her head.

"As of this morning I'm UA. Unauthorized Absence. AWOL. Does that shock you?"

"No. I admire what you're doing."

"Then don't even tell your friends."

"I won't, but they'll figure it out. Daryl has ways of finding out about people. I was with him for awhile when I first got here."

"I know."

"How?"

"I knew as soon as he walked into that room yesterday," he responded.

"You're pretty sensitive. And anyway, Terry will want to hear your story."

"Not if I keep moving."

"You can hide here better than anywhere," she said, resting her chin on her knees. "There's a lot of people on the run around here. Who'd recognize you? All hippies look alike to cops." After a pause she asked, "What do you think you'll do?"

"I'm not sure. Go underground. Go back while I still can."

"What do you mean?"

"If I stay out less than thirty days I'm just UA. I'll get some brig time, maybe some hard labor detail. If the ship gets deployed while I'm out that's missing movement, and that means more shit. If I stay out more than thirty days

I'm officially a deserter and I'll get court-martialed if I go back. Or if they catch up with me."

"Why don't you go to Canada?"

"They say it's hard to get in," he explained, "and the Navy chasers hang around the border. I don't know anybody who got away with it."

"Aren't you going to throw that away?" she asked, nodding at the ID card.

"No. If I'm caught without it I could get five years." After a moment he said, "I'll stay if everyone agrees to it."

David stood up to shove the ID card into his pocket. When he sat down again Diane let her legs straddle the stone wall again and put her arms around him. They kissed for a long time in the high wind.

FOUR

On the morning of June 20, David got up while the house was still quiet, rode a bus downtown to the Wharf, found a bench near the water, and for a long time watched ships riding the trough. Finally he pulled a pen from his knapsack and wrote a letter to his brother Bill, filling two sheets of plain ruled paper, explaining why he hadn't written sooner. The family would probably be getting a letter from Westpac telling them David had deserted the Navy and they should let the authorities know if they found out where he was. He couldn't go back yet; if he did he'd go crazy. He'd write again, but he couldn't tell them where he was living, so if someone came looking for him Bill and his mother wouldn't have to lie. He was in a good place; he had friends and enough money, so they didn't need to worry. The whole time he was writing he turned over and over the arguments for going back or not, still farther in the reaches of his mind knowing he had already made the decision not to return. After re-reading the lines, he sealed the envelope and wrote Bill's address on the front. Somebody Diane knew was driving to LA and would mail the letter there so it wouldn't have a San Francisco postmark. He stuffed the letter into his knapsack and took a bus back to the Haight.

Morning light filtering through trees cast speckled shadows on the faces of people standing in the Panhandle, their voices barely audible above the rustling leaves. Heading toward Oak, David stepped behind a reporter in a sport coat who scribbled notes on a dog-eared pad. He was listening to a gaunt, bearded man with shoulder-length hair and a dark-haired, petite woman whose arm encircled the man's slender waist. Both wore loose-fitting white pullovers, tight blue jeans, and sandals.

"I don't know how long this will last, probably not long," the man was saying.

The woman nodded.

In another group a man wearing a sheepskin vest passed a joint cupped in his hands.

"It's their best, I swear, nobody else is doing anything like it."

"I didn't think they could get any better."

"They should have been at Monterey."

"Were you there? Friend of mine said you couldn't stay straight there was so much smoke in the air."

David passed a man in a T-shirt and Army fatigues standing under the street lamp and heard him say "runaways."

David crossed Oak, climbed the steps two by two to the porch, and walked into the dark living room.

Kneeling on the threadbare red carpet, Terry divided his Tarot deck and turned half the cards around. Rennie sat watching him, surrounded by the folds of her paisley skirt.

"I heard there was another raid on Ashbury last night," Terry was saying.

"Hey, man. Where you been?" Diane asked, leaning back in the rocking chair, her right knee crooked over the arm. Her legs were bare below olive-colored shorts, and she wore no shoes or sandals.

"Walking," David answered.

Terry shuffled the cards. Rennie smiled up at David so widely her eyes seemed to disappear.

"I don't see what you get out of those damn little cards," Daryl said, hunched in his overstuffed chair.

"Man, people have been using them for six hundred years."

"Crazy people," Daryl guffawed as he raised a lighted Camel to his mouth.

"How do you know there isn't something to it?" Diane asked, tapping the end of her Taryton with her left hand on the edge of a clamshell that lay on the floor.

"I know what I can *see*, what I can *prove*. What can be shown *scientifically*."

"Not all truth is scientific," she said.

"What isn't?"

"Artistic," she answered.

Daryl rolled his eyes.

"Scientific theories are always being proved wrong," Terry said. "Didn't doctors put leeches on people to suck out the poisoned blood? And didn't they used to try to tell your personality by measuring your skull?"

"People are always rejecting theories, but they never reject science."

"So why do you drop acid?" Terry pointed his knife-blade nose at Daryl.

"Chemistry, man, science at its best."

"You should've been with us at Monterey," Terry said, looking up at David.

Diane and Terry had driven Daryl's 1963 Saab to the festival, while Daryl rode his red Harley. Afterward they drove through Big Sur to visit some people Terry knew. Late the night before, David heard them stomping in the front hallway as they carried their sleeping bags and knapsacks into the house.

"You should have," Diane said, resting her head against the back of the chair. David could see the ridge of her throat underneath the smooth pale skin. She was wearing a sleeveless white tank top and no bra, and her eyes looked tired, as if she had just awakened. He suppressed the urge to run his hand down her neck and over her breasts.

"I don't like crowds," he answered, his throat tightening.

"The crowd was the best," Terry said emphatically. "It was like the rally last fall."

"I liked Shankar," Rennie declared.

"Commercial shit," Daryl snarled.

"Aren't you going to answer him?" David asked Rennie.

"I thought I'd let it slide," she said, looking down, her long ginger hair falling forward around her face.

"I'll let it slide," Daryl said, narrowing his eyes at her.

"Man, relax," Diane said. "How would you know whether anybody was any good or not? You were so completely stoned."

"Rennie likes Eastern culture," David said, offended that Terry was not speaking up for her.

"Big Sur was great," Rennie declared, looking at David. "Those people have it right."

"Yeah, for two weeks in the spring," Daryl said.

"They looked pretty strung out to me," Terry offered.

"Don't be so down on everything, you guys," Diane said. "Big Sur is a beautiful place." She flung back her head. "You ought to go there, David. How was it here? We miss anything?"

"No," David shook his head.

"Daryl's been giving us his philosophy," Terry said to David. "He doesn't think there's anything in the Tarot. I cast his fortune once and he doesn't buy it."

"What was his fortune?" David asked, stepping closer.

"I turned up two trumps and two court cards," Terry answered. "The King of Cups, Ace of Swords, the Emperor, and the Sun, all the right side up, no reverses. Indications are power and rationality."

"Sounds like Daryl to me," David answered, grinning.

"Bullshit," Daryl said. "I don't need cards to tell me who I am."

"And what about your fortune?" David asked Terry.

"I'm a wanderer," Terry said. "One of my cards was the Knight of Batons, meaning a sudden departure. But it's hard to tell. There's more than one way to read them."

"So what do you know that you didn't before?" Daryl rolled his eyes.

"How about David's fortune?" Rennie suggested.

David shifted his weight as Terry shuffled the cards again.

"There's lots of ways to do it," Terry explained. "I can give you a short reading with three cards or a horoscope with twelve, or a full reading with forty-eight. For hard questions you really need a full reading."

"Just do three," David said.

"You need a Significator," Terry said. "I use the first trump or court card I turn up." He laid a series of cards face up.

"There it is."

"What?"

"The Hanged Man."

David looked at the picture of a medieval page holding a lute and hanging by one leg from a gibbet.

"Uh, oh," Daryl said. "Straight Man's in for it now."

"What does it mean?" David asked.

"Actually the Hanged Man isn't bad," Terry answered. "He's a water sign. He purges his old self to make room for a new one."

"Bullshit," Daryl said. "You don't believe that stuff, do you Straight Man?"

"The cards don't tell your fortune," Terry addressed Daryl. "They just suggest what you might do when you find the powers or the energies aligned in a certain way."

"Oh, SHIT," Daryl answered.

"Hey, what's going on?" Terry asked, his bulging, bloodshot eyes peering through his wire-rimmed spectacles.

"Nothing," Diane said, crushing her cigarette in the clamshell.

"Come on you guys," Terry insisted.

"I used to be in the Navy," David volunteered after a pause.

"That explains the water thing," Terry said. "Maybe the cards are telling you about something that's already happened."

"Oh, give me a break," Daryl said, but his eyes were on David. "So what'd you do in the Navy, Straight Man?"

"Same as everybody else, put up with a lot of bullshit and boredom."

"Didn't it bother you to be part of all that?" Terry asked.

"Yes," he answered.

"Did you get drafted?" Terry pursued.

"Yes."

"You must have gone in young to have finished a four-year hitch," Daryl said. "Isn't it four years in the Navy?"

"Yes, it is."

"And still spent a year in college, didn't you say?" With his right thumb and middle finger Daryl held his cigarette poised in mid-air.

"I don't remember exactly."

"Don't be so uptight," Terry asserted. "You can trust us." He shuffled the cards three times, cutting the pack in half and turning it around each time. Then he laid out three cards near the Hanged Man.

"This one is the Eight of Cups," Terry explained. "It's the first one I dealt, so it represents your state of mind right now. Cups are a water sign, and they're usually lucky. The Eight indicates you've been wandering, but it could be mental wandering."

"And the other two?" Diane asked, swinging her leg over the arm of the chair and sitting up.

"The second one usually tells you what's coming up. The Nine of Swords can be unlucky, but right after the Eight of Cups it could just limit the earlier card. It's reversed, though, so that decreases the unlucky part."

"What else?" Diane insisted.

"Well, it can also mean isolation or independence or something like that."

"Go on." Diane, Rennie, and Daryl were all watching now.

"The last one's the Seven of Batons, which is usually a pretty good suit, a fire sign that also means creativity. The Seven refers kind of to self-reliance. If I were casting your horoscope and it turned up between other cards in the same suit I'd say you were in for a big test of some kind. As it is, I'd just say be really careful what you do for the next couple of weeks."

Terry rocked back on his heels.

"There's something heavy going on," he said. "I can feel it."

"Yeah," Daryl said, still watching David.

"I thought you didn't believe in anything you couldn't prove scientifically," Diane said.

"Bitch," Daryl snapped.

David stepped closer to Daryl's chair.

"What's the deal, Straight Man?" The skin wrinkled around his mouth.

"I don't like you calling her names," David said evenly.

"She's okay."

"I don't care if she is or not."

Diane stood.

"Okay, cool it now, you guys."

"See?" Daryl said.

"No, I don't see," David replied, standing over Daryl, hands at his sides.

"You're selling wolf tickets," Daryl sneered.

"Am I?" David asked.

"Hey, I agree with Diane," Terry said, the Juggler in his hand. "Let's all just be cool."

"All right, all right, Mouseketeers," Daryl said. "Diane's not a bitch. The man from the flatland says so."

🐝 🐝 🐝   🐝 🐝 🐝   🐝 🐝 🐝

Terry peered through round, rose-tinted, wire-rimmed glasses and held the microphone while the biker talked about his trip across the country. A knotted brown bandana covered his head, and his curly beard concealed his neck. His purple, black, and orange tie-dyed shirt was stretched skin tight over his biceps and rotund waist, but his camouflage pants sagged above boots so ragged the soles were about to come off. Behind him, the roofs of houses along Fell Street rose above tall trees.

"When you're in a car, man, you can't see even half what you can see on a bike." The man spoke with a nasal Midwestern tone. "When you stop for a bite there's always somebody to talk to, to hear where you've been and who you've met. Even the old timers, they want to hear. One old timer lady in South Dakota, she told me her parents wouldn't let her marry a biker but she ran off with him during the twenties, man, and she was still married to him, he was standing right there with her, in his faded overalls, and her in this dress like a sack. They were happy; they knew who they were.

"You can tool along for miles across Nebraska, there's nobody in that whole fucking state, the cows take care of themselves, I swear I never saw a soul the whole fucking time, and I know why the tornadoes go there, cause there's nothing to stop um from Texas to North Dakota."

After the man wandered away Terry wrapped the cord around the microphone.

"This part is the best," Terry said. "Random people in the park, spur of the moment stuff, you know. I mean I ran away from home and hitchhiked across the country when I was sixteen, but I didn't meet people like this." He packed the microphone carefully into a black case.

"Didn't your parents come after you?"

"Sure they did, but I never stayed anywhere long enough for the cops to find me. I knew to double back so they couldn't close in. I was gone a month. It finally got to be a drag. I showed up one afternoon and walked right in and said, 'Hi, Mom, miss me?' She almost had a heart attack."

"Were they mad at you?"

"Are you kidding? They nearly killed the fatted calf. My dad smoothed it over with the police. He's a lawyer and knows how to handle stuff like that."

"How does he feel about you doing this?"

"You mean being here?"

"Making movies."

"He's all for it. Thinks I'm going to be some big Hollywood director or something. Hey, why don't you play some music for background?"

"I might."

"How about letting me interview you about the Navy?"

"No way."

"Why not?"

"I don't like cameras pointed at me."

"Yeah, really. Take that shit yesterday with Daryl. He didn't have to go and talk to Diane that way. She's not a bitch; she's just different. Even back at Antioch when she lived with my girlfriend Stacy. A little on the weird side, maybe. She's smart though. Soon as she shows up you know there's somebody you can connect with."

Some time later—David no longer paid attention to the days of the week—he walked alone in the park past the hill when he saw Rennie in her long denim skirt coming toward him.

"What's going on?" she asked.

"Nothing much. Haven't seen you these last few days."

"I've been at Andrea's. The house is getting crowded," she said. "Terry's letting so many kids sleep over."

"I know. It's beginning to bug me, too." He'd seen the squat little yellow house on Del Mar where Rennie's friends lived. He could picture heavy-set Andrea's ruddy skin and wavy brown hair. Everybody in Terry's house went there to use the phone.

"But now even Andrea's letting a bunch of people sleep over. They pay her for a room and she gets more than she pays out." Rennie shrugged.

She turned and walked with him, looking down, hands in her skirt pockets.

"I've been working over at USF," she said finally. "I type there in an office sometimes."

"I didn't know that. Terry doing anything today?"

"I don't know. We don't check in with each other." Rennie giggled, shaking her head.

"He kind of pissed me off when Daryl was giving you a hard time about Monterey."

"Terry's okay. Daryl's a real creep. I don't know how Terry and Diane stand him. She and Daryl were together when she first got here, you know." Rennie tilted her head to look at David.

"I know."

She straightened her shoulders.

"So how'd you and Terry get together?" David asked.

"At the rally last January. I went with Andrea and her friends to the polo field. It was all so great, all these heads and the music and poetry. The polo field was packed and you could hardly see the speakers way down at the end on this platform they had. They set off balloons and the people wandered around like waves of color, most of them high. And I felt like I belonged there somehow, though I stayed straight and I didn't know anybody but Andrea. Anyway, I got separated from her and her friends and was watching the ducks on Spreckles Lake. Terry came up to me and asked if he could take my picture, walking alone in the fog. I was wearing this long cape I have."

"The green one," David said, remembering the flannel cape she sometimes wore.

"Yeah. And afterwards he walked me back and asked me if he could come over, and we started sleeping together, and eventually I moved in. I was at SF State for two years."

"Diane told me."

"Man, I was so excited about getting away from home and going to college." She ducked her head and laughed. "I really thought every door opened into some kind of wisdom." She glanced at him. "What a bunch of shit. I started spending all my time in the Experimental College."

They walked along a narrow path among shrubs and young trees beside the new tennis clubhouse.

"Diane says you dropped out because of some guy you were going with," David said.

Rennie laughed.

"Oh, yeah, Jason," she said. "He was in his last year of graduate school in psych at Berkeley. I was a lot younger than he was. I was *so* gone on him. What an ass I was."

"Why were you an ass for liking him?"

She shrugged. "I didn't just like him. I thought he was this great, deep guy, and he wasn't anything like what I thought. He was just a creep who had me thinking he was somebody. He'd ask me out and then tell me how much he hated women. See, he'd been divorced." She reached up and unfastened a large barrette, letting her glossy hair cascade onto her shoulders.

"He was my first. I could hardly study that term, I spent so much time

mooning about him, and then he graduated and left for his internship in LA."
She ran her fingers through her hair.

"After awhile he wrote and said I should come to see him, so I took
a bus to L.A. one weekend. After that he didn't call for a long time. When I
finally called him he told me he was engaged to the daughter of one of the board
members at the hospital where he worked. Well, I was all down about it, but
you know, somehow, I also had this great feeling of freedom, too." She shook
her ginger hair away from her face.

"What an asshole. Then I met some kids who were studying Zen, and
I met Andrea, who told me she'd been here last summer and the people were so
together and she was getting up a group to share expenses. So I dropped out at
the end of the term and came with her."

"The good thing about Terry is he listens," she continued after a
moment. "He doesn't try to tell me what to do and what to think. Most guys
I know tell me I think too much and study too much. They're always saying,
'You know what your problem is?' And then they lecture me about what I'm
doing wrong. I hate that. I know Terry's going to take off; he's been talking
about it since I met him. Diane told me he has a different girl on each co-op."
Rennie giggled.

They walked out of the woods onto the grass.

"Why'd you go into the Navy?" she asked suddenly. "You had a 2S,
didn't you?"

"Long story."

She looked down and thrust her hands into her pockets.

"My dad died, and I didn't want to ask my mother to pay the tuition,"
he answered. "Then there was the big draft increase."

"Were you real young, like Daryl says?"

"Not really," he said, stopping. Rennie turned toward him, clasping her
hands and raising them toward her chest. "I never finished my hitch."

She stood looking up at him, her head tipped to the left, her face framed
by the long hair. He sat down on a large rock.

"You got out somehow?"

"I'm over the hill," he said. "Absent without leave."

"Diane knows?" she asked, her eyes widening.

"Yes. She's the only one."

"I won't tell anybody. How'd you do it?"

"Just walked away. They don't keep us under lock and key."

"The day you showed up at the house?" she asked.

"Yes."

Rennie stepped up to him, took his face in her hands, and began to kiss him, her tongue finding his, her hands stroking his neck and the coarse, curly hair of his beard. His hands followed the curve of her hips. She stepped between his knees as the voices across the lawn faded into the sound of rustling leaves.

❋ ❋ ❋   ❋ ❋ ❋   ❋ ❋ ❋

"Come and look at this, man."

Inside the doorway of the dark, musty little room Daryl reached for the beaker and shook it under a black light, and David saw what looked like sparks.

"Piezoluminescence," Daryl said. "Totally pure salt, not some junk from morning glory seeds."

"You better be careful where you keep that shit. Terry's been letting some weird characters sleep over."

"It was in the refrigerator all night. What the fuck do I care what that little preppie does?" Daryl shook the beaker again. "A chemist is like god, changing the bonds, fucking with molecular structure."

He poured distilled water carefully from a plastic bottle into another beaker.

"People at Berkeley still get me what I need."

"Why didn't you just stay there?"

101

"Couldn't deal with the shit," Daryl told him, "any more than you could. See that?" He shook the beaker again.

"I see it."

"One little structural change makes something completely different, tryptamines of carbon, hydrogen, oxygen, and nitrogen. People are nothing but bundles of nerves, Straight Man, and all their politics and wars come from sodium and potassium ions pouring through the membrane channels."

"Sounds a little simplistic to me," David muttered, shoving his hands into his pockets.

"Negatively charged neurons become positively charged when the channels open, and sodium ions rush in. After sodium, escape of potassium. Electrical impulses trigger a neurotransmitter that bonds to the receptors on the next one. And then the amides that mess with the neurotransmitter extend their power."

Daryl broke the cake of salt with a spatula and measured it in into another beaker, poured the distilled water over it, and stirred.

"They'll know right away how pure this is; it's going to be as good as it gets. And all because an amide screws around with neurotransmission, light from interstellar space in the vault of the skull, dust from the explosions of stars."

With a medicine dropper he squeezed circlets of solution onto little tabs of paper.

"Aren't you a little careless who you show that stuff to?"

"Not to you, Straight Man." Daryl narrowed his dark eyes. "I know you got a secret, you know I got one. You're not going to rat on me."

David pulled his knapsack higher onto his shoulders, glanced back at Daryl's metallic green Saab to make sure it was far enough off the road, and started up the trail. Diane walked ahead of him, left hand clutching the strap of her knapsack and her right hand poking the ground with a walking stick. She turned off the main trail and followed a dirt path running almost straight up the hill. The lower slopes were covered with snake grass, passion flowers, and lupine, but as they climbed, brambles and lavender tea spread over the pathway. Finally they walked through Monterey pine, buckeye, and oak. A steep, narrow forest trail led to a place where the terrain leveled out. A red-throated quail ran across the path, chirring, and disappeared into the long brown grass waving in the wind. Two splintered fence posts leaned near the trail, and sharp black rocks rose across a meadow like the spinal cord of the mountain. Farther west, feathery wisps of fog floated at the top of the highest slopes.

"The locals call this Old Baldy," Diane told him.

They climbed past Phoenix Lake and up steep trails toward the summit of Mount Tamalpais where the fire tower stood like a pagoda. The cloud-veiled sun was overhead when they looked down on the Pacific. They flung their knapsacks on the ground and sat on a bluff where tiny white wildflowers bobbed furiously in the high wind. Sea gulls circled below them, weaving in toward the mountain and out over the gray water.

From a brown paper bag Diane produced apricots, plums, and two cheese sandwiches with avocado, tomato, alfalfa sprouts, and lettuce.

"You sure are far away," she said.

"Just thinking."

"About what?"

"About how you never expect things to turn out the way they do," he answered.

"It's better just to let stuff happen."

"My mother used to call me her accident. I'm beginning to think she was right."

"We're all just accidents. I mean, when you think about it, if every single ovum and every single sperm has different traits or whatever, and there are millions of them, isn't it an accident when they meet up at just the right time? All our lives together make up some huge tapestry."

"You sound like Daryl," he said.

Rolling her eyes, she struck a match and lit a Tareyton, cupping her hand around the flame before scraping the little wooden stick back and forth in the loam.

"Or look at it the other way: if the odds are so huge against any one sperm reaching the ovum, then the one that does make it is somehow meant to be the one."

She drew on her cigarette again and blew the smoke out onto the wind. David smelled bitter tobacco and sharp pine, enjoying the fragrance but wishing she smoked less.

"What do you think makes us who we are?" she continued, leaning back on her left hand. "I mean, are we born to be this or that?"

"I don't think that's the question," he said, sitting up. "The point is what we've done or haven't done."

"You're talking about the Navy."

"Not really. But all the time I think about what I'll do if they catch up with me."

"I know." After a pause she continued, "What we've done makes us who we are. *We* weave the tapestry. We just think more about what we haven't done." She drew on her cigarette. "So what's going on with you and Rennie?" Diane grinned.

"What do you mean?"

"Daryl told me he saw you and her making out in the park." She sat up, scraped a shallow depression in the loam, and flicked her ashes into it.

"We weren't making out. We were talking and she kissed me. What's going on with you and Daryl?"

"Over and done with. Guy's a walking ego trip. I was stoned most of the time anyway."

"So what's the big deal?"

"She'll fall in love with you."

"How do you know that?"

"You told her about yourself. When she falls, she falls hard."

"She got over that Berkeley creep."

"Sure she did. Now she's ready for another big dive. That calm exterior covers a seething volcano of passion."

"I do think Rennie's too good for Terry," he said.

"You're damn shit right about that."

"I thought you liked him."

"He's okay, but he's not for her. He's on this Renaissance-man trip." Diane rolled her eyes. "She isn't on the same wavelength."

"You don't care if I kiss her, do you?"

"It just kind of pissed me off the way Daryl was gloating."

David took her face in his left hand and pulled her toward him as she crushed her cigarette in the loam. They kissed in the cold wind, and Diane inched closer to David, who lay back and pulled her on top of him. Her hair smelled like clover.

✻ ✻ ✻   ✻ ✻ ✻   ✻ ✻ ✻

The sun glimmered well over the mountain when they walked down the east side of the slope above Phoenix Lake. David glanced at the down on the back of Diane's neck revealed by her braided hair.

"Look out there," David said, "to the right of Tiburon. You see Angel? And the little one, Yerba Buena?"

"Yes."

"See the brown rectangle beside it?"

"Yeah."

"That's Treasure Island."

"It's some sort of military base now," she said.

"It's a naval training center."

105

"Where you were stationed?"

"No," he said. "I was at Alameda and Hunter's Point."

"So what's with Treasure Island?"

"The brig's there."

"Don't worry about that now," she said, reaching around his waist.

"It's Building 222," he said. "Same as my birthday, February 22."

"That doesn't mean anything. It's just coincidence."

"Sometimes I dream I'm inside it, walking through the corridors."

"What does it look like in the dream?" she asked, hugging him.

"Like the passageways on a ship," he answered, looking out over the bay.

Sitar music on the stereo wound through the rose-colored light. Blood pounded in David's ears. People he didn't know reclined on the floor, chairs, and couch. Terry really shouldn't have invited this many.

Diane, sitting beside him on the floor, raised herself to her knees and then to her feet like a bird lifting off a branch. When she stepped to the mantel to light a candle, ghostly radiance followed her and swept upward when she raised her arm. Above the bay window the stained glass shining blue, rose, and yellow in the late afternoon began to vibrate in time with the music, curling along the wall and ceiling. Red fuchsia in a vase poured crimson into the air.

The black stereo speakers on the low table grew larger; six green leaves of sound waves formed from the speakers, spread outward, and morphed into a rotating wheel that changed from green to blue to purple to red.

One thin, barefooted guy wearing a white tunic and loose white pants sat cross-legged on the rug. His long, kinky brown hair was pulled back into a pony tail, but as David watched, the hair fell onto his shoulders and stretched longer, and he became thinner as he held both arms up, his palms parallel to the ceiling. The man's face grew even narrower until he appeared to be mere bones covered with skin; his eyes looked larger, and he tipped his head back and stared upward.

Hearing a laugh or a grumble beside him, David turned toward Daryl sitting on the overstuffed chair. The magician looked back at David and then began to nod his head slowly and then faster, ducking his beard to his chest and throwing it far back so quickly David couldn't tell whether Daryl grinned or scowled. His red beard grew longer and bushier, and his red-brown hair curled massively around his head. The man stopped nodding and stretched his right arm outward until a spear grew out of it and he wore leather wrist bands with tassels, a necklace of animal teeth on a thong, a vest made of sheepskin, and leather leggings. Grinning, Daryl took the spear in both hands, his eyes becoming slits of light.

"Good stuff, eh, Straight Man?" he said, then nodded and pointed the spear toward the corner.

From the darkness a spider appeared, at first as big as a palm, but growing to the size of a fist and then an outstretched hand. At first it looked black, then brown, then red. With its eyes focused on the middle of the room, the spider began to pull a web slowly out of its flanks, the thin sticky fiber floating in the air. Daryl, still grinning, watched it at the same time. The long, thin legs attached the web to the doorjamb and the wall, adding strand after strand in the octagonal shape David had seen as a boy between stems of goldenrod in the fields, but then the spider stepped inside the web, and David saw that it was three-dimensional and would soon take over the room. He raised his hand to hold the strands back but they continued to expand and the spider grinned and blinked. The thin man continued to stare at the ceiling, his arms reaching · upward. David put his hand on the man's shoulder and pointed toward the spider, and the man looked and saw it, too, but the spider grinned again and pulled the strands around itself, disappearing into the darkness of the corner.

Rennie, sitting on the floor, was trying to talk down a guy who seemed to be having a bad trip. As David watched, her ginger hair grew longer and spread outward like a cape that flowed to the floor, and her skirt became voluminous folds of blue and green.

Seeing the orange wheel on the wall begin to turn, David walked through swirling, purple-gray currents toward the Tarot poster. On the wall it picked up speed, detaching itself and growing larger, spinning in mid-air, sending off vibrating bands of yellow, orange, red, purple, and blue. It uncoiled and became a rainbow but coiled up again and slipped back into the poster, and then the room became a kaleidoscope of colors that flowed into his body. The wheel continued spinning, shimmering until it became luminous white. The universe breathed as he breathed, lived as he lived, conscious of its own life. The Tarot poster was speaking to him, telling him he was part of everything in the world and everything and everyone was part of him. The spinning wheel became the flowers of Queen Anne's Lace, a field of blossoms that stretched up a hillside, the wind blowing and flowers uprooting themselves from the ground and flying through the air, white flame rushing up and over a hill like a river flowing into the sky and whirling like galaxies. Waves of light crashed over each other and broke, and points of light flew upward. Wind from the bay was blowing through his body, and everyone in the room was riding the tide of the visible air currents illuminated with solar waves that rushed through the house, and he was treading light that buoyed him up. Now he knew the walls and ceiling were merely part of the outdoors like a bird nest or groundhog den. He realized that all the images were deep in his mind, deeper than he had ever been able to go inside himself. His mind was as vast as the cosmos and boundaries faded into one continuous existence within and outside of him.

David stepped toward the mirror above the fireplace; he saw his hazel eyes in cave-like sockets and the mass of dark hair and thick, bushy beard surrounding his face. Then he saw that he had merged with the image in the mirror and was looking out towards himself; David had passed through the barrier, while Shields stood back and waited. At the same time he felt afraid that he had separated himself from everyone for too long and now he would be alone forever. It was the drug, he knew, but then he wondered, was it really? Hadn't he always been alone? Was he so different from everyone else that he could never belong anywhere?

Then he saw Diane walking toward him, her arms like wings of golden satin. Undulating layers of golden and amber light surrounded her, radiating so brightly he could hardly look at her. Fearful that she might be consumed in fire, he stepped toward her to smother the flame, but then he saw that the light surged outward from some inward source—clear, like water. She knew what he was feeling and put her hand around his, and in that moment their bodies merged, his hand becoming illuminated and then part of her hand. She led him out of the mirror and up the stairs that stretched far away.

When she opened the door to her room and he stepped across the threshold, he knew a door inside himself opened. He thought he might be swept away in the swirling colors, but there was Diane anchoring him, removing his shirt and jeans. Suddenly feeling free now, he wanted to tell her he knew where he was; he belonged to the world now that everything was inside him. She lay down on the mattress and gestured for him to lie down with her. Her skin appeared luminous, and when he stretched beside her, she put her hand on his hip and his skin became illuminated so that he couldn't tell where her hand ended and his hip began. Never before had he felt so much happiness or peace; he knew she felt the same, that their minds were not separate entities but one infinite, flowing energy. He came as soon as he was inside her, not as usual like an explosion that lasted a few moments but like a tidal wave that grew increasingly powerful as it rushed across the surface of the bright ocean that expanded outward forever.

FIVE

Diane stood looking at the brown shingle house on California Street in Berkeley. She'd been in San Francisco three weeks before she decided to go see her grandmother's old place—a New England-style three-story—which she hadn't seen since the funeral eight years before. An oval cut-glass window from the twenties looked out over a wooden porch. Cypresses shaded the front lawn. Diane pulled her cigarettes from her pocket, lit one, and scraped the match against the concrete.

"She sure was independent," Diane whispered to herself.

Diane's grandmother, Birgit Peterson, had been born in Bergen, Norway. Her parents—Niall Pedersen and Margit Lohrs—emigrated to Los Angeles when their daughter was twelve, Anglicized their last name, and bought a grocery shop in Venice. A brown photograph showed tall, slender Margit with her hair fastened up and Niall looking serious in front of their shop. At eighteen, Birgit Peterson married a failed gold prospector nine years older than she was, an Irishman named Cavanaugh, in Los Angeles and had a son and daughter. Her husband worked in shipyards and laid track until he heard they were hiring on the Comstock Lode in Nevada. Leaving his wife and children in Los Angeles, he went to Nevada City, intending to send for them if he could make more money there. He was killed in a cave-in three weeks later. Birgit— married only five years before she was widowed—moved with her children into her parents' house and worked in their store as she had before she married.

Birgit's father died suddenly when she was twenty-nine, leaving her his life's savings. With her mother, nine-year-old son, and seven-year-old daughter, she moved from Los Angeles to Berkeley where she used her inheritance to buy the house on California Avenue. The family occupied the first floor and rented out the rooms upstairs to lodgers—there were plenty in those days. Birgit Cavanaugh chose Berkeley because she was determined that her two children would get an education at the university there. Their lives were cramped, but the son graduated with a degree in architecture and the daughter in psychology. Birgit lived in that house on California Avenue for years after her children were grown, taking in boarders as long as she was able, and living there by herself afterwards.

Birgit loved San Francisco and Berkeley and claimed a large circle of friends, but she never remarried. She also loved Los Angeles and told her children and grandchildren stories about hiking in the mountains, trips to the ocean, and long, dry summers when forest fires raged. She died when her granddaughter Diane was twelve, and her own children buried her beside her parents. Diane recalled the day Birgit sat in a high-backed chair in the front room watching her ten-year-old granddaughter draw and said to her daughter-in-law, in the slight Scandinavian intonation that she never lost, "She'll be an artist like you, Ulana, and she'll come back to California."

"How can you be so sure?" her mother asked.

"Because she has the West in her blood," her grandmother answered.

Diane's father Richard studied architecture with Frank Lloyd Wright at Taliesin West in Arizona and went to Stanford for his MA where he met his wife, an art student on a scholarship who wanted to leave behind her family of factory workers in North Carolina. It seemed the two coasts tugged on them until they moved inland; he took a job with a company in Columbus and Ulana painted portraits on commission and taught art to high school students. Their children—a son, also Richard, and Diane—went to the University School where they both finished before they were eighteen. Richard studied physics at Columbia.

Her brother's success and her own similarity to her mother probably caused Diane to quarrel bitterly with her parents from the time she was eleven. Diane accused Ulana of trying to rise above her family, and Richard's father had been a miner and his mother a boarding-house keeper, so what were they doing now but trying to be something they weren't? She said they wanted to make her into copies of themselves and told them they couldn't know what was best for her because she was different from them, all the while knowing that her parents had always encouraged their children to think for themselves. When they visited North Carolina she overheard her mother complaining one day about Diane's rebelliousness. Her grandmother answered, "Well, you were the same way, Ulana."

Diane walked around to the back of the house where her grandmother used to keep a kitchen garden. Someone had replaced the old cane fence with redwood. Her father still owned the house, now divided into three apartments inhabited by strangers. Although it looked nearly the same as it had eight years ago, Diane felt as if she'd been someone else then, living a different life, like a character in a story she was re-reading. Kicking a stone from the path, she strode to the front of the house and headed down California Street.

"How many of you can find Webster Springs on a map?" the teacher asked the kids one morning on Diane's first co-op job as a teacher's aide during the winter of 1965. Martin Grassman, an Antioch graduate, had come to this school in West Virginia the previous year with the Teacher Corps. Diane watched him, arms folded, thin and muscular, his dark eyes searching the students' faces. His disheveled white shirt was partly pulled out of his loose-fitting pants.

Her first quarter at Antioch College proved to be the favorite time of her life so far. For her second term Diane chose this co-op to find out if teaching might be for her.

"Sixth graders should be able to read a map," Martin said encouragingly rather than admonishingly.

"My pa has a map in his car," one boy said.

"Good. And what does he use it for?"

"Don't know."

"Where does he drive to?"

"Hunnington, sometimes."

"Where's Huntington?" the teacher asked him.

The boy shrugged.

"How many have ever tried to read a map?"

No one raised a hand.

Diane looked up from the felt she was cutting for the children to sew. They were going to make their own costumes for a play the class was writing together. Martin had sacked the dog-eared textbooks and allowed students write their own stories and read them to the class. At the end of the year he promised to bind all their work into a book.

"How many of you know where West Virginia is?"

No hands went up.

"Look here," Martin told them, pulling an old map of the United States down from its holder on the wall. "Here it is. Right below Pennsylvania and Ohio, between Virginia and Kentucky. Have you heard of those places?"

All the heads nodded.

"Anyone visited those places?"

Everyone sat still, eyes on the teacher.

"Okay, no more geography for today. We're going outside to draw a map. Bring your tablets and pencils. Everybody get your coats."

Shouting, they ran for the dark cloak room and grabbed their jackets and hats from hooks on the wall. Some wore short sleeves and no socks, and few had gloves. The girls wore blue jeans underneath their cotton skirts.

Diane followed them outside where Martin was already explaining above their excited talk.

"Tom, you and Wilfred go that way; Bobby Joe, you and Ondine that way. Draw the school building in the center. Put in every street that goes to it. I'm a visitor trying to find the school, and you're going to show me how to find everything."

"What if they don't come back?" Diane asked.

"That happens in the fall or spring during harvesting or planting," he answered, "but not so much in the winter."

"Do you think they'll be able to draw it?"

"Yes," he said, watching them. "They don't know geography, but they do know the layout of their families' farms. They know exactly how long it takes to walk to any stream or pond where they can fish and how many steps to the well because they have to carry the water, and they know how many windrows they can get out of a hay field. They know the lay of the land, but it's in their heads."

"I don't know how you understand them, coming from Baltimore," Diane commented. Only occasionally did Diane hear in Martin's pronunciation the remnants of an East Coast accent leveled by years in the Midwest.

"And being Jewish? You do whatever it takes," he shrugged. "In most ways, teaching here is more fun than a city school. Nobody cares if I don't follow the curriculum. I've never had a parent come in to complain about anything. They don't have time. And they don't even know what their kids are learning. Most of them never went to school beyond eighth grade. Some never went at all. Lots of them don't care whether their kids even go to school or not; when they're old enough to tie their own shoes and pour cereal from a box the parents leave them to themselves, like a litter of pups."

Diane took a few steps in the opposite direction and looked out over the field next to the school.

"Never thought you'd meet people like this, did you?" Martin asked.

When she turned her head she saw him watching her closely, his well-formed hands on his narrow hips, his shirt sleeves unbuttoned and cuffs turned up even though it was February.

"No. I didn't even know people still lived like this," she answered.

"You mean plowing with horses?"

"I mean thinking that because they didn't go beyond the eighth grade, their kids don't need to either."

"That's what I want to lead them out of," he answered, his dark eyes shining.

Martin turned his gaze back to the kids pointing, talking, and scribbling. They all did come back to the classroom, running toward him when he called, noisily throwing their coats onto hooks in the old cloakroom, chattering over their crudely drawn maps.

🦟🦟🦟   🦟🦟🦟   🦟🦟🦟

A pile of snow fell from the white pine branch outside the window of Martin's living room.

His wife Elaine was breast-feeding their two-month-old son Cody in a rocking chair by the bookcase. She was a beautiful woman with dark, shining eyes and lustrous dark brown hair. A Chinese teapot and cups, bought during her co-op in Taiwan, stood on one table, and hand-woven curtains from Honduras covered the windows. Framed pictures of Martin and Elaine in the Honduran village where they served in the Peace Corps, as well as one of their simple wedding in Glen Helen near the Antioch campus, hung on the living room wall.

A log broke apart inside the wood-burning stove, and Martin laid his book on the coffee table, opened the iron door, and pushed a poker into the embers.

"They really learned from drawing those maps of the town," he said suddenly, closing the door of the stove. "One day they'll find a way to get out of here."

Elaine was stroking her sleeping boy's back.

"Is it really so bad for them here?" Diane asked. She sat cross-legged on the floor reading *The Rebel*.

"Would you like to live the way they do?" Martin replied.

"No, because I come from a different place," she answered, sitting up, "but I don't think living without maps and electricity is so bad if you've never had them. Is it so much better having dishwashers and electric can openers? If these people have knowledge 'in their heads,' why do they need to put it on paper? They grow their own food and forecast weather. We can't do that. They know more about survival than we do. And *we're* here to teach *them*?"

"It's my job to help them achieve all they can," Martin explained. "Otherwise they'll be left behind. If they want to stay here, they can. At least they'll have a choice."

"Maybe this life is all they really need," Diane insisted, throwing her head back. "Maybe having choices will only make them dissatisfied with what they have."

"They'll know better than to marry their own cousins and lock their kids up in the back shed," Martin answered, referring to a local man who kept his retarded son imprisoned in a woodshed for five years before the authorities found out and took the child away.

"Instead they'll be locked in some institution away from their families and taken care of by strangers," Diane said, leaning back.

"Strangers trained in their care, at least. I don't believe ignorance is bliss."

"Diane's learning whether or not she wants to teach," Elaine said, shifting Cody gently. "I agree with her that education is never just what we learn inside the school."

"They weren't inside last Monday when they drew their own maps," Martin said.

Elaine and Martin had the ideal relationship, Diane thought at that moment. If she were ever to marry, she would probably choose someone like

Martin who knew what he wanted and pursued it with so much energy.

During spring quarter Diane met a third-year student, Alan, who wanted to be a director and suggested that Diane should help with the set of the play they were doing. The stage was supposed to be bare except for a tree; maybe she could figure out a way to paint the background to make it look more spacious, since the characters were supposed to be standing on a plain. Diane created the shadow of a tree by shining light on an iron pipe that she heated and bent into a contorted shape.

"It's about two guys waiting for God to appear, but of course God never comes because he doesn't exist," Alan told her. They were moving props in the rehearsal room.

"I think that's too easy," Diane argued, shoving a chair across the bare wooden floor. "People wait around for lots of things to happen that never do. The two men are just two parts of the same person. This guy they talk about is whatever is missing from their lives."

"Maybe he's fate."

"Come on," she retorted. "People don't wait around for that."

"How do you see Lucky and the other guy, oppressed and oppressor? The others watch and do nothing."

"One of them tries to help."

"Not very hard, he doesn't," Alan answered. "And in the end Lucky enslaves his master. It's a way of saying that the oppressed will eventually turn on their oppressors and become tyrants themselves."

"Then maybe the other guys are right to do nothing."

In April when Diane turned eighteen, a friend drove her to Planned Parenthood in Springfield and got a prescription for birth control pills. She didn't want Alan to know he was her first, so she locked herself in the bathroom, pulled two tampons out of the box, and shoved them as hard as she could into herself.

"Are you all right?" her roommate Stacy called.

"I'm okay. Got my finger caught in the damn zipper."

Diane swallowed the tablet that Stacy's boyfriend Terry got from someone and waited a long time listening to jazz on Alan's stereo. She and Alan smoked dope with Stacy and Terry in the woods near the campus several times, but Terry said this was supposed to be better than anything they'd tried yet. Rays of light began to follow the movement of her own hands; when Stacy got up to put another record on, a silver-gold shadow followed her. When Stacy started to peel an orange Diane flinched: it was a living, breathing thing; Stacy knew it too, because she put the paring knife down and held the orange for a long time pulsing and squeaking.

In the bathroom mirror Diane saw her own face taking on the pattern of the faded beige wallpaper with black curlicues; as she watched, her reflection became a jigsaw puzzle of the same picture. The walls vibrated with the energy that circulated around all four of them, but when she locked the door and tried to turn on the taps, the faucets and pipes leered back at her, the curving iron stem of an old-fashioned lamp squirmed, and the tiny latch morphed into a large black lever. Suddenly she felt anxious and walked back into the living room where Terry and Alan sat grinning. The colors of a large Pollack-like painting on the wall vibrated and twisted, then burst like fireworks into gold, purple, and green. Diane stepped inside the mass of color that swirled and spiraled all around her.

Snow covered the wet, dark branches of trees in little Gramercy Park in New York behind a tall iron fence in a neighborhood of apartment buildings with neo-classical and Gothic-revival details. Diane climbed the curved, carpeted stairs of the National Arts Club and ran her hand along the smooth wooden balustrade. Oriental vases stood on mahogany tables; the walls were hung with Arts Nouveau, Impressionist, and Dadaist paintings. The opulent rooms reminded her of museums in France she had visited with her family. Guests wore gowns and tuxedos and held tall drinks. She was here with the director and interns of the Harlem Theatre Project where she worked in public relations. It was her advisor's idea; he wanted her to do something different for this co-op. It was hard to find an apartment in the City, so Diane shared a four-room flat on Greene Street in Soho with friends of Terry's who went to NYU. Diane walked behind the crowd in the main gallery decorated with enormous blue and white Asian vases, black and pink striped settees, and a dark red Persian carpet.

Will Federson, the project director, was thirty-two, stocky, and muscular, with a round face, large cheeks, and smooth, dark skin. When he smiled the lines beside his mouth made Diane think of wrinkles in hot tar. All the interns were black. Diane knew Will would never have hired her if the advertising manager, who knew her advisor at Antioch, hadn't said they should get a college kid to work in public relations rather than lay out the money for a permanent hire. Will had a short fuse and bullied his actors and crew, but just when they were about to quit in frustration he knew how to encourage them into staying. He especially wanted this play to succeed—it was one of his own, about a young friend who'd been murdered in Needle Park. Diane loved the dance-like, haunted movements Will taught his actors and that he said were more important than spoken words and expressed the savage in man; a performance wasn't any good, he said, unless it made the audience hurt a little.

"Snazzy place," said a voice behind her, and she turned to one of the actors named Tad.

"*Too* snazzy," she said.

"I don't know; I kind of like a lot of color."

"If you like color why are you looking at me?" she asked, throwing her head back. She was wearing a low-cut red dress with long sleeves buttoned at the wrists that she'd bought in a boutique in the Village, and she'd pinned her hair back in a French braid. Will wanted everyone to look professional tonight.

Tad grinned. "Maybe I like a little variety." Diane wondered whether Tad, who had the lightest skin in the crew, felt on the outs from them. She knew Will thought highly of his talent. Besides acting, he worked as a lighting technician and photographer.

Someone turned the lights down and the projector came on. Will explained the slides—pictures of different productions his company performed. Watching his shining eyes, Diane felt a thrill rise from her stomach as she listened to him describe his project, dropping his usual street slang and explaining in formal English that the actors and technicians also served as the theater's janitors, all the time holding other jobs. When he finished, the people applauded warmly, though she knew they didn't understand him. They were like her parents who always talked about civil rights and racial equality but didn't know any black people. Their faces resembled the petals of jonquils that thrust from tall, cream-colored vases standing on small tables polished to glistening reflection.

※ ※ ※   ※ ※ ※   ※ ※ ※

"Funny how pale white people look to me now," Diane said, studying Will's paintings of African dancers in long yellow and red costumes. They went in his efficiency on Amsterdam after seeing *The Andalusian Dog*. A black and white Art Nouveau lamp threw faint light on the wall.

"You're an artist," he said. "I'm going to have you work on sets from now on. You're wasted in that office." He placed a snifter of brandy on the table in front of her.

"But I'm good at it," she said, turning toward him, "and I like doing publicity."

"Anybody can do that kind of thing."

"Oh no just anybody can't," she said, straightening her shoulders. "Even you should know publicity takes creativity."

"What you mean 'even' me?"

"I mean *you're* the artist. And you should be more involved with what *we're* doing." She leaned slightly back, her hands thrust into the hip pockets of her jeans.

"Let me tell you, Girl, my whole life been public relations."

"What do you mean?"

"My father died when I was fourteen. Started skipping school and would've dropped out of high school if I hadn't met an older cat who heard me play and asked me to sit in at a joint in the Village. I played trumpet Friday and Saturday nights. After a while he told me I should go to City College. Only stayed two years, started doing my own stage productions, and then I met up with these two fellows who had a clothing store, said they'd bankroll my theatre."

"You sure were good with those types at the Arts Club," she said, sipping brandy.

"They're people, and I want to communicate with them. I want their money, sure, but I also want them to see my plays and tell their friends to see my plays. I used to hate white people till I started mixing with them. Found out they have the same worries I do, only more. When I see cats shucking and jiving trying to scare white people, I want to tell them to cut that crap out, they aren't scaring anybody or proving anything except how stupid they are."

"I was in Chicago last year on a co-op," she told him, running her hand along the back of a brocade couch. "I wanted to walk to the lake but I took a wrong turn somewhere and ended up in this black section of town. Some guy across the street was shouting at me, and I didn't know what to do. Some black girls came along and one of them put her arm around me. One of them said 'Is she scared?' and another one said 'Sure she's scared,' but I wasn't, I just didn't know what was wrong. They walked me back to Lake Shore Drive."

"Now don't you go trusting people just because someone been good to you."

She laid her palm against the small of his back and ran it up his spine to his shoulders.

"You been seeing Tad," he said.

"We went out a couple times with some of the others. No big thing."

He put his arm around her waist, drew her to him, and kissed her.

"How old are you?" he asked.

"Nineteen," she answered, reaching her arms around his waist.

"You been with a man before?"

"One."

"You a baby," he said.

"Ever made it with a white chick before?"

"Lotsa times."

"Well I've never made it with a black man. And I stopped taking pills, but I have a pack of condoms."

"Okay. I can wear a raincoat. I already have a son, and I don't want another one with no white lady."

"Where's he?"

"With his mother. I got her pregnant and married her. Never do that again with anybody, white or black."

"I'm not interested in getting married," Diane said.

Putting his hands on her buttocks, he drew her closer.

"You'll get married," he said, kissing her neck. "All the ladies do. But I know: you still 'findin' yourself."

"And I suppose you never had to find yourself?" She pressed her pelvis against him.

"Baby, I done found myself a *long* time ago."

Diane sat upright, immersed in hot water in the old claw-foot enamel tub in the apartment. Steam rose from her shoulders as she felt her blood tingling. The life in her felt like turbulent waves crashing onto the sand of a beach.

In June the cast and crew celebrated the end of a run while Will went to Boston to meet a contributor. Afterwards they drank Heineken and stood near the piano with their arms around each other's waists, singing "You Can't Hurry Love" and "Don't You Want Somebody to Love?" while one of the actors played. In late afternoon Tad announced he had beer, dope, and food at his place and everyone was invited.

About half of them walked in the close, humid heat the few blocks over to Tenth Avenue up to Tad's loft on the top floor of a warehouse. Through the iron grill of the freight elevator, Diane watched the brick wall descending, heard the loud clicking of the hydraulic lift, and felt the metal car vibrate to a halt under her feet. They rolled the gate back, stepped across a narrow, dark hallway, and spilled into the room as Tad held open the gray metal door.

The loft was spacious and filled with poster-sized photographs of Duke Ellington and John Coltrane. At the far end of the room a copper bed frame and sheetless mattress had been shoved against the wall near crates strewn with clothes. A plastic curtain hung from a circular rod was drawn back far enough to reveal the faucet, drainage hole, sink, and toilet that served as a bathroom. In the other corner stood an old formica table with aluminum chairs, portable refrigerator, and hotplate. Purple bed sheets hanging from a rope tied to brackets covered four large windows. The cast members stood drinking Stroh's, joking, and dancing to Ellington. People came and went. As the veiled light at the windows dimmed, a stage hand named Leonard lit a joint and passed it around, and Tad changed the record to Coltrane. Diane knew she wasn't in control and was probably making a fool of herself, the only white person among all these black kids, but she'd worked with them almost six months, and this was the last time she'd be with them. The combination of beer and dope made her feel as if she were drifting half-submerged.

"Gotta go," said Renee, one of the actresses.

"I gotta go too," Diane said. "Wait up, Renee."

"C'mon, stay awhile," Tad said, putting his arm around Diane and stroking her hair.

"Gotta go, honey," Renee insisted.

Tad started kissing Diane and running his hands down her neck. She heard the door slam and realized vaguely that she was alone with Tad. His hands explored her shoulders and hips as he said, "You could be an actress with those prominent cheek bones. Let me take a picture of you." His fingers released the top button on her shirt.

"No," she said, but couldn't get up.

"I've never made it with a white girl," he said. "Just let me look at you. You can be so out to lunch you don't even have to know I'm here." She felt his hands unbuttoning her shirt. When he began to unzip her jeans she sat up and pushed his hands away from her.

"No," she declared. "I'm leaving."

"No you aren't," Tad said, holding her down.

She tried to struggle out of his grasp, feeling afraid for the first time in her life.

"Am I too dark for you, baby?"

"Don't be stupid," she said, pushing at him as he forced her down and straddled her pelvis.

She fought, but he was stronger and not so drunk and held her down as he pulled off her jeans. She tried to scream but couldn't breathe and heard him saying, "No one can hear you. This room been soundproofed and there's nobody downstairs anyway. I know you've been screwing Will, so you can do it with me. All those cunts want to screw Will."

As he forced himself into her she thought she was strangling, and with every thrust she felt she was losing her innocence along with everything she believed in. She concentrated on the hard, bare floor under her head and shoulder blades, thinking if she could only keep breathing she would survive this. Tad finally stood over her.

"There, come in here and say no to me," he hissed.

She pushed herself up from the floor, grabbed her jeans, and ran for the sink, his semen running down her leg. Still dizzy with the wine, she yanked the curtain around and washed herself with a towel that hung on a hook. When she pulled the curtain back he was standing there, hands on his hips.

"Don't you touch me."

"You're a hypocrite. You think because you screw the big man you're cool. Let me tell you, girl, you aren't the only one he screws. He doing it with all the actresses."

Disgusted and angry, she ran toward the door, down four flights of steps, and into the street toward the subway on 126th. When Diane got to the apartment she shut herself in her room. The other girls were away. She couldn't remember why she'd gone to Tad's loft in the first place, except that everyone went there after the cast party. Now she knew she could trust no one; she had been a fool ever to trust anyone.

Diane stayed in the apartment all day Monday but on Tuesday forced herself to go for a walk in Tompkins Park. She used to enjoy watching the people who hung out in there, but now she kept away from them, walking on the edge of the pavement, vowing not to trust anyone again, while they watched her over their shoulders.

On Wednesday Will called her.

"I've been busy," she said.

"What's happened?" he asked. "Something, I know; I can hear it in your voice."

"Nothing."

"If you don't tell me I'm coming over there."

"I'll meet you somewhere, not here or the theater." Her voice wavered.

"Okay, we'll go to the park."

"Too public."

"Baby, what's happened? I'm coming over."

"No." She paused. "I'll come to your place."

Diane took the A train to Amsterdam. In the hallway outside his apartment a single bulb shone from the entrance onto the floor of the vestibule. When Will opened the door she stepped into the living room without looking at him.

"Now you sit down and I'll get us a glass of wine."

He went into the kitchen while she stared at the painting of the dancing woman in the voluminous yellow dress that now appeared alien rather than exotic.

Will walked into the living room and set a glass of red wine in front of her.

"Now what is it?" he asked as he took her arm and guided her to the settee. She sank onto the cushions and began to cry into her hands.

"What happened? Tell me nice and slow." He drew a handkerchief from his pocket and put his arm around her shoulders. Diane rubbed her face and swallowed.

"I went to Tad's place after the party Sunday. A whole lot of us went."

"So I heard. What happened?"

"We were drinking and smoking. I didn't realize when the others started leaving. Then Renee said she was going and I told her to wait up. He said to stay awhile."

"And did you?"

"I didn't want to. I was drunk. He started unbuttoning my shirt."

"Then what?"

"I tried to get away."

"Did he force you?"

She nodded, crying again.

"Did he beat you?"

"He held me down. No, I don't think he hit me. I can't remember."

"Honey, you didn't do anything wrong. You just trust people too much. You'll get over it in time. You need to go back to work and try to forget it. He's not in control of you: you are. Tell yourself nothing like this will ever happen again."

"He told me something else."

"What did that bastard tell you?"

"He said you screw all the actresses."

"Do I got time to screw all the actresses working sixteen hours a day?"

She sat up.

"Did you report this to the police?" he asked.

"I knew Tad. I went to his place. Who'd believe me?"

"You're white. Tad's black. They'd believe you. You got to report this."

"When my roommate at Antioch was raped she went to the police, but they made it sound like it was her fault. She told me never to put myself through all that stuff."

"You should have reported it. Tell you what: I'm going to get rid of him."

"He's important to your project."

"Baby, actors like him are a dime a dozen."

"I haven't cried like this since I was a little girl." She rubbed her face with the back of her hand.

"That's okay, baby, you just go right ahead and cry all you want to. You going to tell your parents?"

"What would I say to them? I went to a party where I got drunk?"

"You're being unfair. They probably understand more than you think."

"You never cry," she said.

"Oh yes I do," he insisted. "I've cried myself a good many times, when I wished there was somebody to cry with me. I hardly knew my father even before he died. I never told you this, but my stepfather raped me more than once. When my mother tried to stop him he beat her up.

"I saw a guy set fire to a homeless man lying drunk in the street," he continued. "My friend and I were coming out the back of a club where we'd just played. We saw this man laughing at the one who was on fire lying there screaming, and when he saw us he ran away. We rolled the poor guy and put the fire out, but his neck and arms were burned, and half his clothes were burned off. There's nothing people won't do to each other."

"Did you call the police?" She sat up.

"Course not. Two young black guys going to call the police? There wasn't no law going to protect us. Eventually you learn who you can trust, and you learn to protect yourself. It's the price you pay for living. Finally, there's nobody responsible for us but ourselves. But I know you. You're not going to let anybody stop you."

He made love to her that afternoon, talking to her the whole time, telling her Tad was just a bad dream, she should forget him, he wasn't worth thinking about, she was a real woman and strong, he knew she would make it; she had talent, brains, and drive; the world was just opening up for her and she could do anything if she put her mind to it; she would be able to face any difficult thing now without fear.

※ ※ ※   ※ ※ ※   ※ ※ ※

Diane sat naked on the commode staring at the reddish-brown stain in her pants, four days late. Always very regular, she spent the last three days trying to keep her mind off her fear she might be pregnant. Laying her arm on the wooden windowsill, she rested her forehead against the soft skin of her inner elbow, closed her eyes, and sobbed a few times without tears. Every muscle in her body relaxed as she expelled all the air from her lungs, then slowly drew in a long breath. She ran the palms of her hands up and down her arms, around her breasts, and along her thighs.

Sitting up, she said softly, "I will never be afraid of anything ever again. *Ever again.*"

Some bird chirped a three-note song outside above the low rumble of a car on Greene Street. Through the window she saw steel fire escapes descend the opposite wall like a zigzagging black sculpture above thin locust saplings that somehow survived in that canyon of concrete.

✳ ✳ ✳   ✳ ✳ ✳   ✳ ✳ ✳

They sat at an outdoor table at Sixth Avenue and Twelfth Street under an old maple. The waiter placed a glass of whiskey in front of Will and red wine before Diane, who used a fake ID.

"Suppose I just stay in New York and work for you?"

"Nothing doing, baby, you got to finish your degree. Remember, we come from different places."

"I'll transfer to Pratt."

"No, baby, you're too young for me."

"You told me I was strong." She raised her head.

"You are, like a young tree that stands up to the wind. I'm like a big old tree with tough bark."

"Bad comparison. You're only thirty-two."

"I've lived a lot in those years."

"So have I."

"Not like I have," he said, shaking his head. "And I don't want you to live the way I have. You're going home and finish that degree."

"You know I love you," she said.

He raised his drink and tilted it at her.

"Do you know what you're talking about?" he asked.

"Yes." She straightened her shoulders.

He swallowed the whiskey in one gulp.

"You think we won't ever see each other again, but you're wrong," he said, setting the glass down on the red-checked plastic tablecloth. "We'll see each other again. That's why I'm not going to say good-bye. It's the way things work out. You part of my life now, and I'm part of yours."

During her third autumn quarter at Antioch in 1966, Diane lived with

Stacy in Terry's apartment off campus while he was in San Francisco. Most of her friends had taken extended co-ops or gone to the other division. She took no theater courses and didn't volunteer to work on the production, instead spending long hours in the art building throwing paint onto large canvases and trying her hand at whole-body portraits.

On December 13, Diane paced along the brick walkway in falling snow to the student union. She hadn't found an interesting co-op for next quarter, so she considered staying on campus for the winter. Inserting her key, she opened the tiny door and withdrew the pile. A letter lay among the glossy ads for sweatshirts and rings. Since she was no correspondent, she received few letters, even from Will, and she turned the envelope over to see in the upper left corner the name of one of the crew from the Harlem Theater Project. She opened it slowly and read the large loopy scrawl that told her Will had been killed by armed robbers. He'd been out walking past midnight and two guys jumped and knifed him. The funeral was Monday.

Diane crumpled the letter into her left hand and walked the perimeter of the campus before she headed back to the apartment. As she started to take her jacket off she realized she hadn't zipped it up before leaving the union. She had walked a mile through snow without noticing the cold.

"What's happening?" Stacy asked, not looking up from her book.

Diane stared at the crumpled paper in her hand. "Will's been killed. I just got the letter."

"Oh, Di, no," Stacy said, laying her book on the table, getting up, and putting her arms around Diane.

"How'd it happen?

Diane began to smooth out the letter she still held.

"It was a robbery. He was by himself . . ."

"Come over here and sit down," Stacy said as she led Diane to the sagging couch.

"Do you want me to get you anything?"

"No."

"You going to the funeral?"

"I'd have to ask my parents for the money. I never told them about Will. I could hitchhike." She was talking to herself more than to Stacy, slumped forward and running her hands through her limp, wet hair.

"You can't hitchhike in December," Stacy said.

"Maybe I could take a bus."

"I'll run over and check the schedule," Stacy said. "We sure could use a phone." Stacy stood up and grabbed her coat. "You stay here now," she said. "I'll be right back."

Diane sat staring listlessly at the closed door through which Stacy disappeared. She was a good friend, the only one Diane confided in about the rape or her affair with Will. Diane walked slowly into the room where she slept and found the one picture she owned of him.

"Why did you send me away?" she asked aloud.

Only then did she cry—furiously, into her hands until she stopped from exhaustion. Her head hurt, but a walk might cure that. Where was Stacy? She said she'd be right back.

Diane pulled on her jacket, walked quickly down to the main street in town, and crossed the campus to the woods. Someone waved to her as she hurried past the nature center perched on the edge of the ravine and followed the stone steps down the hillside to the stream. From the path she took a side trail through some tall pines to a sedimentary outcropping overlooking the Little Miami. She scraped the snow off a large flat rock where she sat with closed eyes, turned her face to the starless sky, and felt the snowflakes falling on her skin, melting, and running down her neck.

"Do you know where you are, Diane?" someone asked. She tried to answer, but she couldn't move her lips. She was lying in a bed.

"Diane, do you know where you are?" the voice asked again.

"New York," she answered.

"No, not New York. You're in Columbus." The voice belonged to a man.

"Do you know what day it is?"

"No."

"Do you know why you're in the hospital?"

"No."

"They found you in the woods. It's a miracle you didn't contract pneumonia."

The woods were in Central Park. How had she gotten from New York to Columbus?

"You've been here three days. You're getting better. You're lucky you didn't freeze to death."

She saw a white coat and a long white face framed with brown hair.

"We're sending you to Dr. Mahalik tomorrow. Do you know where Upham Hall is?"

It was the psychiatric ward at Ohio State, a rectangular box all glass and steel on stilts over a parking garage. They were wasting their time: she wasn't crazy.

She must have slept because she woke up in a room that seemed transparent in the sunlight. An IV was attached to her hand.

"You haven't eaten anything for almost a week," a nurse explained. "Are you hungry?"

"No."

"The doctor'll be in to see you tomorrow. Your parents come every day."

The doctor did come the next day, a young man with pale skin and hair and green eyes that were moist at the corners. Diane sat up in bed while he sat in a straight chair. He asked her if she knew the date and where she was.

"Columbus," she replied. "December."

"December 16. Friday. Can you verify your name for me?"

She repeated her first and last names, though she resented his asking. Who was he to make demands on her?

"Last week you sat in the woods for hours after dark, and it was below freezing. Diane, why were you sitting in the woods?"

"I was watching the snow." Damn him. What business was it of his?

"In the dark? Your mother says you haven't eaten much since you came back from New York last summer, and your roommate at college said you hadn't eaten anything the day they found you. You're ten pounds under weight. Can you tell me why?"

Diane looked at the moist eyes and pink lids. Why hadn't Stacy come back that day?

"We're trying to help you, Diane," he said.

"Do you know," Diane began, "that I'm nineteen? I'm supposed to be having the time of my life."

"Why aren't you having the time of your life?" the doctor asked. "What's stopping you?"

She didn't answer.

"Do you have a boyfriend?"

"No; not now. I used to."

"Where's he now?"

"New York."

"Was college going okay for you?"

"Yes," she answered.

"Do you want to go back?"

"No."

"Why not?"

"I just don't," she shrugged.

When the doctor left, the nurse came in and disconnected the IV tube.

"You can get up and walk around," she said. "There's a library and a game room downstairs." And the outer doors are all locked, Diane added to herself.

"Your clothes are here in this closet," the nurse said. "Your mother brought some things for you."

After the nurse left, Diane swung her legs over the side of the bed and walked to the bathroom. In the mirror she saw large, hollow eyes and dirty, limp hair. Slowly she drew on the aquamarine cotton dress with long sleeves that she hadn't worn for years. There was nothing wrong with being in the loony bin, she told herself. Her mother always said that mental illness wasn't anything to be ashamed of. Her aunt was a psychologist, and she said the same. But Diane wasn't mentally ill. She needed to figure out a way to get out of here without telling these doctors anything. Will's memory was too important to share with people she didn't know or trust.

Diane wore that dress and pinned up her hair the next time the doctor visited. She was sitting on the side of the bed, imagining how she would paint the mass of shimmering metallic color in the parking lot.

"You look great," the doctor said, walking into the room. "Okay if I sit?"

Diane nodded once. He sat in a chair near the bed and laid his folder on the medicine table.

"Are you ready to tell me why you were in the woods all night?"

She saw his pale green eyes, the pale neck with blotched skin emerging from his white coat.

"I went there to think," she said.

"You mother says your roommate told her you'd gotten a letter about a friend who died."

"Yes, I did," she said, nodding. So Stacy told them her secret.

"And you were close to this friend?"

Tell him just enough to get him out of here.

"He was director of the theater where I worked. It was just a shock to hear that somebody I'd worked with every day was dead. That's all."

"And that's why you sat all night outside?"

"No."

"What else might have been on your mind?"

"It was the shift from New York to Ohio," she stated. "They're just too different."

"You told me you had a boyfriend in New York. Was he the one who died?"

"No," she shook her head.

"Do you want to tell me what happened?"

"He had a job there. I went back to college." She shrugged.

"Has a boy ever tried to get rough with you, Diane?"

She focused on the folds of pink skin around his eyes.

"No."

"Maybe what you need is a little less excitement," the doctor concluded, closing his folder. "Tell you what: let's see if we can get you out of here." He stood, tucked the folder under his arm, and put his palm against the flat handle of the door.

"You stay pretty for me now," he said, pushing the handle down. After he left, she raised her middle finger at the door.

That afternoon when Ulana and Richard came to see her, Diane asked for some more of her clothes, and she washed and braided her hair. The doctor discharged her after one more day and sent her home, where she spent the time walking around the house and garden. There was a letter from Stacy telling her how worried she'd been and how bad she felt that she hadn't come right back after she went to the union. When she left Diane, Stacy tried to find a bus leaving sooner than the ones listed on the board; she had to go get change to call the station in Springfield. She felt responsible for what happened. Diane realized she probably hadn't waited long enough for Stacy to come back and she shouldn't blame Stacy for trying to help. Tears rose to her eyes.

On Christmas Eve Diane's brother came with his new fiancée Sarah, so for three days Diane didn't have to be bothered answering questions. Ulana talked to her future daughter-in-law about their plans; Richard talked to his son about his work. Neither Diane's brother nor Sarah pried into her business, asking her only how she liked Antioch and being satisfied with brief answers. She was relieved they didn't want her to talk about being in Upham, and she knew they didn't want her trouble to interfere with their happiness. She didn't resent their indifference; they had a right to their own life.

Diane watched her mother taking the ornaments off the tree the day after Christmas, packing them carefully in tissue paper, and laying them in boxes. Her mother's hair was graying but was still mostly blond. She wore it long and wound in a French twist like Diane's grandmother, and although her fair skin no longer looked youthful, Ulana was still beautiful. What would Diane look like when she was forty-five? She walked across the room and began lifting the ornaments off the tree. Diane held one they brought back from Switzerland, a clear globe with a tiny, painted wooden chalet inside. For a moment she wanted to tell her mother about Will, about everything. She drew in a breath, and just then Ulana asked, "Do you think you want to go back to Antioch winter quarter? You know, you can go to Ohio State instead." Diane saw the tiny lines at the corners of her mother's eyes.

"I don't know yet." Swallowing hard, Diane watched her mother wrap ornaments in tissue paper and insert them into little cardboard holders. She took a step back. No one knew anything about what happened in New York except Will, Stacy, Tad, and herself. Will was dead; she'd never see Tad again; Stacy hadn't told them very much. If Diane didn't say anything about it, it was like it never happened. All she needed to do was forget about it. Will wouldn't want her to waste her time feeling sorry for herself; he'd want her to do something with her life.

In the evening Diane sat down at the desk in her room and wrote a letter to Martin and Elaine telling them she wouldn't be going back to Antioch. She sealed and addressed the envelope, surprised at herself for filling a whole page. Then she wrote to Stacy explaining that she certainly didn't blame her for anything; it was Diane's own stupid decision to go walking in the woods in the snow.

After New Year's Day she found a letter from Martin in the mailbox. She'd written to the address in West Virginia, but he'd received it at their new place in Fort Collins where he was in a graduate program. Elaine was a teacher's aide in an elementary school but took a leave of absence after the birth of their second child in November. They were sorry to hear about Diane leaving Antioch and invited her to come and stay with them in Colorado. Maybe what she needed was a change. She could help with Cody and their new daughter Tess.

"She's had too much change," Ulana said to Richard when Diane showed them the letter. They were sitting at the big wooden dining room table. "We let her go to college too early, and after what's happened . . ."

Richard was tall, his hair mostly gray now, distinguished-looking in a brown V-necked sweater buttoned over a tan shirt. The room smelled like candle wax.

"She knows Martin," he said. "She talked about nothing else when she came back from West Virginia but Martin and Elaine. Diane, what do you want to do?"

In the evening of January 12, 1967, wearing her dark green parka, Diane climbed the steps of a Greyhound bus in downtown Columbus. In the middle of the night in Chicago she changed to one for Denver. She slept with her head against the window and woke at dawn as the bus drew into the station in Des Moines. Crossing Nebraska the second night, Diane awoke to see Orion and the Dipper in the clear winter sky. Before daybreak on January 14, she got off the bus in Denver and boarded another one for Fort Collins. No longer able to sleep, she watched the sun come up as the bus rolled past meadows, stands of pine and hardwood, and, in the distance, snow-capped peaks. The bus pulled into the station at about ten in the morning. She slung her backpack over her shoulders, collected the two green vinyl suitcases she had taken to Yellow Springs, West Virginia, Chicago, and New York, and walked through the turnstiles to the lobby. Picking out Martin's dark hair and eyes in the crowd,

Diane raised her arm and waved. Elaine held her sleeping daughter while between them Cody stood sucking his thumb. Martin stepped toward Diane, his arms outstretched, smiling broadly although there was something strained in his expression. She set the suitcases on the floor and felt herself swept into Martin's coat that smelled like snow. When she stepped back from him, Elaine handed Tess to Martin and hugged Diane.

"How you guys doing?" Diane asked, stooping to hug Cody who stood between his parents, fingers in his mouth. "What a big fellow you've grown into."

"We're doing great," Elaine said, taking Tess back from Martin.

"Come on, let's head for home," he said, picking up the suitcases. Diane led the way and opened the doors for him and Elaine.

They walked outside into the cold air toward the parking lot. Martin set the suitcases into the back of his sand-colored Volkswagen and they all piled into it, Martin driving, Elaine in the front holding Tess. Diane sat in the back seat beside Cody, who slept during the entire trip home. Piles of snow at the edges of the parking lot gleamed in the light.

Diane leaned on her right leg and looked up at the vertical brown Horsetooth Rocks rising high above the cedar trees and tamarack. Even though it was April, the soil was dry and dusty, and the sun shone hard and bright. She pulled her canteen from her backpack and took a long drink. Cottonwood and aspen leaves shimmered in the mountain wind. She shoved the canteen into her backpack, pulled the straps over her shoulders, and started up the trail.

Martin and Elaine rented a stucco and shingle house on Linden Street, near the Colorado State campus. Walking through the front door, Diane saw the same Chinese teacups on the table, Honduran curtains, pictures of their wedding, and Martin and Elaine in the Honduran village. They tried to get Diane to enroll at Colorado State and live with them; they'd be glad to have her help with the kids.

Diane spent one morning in the house before leaving and walking quickly to the campus and across the large grassy quads, glimpsing in the distance the peaks of the Rockies shrouded with the blue clouds of a winter storm. At the bookstore she filled out an application for work and afterwards bought presents for Elaine, Martin, Cody, and Tess, and postcards for friends.

Two days later the bookstore manager offered her work shelving art and theatre books. Diane began to draw again in pencil and ink. In April she'd be twenty and had no time to waste. She didn't want to ask her parents for money any more, since they'd already spent so much on her, and she was sure now she wasn't going back to Antioch. Instead, she'd work to make money to go to CSU.

One day in February she stepped out onto the porch to take in the mail and saw among the bills and ads an envelope addressed to her. The return address was Stacy's in Yellow Springs. Diane tore it open as she stood in the wind.

> Dear Di, I got your postcard from Fort Collins. Glad to hear you're in Colorado. I've never been. You know what? Terry wrote to me. He's still in San Francisco and loves it. Well, I thought maybe you might like to go since you're already so far west. Terry's living in a house with some people and I wrote and asked if he would have room for one more and he wrote back and said yes. Can you believe that, he actually answered my letter! His address is at the bottom. No phone. I have a new boyfriend named Mike and am going to Finland for the summer. Love, Stacy

Diane shoved the letter into her pocket. She had only two years of college to finish; why should she be in a hurry to leave?

Was it an eagle? A large bird with a wide wingspan circled outward from a tamarack on the hillside. Fishing Martin's binoculars from out of her pack, she found the bird in flight and distinguished the light brown neck feathers of a golden eagle. It circled and dipped behind some tall pines. Behind her the trail wound down the slopes like a shaded pencil line while ahead it entered a grove of low conifers thin and stunted by the wind. Shoving the binoculars back into her pack, she headed toward some trees that stood at the base of the high rocks.

The evening before, Tess shrieked and screamed when Elaine tried to put her to bed. Diane got up from the couch where she'd been reading *The Glass Bead Game* and climbed the steps to the children's bedroom. Diane opened the door to see Elaine with Tess in her arms. The baby's face was purple, and her tiny hands wet with tears and saliva.

"Can I do anything?" Diane asked. Elaine smiled, and Diane saw for the first time lines at the corners of her eyes and a strand of gray in her hair.

"Colic," Elaine explained softly. "It just has to pass."

Diane looked in on Cody, who was asleep on his parents' bed, and walked back down stairs and into the dimly lit hallway. The door of Martin's study opened and he strode toward the kitchen. When he passed her, his knuckles brushed her hand, and she could feel the warmth of his body and smell his wool sweater.

Now Diane found the hiking more difficult, going up over boulders beyond the tree line. She looked down on the tops of cottonwoods and tamaracks she had hiked through earlier and up at the high reddish rocks forming the last barrier to the summit. At the very top, the sheer cliffs of the Horsetooth rose to 7,000 feet of altitude. She rested at the foot, wondering whether she should attempt the summit alone; if she lost her footing on those high crags, she might get hurt and not be able to get down the mountain by herself. By the time Martin and Elaine missed her it would be dark, and she didn't have the right clothes to spend the night at that altitude.

She remembered Terry's answer to her letter. In San Francisco there was something going on all the time, like music and street dancing. He was living with a girl in a house near the park and could use another renter. Diane thought she might hop a ride with somebody. There were lots of names pinned on the ride board in the student union, and there was a crash pad on Remington a few blocks from Martin's where people stopped when they were driving west.

Squinting, Diane looked up at the sheer rocks. She pulled herself up over the large boulders and stood at last on top of the mountain in the burning air beneath the cloudless blue sky. The landscape sorted itself into dark trees, lighter green meadows, and gray-blue ovals of sparkling lakes. Diane paced the top of the rock to the end before retracing her steps to the trail head. There she looked out over the vista one more time, thinking Will had been right: she was in control of her life.

SIX

The tires of Daryl's Saab zinged over the steel webbing of the bridge. From the front passenger's seat, David watched the mountain rise before them out of the fog. To his right he saw the wooded crown of Angel Island, California gulls skimming the sparkling water in the angle of the sun, and a man standing near the side of the bridge looking down at the water.

"How's Daryl going to find us?" Terry asked from the back seat.

"We told him McClure's Beach," David said, glancing toward the rear. Rennie smiled at David.

The bridge that bore them across the water set them down on Highway One, and they drove toward Inverness and headed due north on Sir Francis Drake Boulevard. Shafts of radiance streamed through the high branches of Douglas fir and pine as Diane drove the car onto the Point Reyes peninsula and then a smaller road that snaked through marshes where white egrets stood, motionless, watching for fish. Before them they saw undulating bluffs covered with yellow grass. Diane pulled the car into a small graveled parking lot.

She and Rennie carried sleeping bags across the sand to a campsite secluded by a high grassy mound. David and Terry carried boxes of food. Rennie used an old board to clear debris out of the fire pit.

"Where you going?" Rennie asked.

"Find some wood," Diane answered as she strode across the dune.

David followed a narrow path that ran along the ridgeback down into a depression and up the far side. The bluff rose toward a point where rocks jutted from the patches of rough, gray-green grass above a sheer cliff falling to the beach below. The sea wind tossed the branches of scrub knobcone and southwestern pine. On a mound to the east a small band of tawny brown tulle elk stood among tall yellow grass. A buck lifted his head, watched David with mild curiosity, and returned to browsing among the shoots. Bloody cranesbill and Indian paintbrush waved in the strong wind beside the wide silver leaves of sand moss on the bluff. He strode up and across a dune and slid down the other side. In a large cove formed out of the black granite cliffs near the water's edge, he unlaced his shoes and poured the sand out of them. After he laced them up again he began collecting a few pieces of driftwood from the beach.

It was August. They'd come here to get away from the crowds. David shuddered when he remembered the house on Oak Street, the garage door that had almost never been opened now standing wide, people inside on sleeping bags spread out on wooden pallets on the oil stained, concrete floor. Dry leaves clustered in the corners, and cobwebs hung from the rafters. One day when he walked through the archway to the living room, a boy with disheveled hair lay on blankets spread on the floor.

"How you doing?" the boy said.

"Are you a friend of Terry's?" David asked.

"Who's Terry?"

"How about Rennie?"

"That chick with the long red hair?"

"Yes."

"Wow, I don't know where she is. Does she even hang around here anymore?"

"How long have you been here?"

"Don't know," the boy answered, rubbing his eyes. "Who are you?"

Standing with his hands in the hip pockets of his jeans, David watched the reddened sun descending toward the horizon and listened to the cacophony of crashing waves and shrieking gulls.

"You're a hard person to find," Diane declared, walking up beside him and dropping her load.

"Where'd you find all that?" he asked.

"That way under a stand of trees." She gestured across the dunes. "You look far away."

After a pause he responded, "I keep thinking I could have done something about that pilot whose plane went down. Maybe I made up an excuse for not diving in."

"You did everything you could." She ran her hand up and down his back.

"The truth is I felt relieved when I couldn't see anything, because I could tell myself I didn't have to go in."

"He'd have drowned before you got to him," she answered.

"Does that make up for not trying?" he asked, thinking women could never understand.

She put her arm around his waist. He pulled her close and kissed her. Her lips tasted of salt, and her skin felt gritty with sand.

"We should probably start back," she said finally. "It gets pretty dark out here after the sun goes down."

When they found the campsite again, Rennie already had a fire going and was heating beans in a pot. A motorcycle engine roared out of the dusk, and Daryl cruised over the dune on his red Harley, kicked the stand down, and killed the engine. Swinging his right leg over the saddle, he lifted his helmet off and hung it on the handlebars. His hair was matted with sweat.

"Nice of you to show up just after we do the work," Diane called to him.

"Least I brought the important stuff," Daryl answered.

Sitting on logs, they ate beans with hard-boiled eggs, brown bread, and slices of melon on old blue Melmac plates that Rennie had rounded up somewhere.

"What you looking at, Daryl?" Diane asked.

David roused himself from a reverie and looked at Daryl, whose cigarette glowed in the dark.

"How do we know you aren't a Navy spy, Straight Man?" he asked, firelight playing on his face. "Why is it you never use your last name?"

"No reason to. Why don't you use your last name?"

"McQuig," Daryl said.

"A spy would have informed on you by now."

"Maybe you already have. Lots of snake-in-the-grass narcs around. They used to infiltrate the students at Berkeley."

"Daryl, you're paranoid," Diane said.

"We know David well enough," Terry said.

"None of you knows me," David said quickly. "But I'm not spying for anybody."

"Don't be melodramatic, Straight Man," Daryl said. "This isn't some encounter group."

"I'm not being melodramatic. And I'm getting tired of being called Straight Man."

"Hey, what's up?" Terry asked. "C'mon."

"I'm not spying for the Navy," David said. He watched the yellow and red flames leaping over a redwood cone Diane threw onto the fire. Rennie, sitting on a log farther back out of the flickering light, turned her face away.

"I'm hiding from it."

Now he had no choice other than to trust them.

"What do you mean?" Terry asked.

"I mean I never finished my hitch."

"So?" Terry persisted.

"I'm absent without leave. A deserter."

"Wow, now I know why you're so camera-shy," Terry said, clasping his hands.

"So if we're David's friends we need to keep quiet about it," Rennie said from the shadows.

"Why'd you even join the pig military?" Daryl asked, still staring at David from across the flames.

"I told you I was drafted."

"Why didn't you just stick it out?" Terry asked. "Get it over with?"

"Too much chicken shit. Too many lies. The whole thing's a lie."

"How do we know *you* aren't a spy, Daryl?" Diane asked. "What exactly did you do at Berkeley?"

Daryl guffawed.

Blue and yellow tongues of flame licked from underneath the charred driftwood. David's face and arms felt hot, but his back was cold.

"If there were a just war there'd be no need for a draft," Rennie said.

"It's easy to be anti-war," Daryl sneered.

"Pretty soon there'll be no more draft at all," Terry asserted.

"How would you know that?" Daryl turned on him.

"Things are changing," Terry answered. "Even straight people are starting to oppose the war *and* the system. I think we can change this country without violence."

"And just how's *that* going to happen?" Daryl demanded.

"We change ourselves. The real struggle's inside."

"If everything's internal like you say," Daryl began, "then any attempt to change things is delusion. Besides, the system destroys anybody it fears or doesn't like, or it neutralizes what it can't get rid of."

"They can't neutralize everybody," Terry insisted.

"This country either gets rid of splinter groups and nonconformists or it absorbs them," Daryl continued. "Look at what they did to the asshole Beats—the right-wing media turned them into a cartoon. McCarthy threatened the little lily-livered communists into submission. Roosevelt's New Deal bought off the revolutionaries in the thirties—the ones they couldn't kill. That was the biggest scam in history—buy off the radicals with groceries and shit jobs. Look at the unions. They're as fat as the government."

"What about the Civil Rights movement?" Diane asked. "Those people put themselves on the line. Some even got killed, but they didn't give up."

"And in 1964 the history of race ended," Daryl responded. "The only reason Johnson passed the Civil Rights Bill was to kill the movement, and he succeeded."

"Then what was Detroit all about?" Diane challenged him.

"It's the beginning of the next phase."

"Oh, come on, what do you know about it?" Terry asked.

"The end of imperialism," Daryl continued, "which will come when we lose that fucking war. Then we'll have confrontation and, if we're lucky, revolution."

"And afterwards?" David asked. "Who'll lead the new country after your revolution? You?"

Even in the semi-darkness, David could see Daryl's narrowed his eyes.

"Really," Terry said.

"You spew out a lot of shit," Diane said to Daryl, "but you can't deny you have it better than your father had it. And you can go home any time you want to. Any one of us could—except David. So who's playing for keeps here?"

"Maybe they'll just forget about David," Terry offered.

"Or there'll be some kind of general amnesty," Rennie suggested.

"Do you ever think you'll go back?" Terry asked David.

"No. I can't even imagine it."

"You are not *being*," Daryl said, watching him. "You are *not*-being."

"Bullshit," Diane said. "We are who we choose to be."

"Now *that's* bullshit. None of us lives entirely free from this fucked-up culture."

"Then what the hell does it matter what any of us does?" she asked.

No one spoke for a long time. Daryl lit the joint he had been rolling, toked it, and passed it to Terry. Sticks in the fire pit exploded with a popping sound like intermittent gunfire. It was nearly midnight when they went to sleep, Daryl in the Saab with the seat tilted back. The other four laid their sleeping bags out under the stars.

"You know there are mountain lions around here," Terry said.

"The fire will scare them away," Diane told him. "It would be great to see one, though."

"It's creepy here since that drug dealer guy was found stabbed," Rennie said.

"That was all the way down by the lighthouse," Terry said, "and anyway, there are three guys here."

"Two, you mean," Rennie answered.

The next morning David woke to the sound of waves crashing against the sand and climbed out of his sleeping bag. Flies crawled on the dirty plates they'd used the night before. He started walking north along the shore. When the sun was at its height he found Rennie in a cove near the beach sitting on a large, round piece of driftwood, looking out over the water. She was wearing a man's brown shirt she'd picked up somewhere and a blue and lavender scarf around her hair.

"Where's Terry?" he asked, crossing the sand toward her.

"Don't know. Went somewhere with Daryl on the bike. Where's Diane?"

"I don't know. She was still sleeping when I got up. You know," he continued, "they say it's dangerous to walk underneath these cliffs. Rocks fall."

"And people get trapped by tides," Rennie replied. "If I see the tide coming in I'll go."

"You may not be able to see it turning."

"I guess you do know something about tides," she said, grinning.

They climbed over boulders and found a grassy place between two hillocks where orange poppies and purple irises managed to sink their roots into loose, sandy soil. A northern harrier lifted off from a decaying log and winged its way over the undulating land. Far ahead, they could see the coastline bending to the west.

"I've always thought you looked like a rabbi with your beard," she said, reaching up and touching the curling hair near his jaw line.

David sensed she felt a little disappointed in him for sharing his secret with Terry and Daryl instead of only her and Diane. He cupped her face in the palm of his left hand and pushed her hair back with his right, then gently pulled the scarf off. She shook her hair free.

"It looks better that way," he said.

"Hair gets in my eyes when I'm walking."

He drew her into the shadow of the hillock and kissed her. She ran her hand down his back, and he unbuttoned her shirt and jeans. She slipped them off and stepped out of her sneakers. They lay on the sand, and she sprinkled a handful on his chest and blew it off. His mouth sought her breasts. Then he pulled her on top of him and she laid her head on his shoulder, the gritty sand rubbing their skin. He waited for her while her hips undulated around him, and when she relaxed he gripped her hips and pulled himself into her again and again until the world imploded.

Afterwards they washed in the cold water and sat half dressed on the beach in the wind. He rubbed her shoulders. The sun had crossed the mid-point of the sky when they got up and followed a path across the dunes.

"We came this other way," she called out at the top of a hillock.

"I want to take a different way back," he answered, and they walked in silence listening to the wind. When they reached the stream they saw Diane striding along a higher ridge.

"Where you been?" she called.

"Down on shore," David answered, waiting for her to cross the sand. She stopped a short distance away and raised her head so that David saw the long expanse of her neck. Diane grinned, turned, and strode away from them.

David and Rennie followed a trail above the shoreline.

"Why so quiet?" he said.

She shrugged.

"Just thinking."

"Why'd you take off just now when we saw Diane?"

"Just wanted to be alone."

"Do you want me to leave you alone?"

"No."

"Is it Terry?"

"No. Terry's always been way out front that he doesn't want commitment. I like him, but there has to be something else. Love isn't just fucking."

She paused, looking out at the waves. "You told me your secret," she said, "and now I'm going to tell you mine." She inhaled. "I told you about that jerk I was with back at SF State. I didn't tell you I got pregnant by him. We got a little careless a couple of times."

"You had a baby?"

"No. I went to the clinic for the test. Then Andrea got me the drugs."

David looked down at her windblown ginger hair draped over her right shoulder and the muscles of her neck firm under her smooth skin.

"She stayed with me through it all. Found out I'd been pregnant with twins."

"Is it bothering you now?" he asked. "Is that why you want to talk about it?"

"No. I told you because you told me your story. I never even for a minute thought about keeping it—them. Would have if I'd thought Jason wanted it."

"He didn't want a child?"

"I didn't tell him. Why would I? He was already engaged to this other woman. I'm glad now. He wasn't worth it. She can have him."

Rennie grabbed her hair in her left hand and tied it back with the scarf.

"So now you know. Does it change anything?"

"No. Only if it were mine I'd want to know."

"Don't worry. I take pills. By the way, Diane doesn't know what I just told you. Nobody does, except you and Andrea."

She turned and ran up the side of a hill. He followed and caught up with her at the edge of a sheer cliff that rose high above the waves.

David rolled the hard tablet onto his tongue and swallowed it as he started up a path toward the fire trail that zigzagged up the slope to the back of the mountain. It was late afternoon, the sun descending at a right angle above the trees on the hills to the north, and as he climbed it seemed that evening ascended with him. Terry, Rennie, and Diane left David at the bottom of the hill and drove to a concert at Muir Beach; they said they'd come back for him when it was over. David told them he didn't want to risk being among that many people, but the truth was he wanted to be alone.

He was nearly up to the ridge trail when he felt the earth losing its hardness and breathing as he did. Mariposa lily blossoms radiated like tiny suns, and the seed tips of snake grass rattled to him and turned into a nest of vipers on the ground warning him not that they would strike but that he should choose his way with care. Blossoms of Alpine forget-me-not opened their tiny yellow mouths and sang to him, and bloody cranesbill poured its purple into the air. Under a holly bush David saw a golden columbine, its five narrow sepals reaching high and dancing like tentacles, the five petals spewing golden coins onto the ground at his feet. A red-winged blackbird on an azalea branch called out with a sound like a jazz riff.

The fire trail continued across a paved road winding its way up the slope. Beside him a gully yawned like a chasm, but exposed tree roots offered themselves as steps, and a root snaked out of the side of the hill, coiled before him, and entered the earth again. He gripped the scaled bark and pulled himself up the steep incline to the top where dry, tawny grass bobbed in the wind and the path widened to the pebbled main trail that ran further up the mountain. The north end of the bay burned like blue flame. At the edge of the trail the long green stem of a tiger lily swayed to Oriental music; the upturned petals wrapped around each other like a turban. David looked out over the valley and felt the vastness of the earth and the mountain calling to him. Below him he saw a gnarled buckeye raising four angled limbs and gesturing wildly. Farther down the trail a small spruce waved its branches, a dark hole forming in the middle like a mouth crying silently; he knew the earth was speaking to him, and if he could walk farther into those woods, following the waving tree limbs into the darkness, he might become part of the wilderness, like the hawk and coyote, living by instinct, not thinking about the next day but only this one. The wail of the wind in the mountain tamarack echoed through him, and he could feel the trees sighing. They wanted him to give up his name and live among them in the shadows.

Beside him, rough bark on the two leaning fence posts he and Diane passed on their way up Tamalpais months before became frowning faces warning him that if he stepped beyond them the mountain would take him into its own wild heart, and the watcher inside asked wordlessly whether he wanted to become part of the wilderness or remain human. His mind returned to that place long ago before he could speak words, before he was an individual, and he could feel more than ever that his energy was part of the earth's great magnetic field circulating around and through his body. High in the trees the wind howled his name, inviting him to follow a path deeper into the woods.

In front of him, four mountain lions climbed out of a ditch beside the path and paced in a circle, their muscles rippling beneath tawny coats, distinctive black stripes around their mouths, black tips on their tails. They were not going to attack him. They glanced to the treetops and knew the name whispered there was his, their green eyes turning to look into his own with feline cunning, as if they could read his thoughts even before they were fully formed in his own mind. They paced patiently in slow circles, the pads of their feet soundless on the brown dust of Tamalpais. Silently, their eyes invited him to join with them and become part of the wild, and as he watched they circled again and again, each one raising its head to him as it passed. Trees became shapes to peer through. Deep inside his chest, his breath formed into a barely subdued catlike snarl, his fingers became claws, his eyes delved deep into the waving grass as his body poised to pounce on and devour anything crouched there frozen in terror.

He didn't know how long he stood watching the lions and listening to the wind, but suddenly he felt something near and started, ready to leap. A voice repeated his name. He turned to see a deer walking toward him up the path, but as it drew nearer, entirely unafraid, it took the shape of blue flame, and then he recognized Diane. She had come for him as she promised. She approached slowly.

"David, leave this place. Come back with me."

The lions circled, and the spruce limbs flailed wildly, the dark hole among their branches emitting a soundless, unwavering cry of terror while the wind howled in David's ears. He hesitated, still alert and poised to spring. Did he want to go with the lions and let go of everything that bound him to civilization—including love?

"Come with me." Diane took his hand; the stored hiss gushed out of his lungs, and he stepped away from the lions which turned and slunk back into the woods, the black tips of their tails disappearing into the brush, while the tree branches flailed above them.

"This way." Diane gripped his hand as she guided him down the trail toward the road, and with each step the howl grew fainter, the wind less strong. He felt sad to lose the lions and his chance to bound off into the trees, but her hand on his was stronger than his desire to be part of the wild earth. As they stepped around a bend the path became a rainbow of pastel colors, and at the side of the hill, next to a stone beehive oven and a sluice gate with an overflow tank, two Indians wrapped in striped blankets squatted beside the road. He stepped closer to them, but they stood and walked into the trees, and David knew they were spirits of people who lived here long before.

When his feet touched the hardness of pavement, his body felt solid again, although he could still hear the earth breathing. Diane put her arms around him, and he knew he *had* come back; maybe this was what it felt like when he first knew himself as a child, stepping from the oblivion of unconsciousness into the light of memory and loneliness.

But now his friends were here; he was not alone.

SEVEN

Westerly wind carried sand across the dunes at McClure's Beach.

"Where's Daryl?" Diane asked as she stacked the Melmac dishes into a cardboard box.

"Haven't seen him for awhile," Terry answered, rolling his sleeping bag into a cylinder.

"I saw him this morning," David said.

Rennie poured sea water from a glass jar onto the ashes of the campfire even though they had been cold for hours.

Although they'd gotten up late, the sun was still high; they'd easily make it into town by afternoon. David rolled a pair of jeans along the seams and stuffed them into his knapsack.

A black Impala drove up the road and pulled in beside Daryl's Saab. David smelled the gravely dust and exhaust smoke as three men got out, slamming the doors hard. Although he was at least thirty feet away from them, David could sense they were doing speed. Large sunglasses obscured the eyes of the one in front. A bearded man, his hair pulled back in a ponytail, wore a green tank shirt. The biggest one sported a wide red bandana.

Daryl paced toward them with long strides from the direction of the beach. David heard their raised voices but the wind drowned out their words.

"What's going on over there?" Diane asked.

"Who knows?" Rennie sighed, irritated.

The three men climbed into their car, started the engine, and peeled away, raising a cloud of dust. Shaking his shaggy head, Daryl strode toward the campsite.

"Sons of bitches," he muttered.

"What were you doing with them?" Diane demanded, standing with her hands on her hips.

"None of your business."

"It'll be our business if you start trouble," she shouted.

"I'm not starting trouble," Daryl sneered. "They started it."

"They're high," David said.

"Yeah, well maybe I didn't know that."

"We don't want crazies here," Diane shouted at him.

"Well, you'd better leave," Daryl sneered.

He turned, kicked a rock out of his path, and paced toward some rocks that jutted from the dunes.

"Are you okay?" Diane asked, reaching for David's hand.

"Yes. Don't say anything," David said, keeping his eyes on Daryl's back.

"Hey, why don't we cool it?" Terry suggested from his crouched position. "Let's pack this stuff up and split."

A few minutes later the Impala pulled up onto the gravel again and came to a stop next to Daryl's bike. The three men got out, slammed the doors, and headed toward the camp.

"Where is he? Where is that son of a bitch?" the one in the red bandana demanded.

"You guys get out of here before we call the cops," Diane shouted at them.

"Oh yeah? A bunch a hippies gonna call the pigs?"

"We don't want any trouble," David said, stepping in front of Diane.

"Yeah," Terry said, still kneeling on the sand.

"Then stay out of my way." The man in the green tank shirt stood square in front of David.

"I'm not in your way."

The man grabbed David's shoulders and shoved him aside. "Not now you aren't." Clenching his fists, David regained his balance to see the three of them striding across the sand.

"We don't want you here," Diane was saying as she followed them. "Why don't you guys just go back where you came from?"

The one with the sunglasses pushed her sideways onto the sand. Rennie ran toward her.

"Stay here," David said, walking past Diane and Rennie after the three men. "Keep out of this."

As if he'd been waiting for them, Daryl stepped from behind one of the boulders. The one wearing the red bandana threw his burly fist into Daryl's stomach, but it landed against the heavy belt buckle. Daryl punched the man in the jaw, throwing him off balance, but he recovered and lunged again at Daryl, who pumped a fist into his face. This time the man sprawled on the sand, but the one in the tank shirt stepped up and tried to hit Daryl, who raised his arm and caught the man's fist. He staggered back as David grabbed the beardless man and pushed him over. The man yelled as he fell hard and his sunglasses flew off his face, revealing dark, narrow eyes.

David stood over the two heaving bodies and watched Daryl and the man in the tank shirt locked together. They lurched against a trash barrel, turning it over, spilling metal cans, wadded paper towels, aluminum foil, beer bottles, and coffee grounds out onto the dirt. Daryl finally pushed the man down. David stepped over to Daryl who yelled, "Look out!" and pulled David forward by his right arm. The beardless man was up and heading toward David. Daryl lunged at the man's stomach, sending him hard on his back.

"Behind you," Daryl yelled as he straightened. David spun again and saw the big man with the bandana coming at him with a large-bladed knife. Daryl jumped between them, grabbing the man's wrist. They grappled like one big unwieldy animal through the trash.

"*Fuck head*," Daryl shouted, and with a downward thrust twisted the man's hand. The knife flew in an arc and landed on a small patch of grass. Daryl dove, grabbed it, and stood, legs spread, facing the man who fell back against the overturned barrel.

"Give it up, asshole."

"I'm going to kill you, man," the guy bellowed, got his legs under him, and catapulted himself toward Daryl. The knife went deep beneath his ribs.

The man yelled and staggered back, holding his hands against his bleeding belly, his eyes wide beneath the red bandana, his mouth in an O. The man in the tank shirt grabbed his arm and steered him toward the Impala. The beardless one picked up his sunglasses from the sand, put them on, and grabbed the injured man's other arm.

"You better get him to a hospital quick," Daryl said to the bearded one in the tank shirt. "He's hurt bad." The man spat in the dirt but kept hold of his buddy.

"Crazy son of a bitch," Daryl muttered as the car turned around and sped down the road. "What did he think he was going to do?"

"What if that guy talks, Daryl?" Terry spoke up, standing now. "What if he dies?"

"There'll be one less moron in the world."

"Did you egg him on, Daryl?" Diane demanded.

"What if I did?" Daryl sneered.

"Are you on their turf?" she insisted.

"What if I am?"

"We don't want your trouble," she shouted, her face flushed.

"Yeah," Rennie said.

"Bitches," he snarled and turned toward Diane.

David stepped between her and Daryl.

"Don't you touch either of them."

Daryl scowled.

"Bitches," he muttered again before he turned and strode toward his Harley.

Diane put her arms around David from behind. After Daryl reached the bike, David unclasped her hands and faced her, holding her upper arms tightly.

"Don't cross him again," he said, gritting his teeth. "I may not be here when you do."

"He wouldn't have done anything. I know him."

"You saw what he did to that guy," David said, shaking her. "And you don't know him as well as you think you do." He let go and turned toward the sound of the motorcycle engine starting up. Daryl backed the Harley out of the parking area and tore down the road.

Rennie set the barrel on its end and began to pick up the spilled trash. Diane massaged her upper arms where David had gripped them.

"Suppose they do talk?" Rennie asked no one in particular. "Suppose some doctor talks?"

"We'll deal with it," David said.

"Daryl had no business bringing guys like that around here," Rennie insisted.

"He tried to get rid of them," Terry answered. "We have to call the police, you know. If we don't, we could be the ones in trouble."

"I agree with Terry," Rennie said.

"There's a pay phone at the lighthouse," Diane suggested.

David strode away from them across the sand, irritated with Terry for letting those speed freaks push Diane down right in front of him, and angry at Daryl for letting this happen to all of them. Those guys knew Daryl's name even if they didn't know anyone else's. Maybe they knew the Oak Street address. He was even angrier at Diane and Rennie for interfering. Women should stay out of men's fights. His throat tightened and he clenched his fists as he took longer and longer strides. But what was little bug-eyed Terry supposed to do anyway? Diane wouldn't have listened to him. And Daryl had risked his own life to step between those goons and himself. As David stood watching the sun on the Pacific waves he realized he was angry most of all at himself, because he was impotent to do anything.

Turning around, David walked back where Rennie, Terry, and Diane were packing things into the Saab.

"I have to get out of here," David announced.

"We're all going to be in trouble if the cops find out," Rennie answered. "Especially Daryl. You didn't do anything."

"Let's stop wasting time and figure something out," Diane insisted.

"Where can we go?" Rennie asked.

"You don't have to go anywhere," David said. "I just need to leave."

"You wouldn't need to be gone very long," Rennie suggested.

"I might," he answered. "I might have to be gone a long time."

EIGHT

Heavy fog rose before dawn from the lake, trailed the edge of the water as the sun climbed above the peaks, and melted into patches of snow on the sides of the mountains. Warren Lake lay at about seven thousand feet, just below tree line, surrounded by a meadow of tall grass and purple and white lupine, yellow mountain sunflower, and red poppy. Beyond the meadow, tamarack and hemlock reached straight and tall. In the dawn light the lake was steel gray, but the color changed to deep blue by late morning, then silver in afternoon. David woke early, built a fire from sticks and pine cones, and boiled water for coffee, afterwards setting off on the trail until the sun was high, then turning around and heading back.

He marked the passing of days by the waxing moon. Time no longer progressed in minutes and hours but in the brightening sky, silver at the tree line, rose and coral before the sun blazed high overhead and crossed the horizon. In the afternoon it turned the valley into gold before the mist rose again and light glimmered beyond the western ridge and died.

As lean as his life had been in the Haight and on board the *Loyola*, that life now seemed filled with superfluity. Even the food he brought with him had little taste; he wanted very little except water that he drank untreated from the lake, reasoning that snow melt would be pure enough. Although he had iodine tablets, he figured he'd better save them for the climb down the mountain.

On the afternoon of the stabbing at McClure's Beach, Rennie, Terry, and Diane burned all their cigarette papers, buried their remaining stash in a pit far from their campsite, and took David to Tomales Point while they drove to the lighthouse and called the police. Two patrolmen showed up at McClure's Beach to take their story and look around, Diane explained to David later. Daryl came back and told the officers he'd been able to fight all three of them because they were so high. He didn't know their names, only that they were dealers and had threatened him before. The police searched the car, bike, and all their equipment, and Daryl went with them back to the Inverness station. By the time Diane, Terry, Rennie, and David got back to Oak Street, Daryl had moved all his stuff to his apartment in Berkeley. Terry told the kids who were sleeping over to find other places to live; Diane and Rennie searched the *Chronicle* every day but found no mention of any stabbing. Nobody who lived around there asked where Daryl went; they were used to people leaving without a trace.

After a few days Diane borrowed a car from someone at Switchboard and drove David to a trailhead in the Sierra Nevada. From there he hiked seven miles into the national forest to Warren Lake. The plan was for him to stay here for a week or ten days, when he'd hike down the mountain to a gas station and call Andrea's number to let her know where Diane should pick him up.

During the fifth or sixth night—he'd forgotten how many days since Diane left—he woke to the eerie half-bark, half-howl of coyotes. He lay motionless in the sleeping bag, staring into the darkness. Unable to sleep, he pulled himself out, slid his arms into his jacket, carefully unzipped the tent flap, and peered out. Cold droplets fell onto his head as he stared at the silver reflection of the bright half moon on the lake.

He lay awake the rest of the night, sleeping only toward morning, and woke up after the sun was well above the trees. Without eating or drinking anything he walked to the water's edge and sat on a rock, facing eastward across the lake toward a line of snow-covered peaks, keeping as still as he could. After a while he heard rustling and turned to see a chipmunk darting along the rocks at the edge of the campsite, taking the measure of his stillness. A red-tail circled above the water and dipped out of sight behind the tamaracks at the far end of the lake. David sat until the sun was just above the mountain to the west, shining with hard brightness on the rocks. When dusk came he realized he'd eaten nothing and drunk nothing all day, but instead of feeling hungry he felt light, empty, and free.

David started. He narrowed his eyes to make out a hiker negotiating the crevasse. Then another one appeared from behind the bend, dressed like the first in olive-green fatigues. David stayed among the trees, watching the men as they walked the rim of the basin, and kept hidden for a long time after they disappeared over a rise. They couldn't have seen him or his tent, but after a few minutes he spotted them again, trudging along a trail that led down the mountain, hiking about five feet away from each other, both weighed down by bulky packs with sleeping bags and tents lashed to frames. Their voices sounded distinct among chirring cicadas, and, as they came closer to where he hid, he could hear the heavy thud of their boots. As they passed him, David saw their fatigues were not olive-green but brown, the color of deer hide.

"How far now?" the second one asked his companion. His face was flushed deep red.

The one in front stopped and pulled a map from his pocket.

"Half mile," he said. He wore a blue bandana over matted blond hair.

"Man, this is a *long* way." He pulled a candy bar from his pocket, unwrapped it, and let the paper fall to the ground.

When he could no longer hear voices or the pounding of their boots, David stepped onto the path, retrieved the candy wrapper, and shoved it into his pocket. When the position of the sun over the mountains told him it was late afternoon, he walked back to his camp, struck the tent, and moved it, his sleeping bag, and his knapsack into the trees. He stirred the cold remains of the fire and kicked leaves over the site, working quickly even as he told himself neither of those guys looked like an Army man or a Marine. Lots of people bought fatigues at surplus stores. Even if they were military, they weren't looking for him. What did he have to worry about? Finally he realized that he was upset because seeing those hikers had shattered his solitude. He wasn't as far from civilization as he thought.

That night he slept fitfully and towards morning dreamed that someone threw back the tent flap. Instantly alert, he sat up, climbed out of the sleeping bag, and pulled on his jacket. Just above the trees at the far end of the lake, the sky was beginning to brighten. David used the candy wrapper to light kindling for a fire, heated water, drank his coffee quickly, and packed up his gear. Striking the dew-streaked tent, he rolled it up wet and strapped it to his backpack. He kicked dirt and rocks over the level place where the tent had stood, and, turning once around to take in the view of the lake and mountains—his home for more days than he could remember—he set off on the trail, walking north.

At the far end of the lake the water formed a cove, and just beyond it up an incline, David saw the mouth of a cave set back from the edge of the water far enough that no casual hiker would notice it from the main trail. David stashed his tent and gear inside and dug a fire pit.

After the sun went down, in the flickering fire light he thought he saw movement just beyond a bush near the lake. It wasn't a grizzly—brown bears no longer lived in this part of the Sierra—but the trailhead signs warned of lion sightings, and he had no gun, only a knife. He threw big cones onto the fire to make it blaze higher, realizing he was not afraid the big cats would attack him, but still uneasy about losing himself to them.

Nothing crouched near the campsite that night, but as David lay awake a wolf raised its solitary howl to the full moon.

In the morning he set off back up the trail leading toward the summit called Castle Crag. He walked through an Alpine meadow where tiny red, yellow, white, blue, and purple wild flowers seemed to rush down the mountainside along the stream, and for a moment David thought he was having a flashback, that these colors were too vivid to be real. He blinked and looked back at the flowers that were still radiant. The wind high in the leaves sounded like water rushing over stones. A red-tailed hawk shrieked.

David climbed the trail past increasingly stunted trees. One gnarled, leafless trunk seemed to twist around itself, the broken branches reaching outward and upward like a man drowning. David followed the ridge toward the huge rock that jutted outward at the summit. He stepped carefully, making sure of every foothold, taking no chances with loose scrabble. Finally, at the base of the biggest boulder, he crept carefully around to the back where smaller rocks afforded footholds to the top, and he stood looking out over the Sierra peaks, patchy glaciers, wind-stunted trunks near the tree line, taller fir lower down, and glassy surface of small lakes far below. Chilled by the icy wind against his sweat-soaked shirt, he pulled on his jacket and red woolen cap.

He slowly placed his boots into the same footholds he used to climb up and found his way down to the high ridge, keeping to the side of the mountain above the waterfall, his landmark. A cloud sailed up the mountainside, and all at once swirling snow enveloped him and concealed everything. He hunched behind a rock to wait it out.

Just as suddenly the snow stopped; he could see the sun again in the blue sky, and only a thin covering of snow remained on the rocks. Wind, cries of hawks, rushing streams, and chirring insects created music more beautiful than anything people produced. Here, where all he needed was water and shelter, his life seemed incredibly simple. At that moment he was sure he loved Diane, and knowing he loved her would be his reason for everything he did from now on. He loved Rennie too, but Diane more because she was fearless. Terry was right—as soon as you were with Diane you knew you had someone you could connect with. She had led him down the mountain when David nearly stepped out of his own skin into the wild. Now extraordinary peace filled his body, he grinned, and he wanted to cry out how much he loved her.

Instantly he saw clearly what he had to do: go back to San Francisco and find a way to free himself from the Navy. He wouldn't be able to offer Diane any kind of life if he stayed in hiding, if he couldn't be himself, if he was not-being, as Daryl said. He would go back to the base on TI, get himself into the dispensary, and convince them he was so crazy they wouldn't want him, like the man Terry told him about months ago when he first arrived at the house on Oak Street. There'd be no need to try to get across the Canadian border. It seemed so easy he wondered why he hadn't thought of it earlier.

David pulled on his pack and started back down the trail, the high wind dropping off as he descended through the Alpine meadow loud with the sound of rushing water. He kept moving after that day, walking along the back of the mountain, staying only one night at each campsite. When his food ran out he left the trail and headed westward down the mountainside over rocky, mossy ground into the first stands of short, wind-blown trees. He drank from his canteen sparingly, taking one sip each time he stopped to rest, not knowing when he would find water again. The temperature climbed, and tall firs blocked the wind, although he was still at a high elevation.

He couldn't even remember how many days he'd been walking after leaving Warren Lake when he stepped out of the woods, crossed a level, grassy field, and stood on a narrow paved road. He drank the last water in his canteen and headed north, telling direction by the position of the sun. His mouth felt gritty and dry. If he didn't find water soon he might not make it. It occurred to him suddenly that Diane could be pregnant, and he wondered why he hadn't thought of it sooner. She said she always used an IUD she'd gotten from a doctor in Fort Collins. A vague worry plagued him that she might think he had enough on his mind and not tell him if she was. He knew that what made him uneasy was the possibility of never seeing Diane again, and he shuddered realizing he'd left her and Rennie alone in the Haight that was getting scarier every day, with no one but weird little Terry to help them. Those drug dealers may have found them, or Daryl might do something, angry at Diane and contemptuous of Rennie. David knew he should never have left them, that he did so because he was thinking about himself and couldn't think about anyone else when he was as good as not even there. "ARE YOU MAN ENOUGH?" the Navy posters read, but it had made him less than a man. It made him no one. He was not-being.

The sun was high overhead when he saw a small shack ahead of him, almost like a storage shed. Spirals of wavy air danced above the pavement as he walked toward the structure, which turned out to be an old store made of wooden planks with a porch and broken steps. The windows had long been boarded up and even the slats were mostly fallen out by now. He turned the knob, opened the creaking door, and walked through, easing his weight with each step to test for rotten floorboards. Inside, there was an old counter and behind it shelves, cobwebs heaving with dust, and another door, this one standing ajar.

He pushed it open to see a sink and toilet, dirty with mineral stains. Exposed pipes ran the length of the wall and reached up under the cracked porcelain. He tried to turn the old metal tap that spun on its hinges. Then he forced the toilet handle down, and water drained from the tank into the commode. Some well or septic system still worked underneath this dead building. In the weird quiet of the shack the whooshing sound of the water seemed deafening. He twisted the cap off his canteen, plunged it into the water, and wiped it on his jeans. Finally he dropped his last two iodine tablets into it.

The road was wider and no longer cracked and full of potholes, and David thought he could hear, when he knelt and placed his ear against the hard surface, the groan of engines and shrill of tires. The pavement curved around a bluff, but he could see a stand of woods behind it, mixed deciduous and conifer.

As he walked around the bend he saw a small lake where the road turned sharply to the right. Three pickup trucks, covered with the dust of the mountain road, were parked along the side, and, standing on the grassy bank, a group of men fished from a small wooden dock. He counted seven of them—one young boy, two older men, and four in their thirties or forties—all either watching their lines, baiting a hook, or casting. When the wind died down for a moment he heard their muffled voices. One line tightened; in hip waders the man reeled the fish in as a soft cheer rose from the others. The sun threw purple light on the clouds and turned the lake water gold, and from the highest branch of a Douglas fir, a red tail rose into the air, circled, and dove behind the trees again. Although David stood on the road only about thirty yards from the fishermen, they hadn't even noticed him.

NINE

The sun hung low above Tamalpais on September 21st when the 108 rolled across the Bay Bridge from downtown, swung around a sharp curve, and started the ascent into Yerba Buena. David ran his hand across his close-cropped hair and brought his palm underneath his shaved jawbone telling himself this journey did not have to be final—it could be a dry run, he wasn't doing anything irrevocable—all the time knowing his mind was made up to go back and face whatever he had to face. The bus swung beneath the limbs of silver-green eucalyptus and shuddered to a halt before the white Victorian houses where officers lived. He stepped down into the dust and exhaust from the bus and watched it roll down the road and across the causeway, stop at the gate of Treasure Island, and continue down the Avenue of Palms. The handles of a plastic bag holding two soda bottles full of water dug into his hand. David followed a footpath into the trees on the other side of Yerba Buena until he was well concealed from the guardhouse—not that anyone at TI watched very carefully—and worked his way through the brambles to the gray torpedo hut set into the hillside opposite the pier. There he squatted on dry brown leaves and watched the sun sink beyond the magenta bridge, throwing a silver-pink glow on the bay.

At dusk, David stood and walked across the causeway and up to the guardhouse—a thrill rising from his stomach as he waved his ID card at the bored young sentry—and strode through, adopting an unhurried gait. Lots of sailors walked back from liberty dressed as he was, in his green plaid shirt and jeans, carrying things they'd bought in the city. He sauntered all the way down the Avenue of Palms next to the shoreline, turned up another street, crossed a grassy strip and parking lot, and walked past the electronics school. The dark hulk of the brig stood across from the dispensary. He shuddered as he peered through the lighted entranceway. Building 222. No matter what happened, he would have to go there. Trying to shake off his uneasiness, he continued up Eleventh, caught sight of the sawtooth roof of the retail exchange in the failing light, and crossed the yard behind the gym to the empty athletic field. Two men turned a corner heading for the theater or bowling alley. The girders of the Bay Bridge rose like the spokes of an enormous Ferris wheel behind the naval training center. Walking toward the shoreline, David made out the Berkeley campanile across the water; finally he crouched among lilac bushes and eucalyptus trees behind a storage shed with double pointed roof. Darkness had enveloped the island when he took one of the bottles out of the plastic bag, twisted the cap off, and drank, letting the water run down his neck and onto his shirt.

As the shell of the waning moon appeared above the Contra Costa hills and Berkeley became a constellation of lights across the water, David left the thicket and crossed the street to a row of round metal supply lockers like squat gray silos standing under the bleachers on the east end of the athletic field. One had a hole in the roof, so he climbed the bleachers to the back row, separated the footboards, lowered his bag of water bottles, eased himself into the darkness, and pulled the boards back into place. Ropes and wooden pallets took up most of the space, but he was just able to stand up inside the locker.

He would fast for as long as he could while he worked up the nerve to try to convince the Navy he was so crazy they'd have to discharge him. The first night and the next day he lay shivering in the cold air off the bay, unable to sleep, so at dusk the second evening he pulled himself out of the locker and walked to the supply salvage shed beyond the deserted pier where he knelt behind the building. An open padlock hung on a hasp between the double doors. When he was sure no one was around, David lifted the padlock and pried one door open. Thin ship's mattresses, blankets, and other stuff lay stacked on the floor; he dragged two narrow mattresses and a blanket outside. After it was completely dark he carried them one by one to the storage locker and shoved them down inside. That night he slept on one, pulled the other over himself, and managed to fall asleep.

During the day he stayed inside the locker, sometimes sleeping, sometimes lying awake listening to the cries of gulls, groan of freighters and tankers, bark of car horns, shouts of men on the playing field, clack of shoes on pavement, and rumble of slow tires on Avenue N only a few yards from where he hid. He knew the time of day by the slight variations of pitch and duration. The rhythm of the base pulsed in the changing light like a beehive with creatures coming, going, and swarming with instinctive precision. Sounds were most discrete at dawn; as the sun rose to the meridian, they grew louder and more frenzied; toward sunset they leveled out, decreasing in intensity, becoming distinct again but more plaintive. He was aware of any man who came within twenty-five yards of the locker, hearing him before smelling him, finally able to feel when someone was coming even before hearing the thud of shoes or slap of trousers. Before dawn and after dark, when he had to leave the locker to go to the latrine or fill his soda bottles from a spigot near the pier, David gripped the edges of the hole in the roof, pulled himself out, and leaped lightly to the ground. Where there were no streetlights he found his way by touch and smell, learning every bush and tree, walking with loose, unhurried strides while watching every movement and shadow.

On a warm afternoon when he'd been in the locker a few days, he heard muffled voices of two men ambling across the athletic field. He knelt quietly, inhaled short, shallow breaths, and watched them from a knothole in one of the boards. Their sneakers shuffled on the bleacher steps, and they sat nearly above him, looking across the field at the back of the building that housed the swimming pool and bowling alley.

"What do you hear from home?"

"Not much."

"Why don't you just come out and ask her? Afraid of the answer?"

"Maybe."

The questioner took two packages of Hostess cupcakes out of a small brown grocery bag, tore off the cellophane wrapper, and let it blow away on the wind. David could smell the heavy chocolate aroma. The man offered one to his friend.

"You still thinking about re-upping?" said the second man, taking the cupcake.

"Yup, think I'm going to do it."

"When did you make up your mind?" He stuffed the cake into his mouth in three bites and wiped his lips on his shirtsleeve.

"Last tour for sure. Think I knew in boot camp I'd probably stick it out."

"Okay for you, up there with the pilots. I'm cleaning floors in the hold."

"Another one?"

"No. Thanks."

The benefactor put the white cardboard and paper cupcake holders back into the bag with the uneaten package.

"Never had you figured for a lifer."

The man shrugged. "What else is there to do?"

It was his companion's turn to shrug.

"Too much goddamn chicken shit for me," he said. "You re-up and then at the end, if you don't like it, you're an old man and what are you good for on the outside?"

"Guess I'll find out."

The heavy odor of chocolate and cream disguised the smell of dirt and hemp that usually pervaded the locker.

"What do you want to do now?"

"Feel like bowling?" asked the one with the cupcakes.

"Okay."

They stood, clumped heavily down the wooden steps, and strode across the athletic field, leaving the brown bag behind them. David could hear the squish of their sneakers on the grass. As the sound of their voices and footsteps faded he wondered why he was so different from them, why he could not just finish the hitch he signed on for, why only a few feet separated him from them and yet a chasm of difference spread between their lives and his. Why was he unable to be like the people in this city who did what they had to do, belonged somewhere, went to work, returned home? Was it his fault or the fault of his parents, teachers, or the Navy, that he could never fit in anywhere? Shivering, he realized the people in the Haight also tried to separate themselves from everyone else and in the end couldn't do it; he'd gone there as someone uncomfortable in his own skin looking for people like himself and never quite finding them. Tim was the only man who'd really understood him, and yet he knew he could never fit into Tim's world any more than Tim could fit into David's—assuming he had one. Diane understood him, but even she couldn't know what it was like never to be able to say who you really were. She and Rennie had tried to persuade him not to go back, but he was going to be free, no matter what it took.

After dark when David pulled himself out of the locker and found the paper bag still lying on the bleacher, he knelt on the grass, tore the wrapper open, and devoured both remaining cupcakes. As his stomach began to digest the sugary cake, he felt somehow connected to the life that was going on all around him—not only on the base but in the cities surrounding it—and he thought he might become normal again, walk across the island to the Comwest Seafron building, and just turn himself in. Then he felt sick and disappointed that he compromised his vow to fast until he was ready to face them, and he strode across Avenue N. When he reached the huge granite rocks along the shore, he forced his fingers into his throat until he gagged, then farther still until the bile rose in his stomach. When he could taste the acid in his mouth he pushed his fingers into his throat a third time, finally heaving and vomiting up the dark brown, half-digested cake. He rinsed his mouth with one of the soda bottles and spit out the water again and again, until the pieces of undigested cake were gone from his teeth and gums. Then he drank deeply from the bottle to soothe the burning in his throat and sat down on the rocks, leaning over to put his head between his knees. After a long time he sat up and studied the lights of Berkeley like a galaxy to the east. He felt light, empty, and alone, purged of contamination but in control of himself.

One evening, he had to leave the locker earlier than usual. First pushing the boards back and reaching around the edge of the entry hole, he lifted himself in one fluid motion as he might have jumped to put a ball through the net, swung his rear onto the bleacher seat, and lifted his legs through the opening. Glancing around, he replaced the boards and leaped over the railing, landing lightly and soundlessly on the grass. He listened but heard no words or footsteps—a sound that had become very loud to him—and so walked silently toward the latrine at Fifth and M. He was almost behind it when he sensed someone approaching and stepped back among some small maple trees. Then he heard shoes clacking smartly on pavement. There were two of them.

"I have to stop in here," one said, slamming the door loudly.

The other struck a match, lit a cigarette, took a long drag, and exhaled slowly. David could smell the man's smoke, the phosphorescence from the match, and the aroma given off by his clean clothes.

The handle clanked, water gurgled in the pipes, and David shuddered, remembering the brown toilet water in the shack near the mountains. The wooden door slammed again.

"Ya gotta go, ya gotta go," the sailor said, and the two continued down the sidewalk, their shoes clacking into the darkness. David had been so close to them he could feel their breath and yet they had not seen him. The smell of urine and cigarette smoke hung in the air long after they left.

Feeling invisible, he walked down the street past the brown and gray legal office building that stood at an angle from the street, dark now like some crouching predator. He turned onto another street and followed it to California, where in the light of street lamp he saw the white stone relief of Mercury on the front of the hangar that had been a pavilion for the world's fair in 1939. Continuing toward the bay, he stood on the grass in front of the horseshoe-shaped Comwest Seafron building where officers decided the fate of everyone in this part of the whole, huge, crazy, impressive mess that was the Navy. He gazed at its long, elegant windows and curving façade, thinking it might be possible to feel proud of being in the service if everything were as ordered and rational as this structure promised. He felt like vomiting again, but he had nothing in his stomach. To clear his head, he walked across the Avenue of Palms and stood in the strong, cold wind watching the tankers drifting up and down the trough in the middle of the bay and the lights of San Francisco like a field of stars below the scimitar moon. The lamps on the Golden Gate looked like strung jewels flung out across the strait. At night the busy city appeared peaceful, ordered, sane. How easily he could give up his plan, steal away from the island, go back to the Haight, and never have to give up love or freedom. There may be some kind of general amnesty, as Rennie had said, but how long would he have to wait for it? If he ran away again, the Navy would always "have" him. He heard Daryl's words, "You are not-being," and realized he had chosen the only way possible: he would have to make the Navy think he was crazy and make them not want him. He would receive a discharge first and then he could go back to Diane.

He kept walking down the avenue past the chapel, PO club, Marine barracks, and general barracks that looked like an apartment building. When he was almost at the end of the island, he turned up another street toward the playing field and passed the exercise yard of the brig with its high wire fencing visible in the glow of the street lamp. In the shadows he faced the archway of the brig, wondering whether he had the psychic strength to face the cumulative power of what lay inside those walls—the battle-tested Marine detachment who guarded the prisoners, the entire naval command whose ships had more firepower than all the Allies unleashed in the whole of World War II, the US government that could subdue any country on the globe and could certainly crush him. Here he was, one unknown person, thinking he could stand against that gigantic power and prevail.

He must be out of his mind to think he could do it. Did he have the nerve to pay the price, to go through with it? When it came to the moment when he faced the JAG, would he prove himself? A couple of storms at sea, fist fights, and the prospect of dying of thirst in the mountains seemed like nothing now. He might forever be branded a defective person, and that would affect his whole life and Diane, if she were willing to stay with him. If they gave him a long sentence—as he knew they would—he'd be walking willfully into it, giving up the life he'd known since last spring, the best he'd ever had, and the only women who'd ever loved him.

The wind was blowing hard. Like a wave, the longing to own his own life again overwhelmed him, and he would never own himself until he had faced whatever he had to and come out on the other side. Turning from the brig he walked back up the pavement toward the athletic field, his fists clenched and his jaw set.

Who was he kidding? He was no actor; he would never convince anyone if he tried to pretend, so he spent most of the time seeking darkness, searching for the seeds of insanity, fixing in his mind the images of his nightmares—the drug dealer with his eyes wide open beneath the red bandana, his mouth a perfect O, clutching the bleeding hole in his stomach; the mountain lions calling him to join them; dark branches on Mount Tam gesturing to him to walk deeper into the woods; dark water where he tried to see where another pilot went under; two halves of a Skyhawk breaking apart on the round down and spiraling along the flight deck in a sea of flame; water hammering the prow, a wave rising so high it obscured the destroyer escort; the great dark emptiness of the *Loyola's* hangar; his father nearly shooting his mother; wings of an unseen bird beating against high rafters of the old Snyder place where the widowed farmer died in the house and lay there undiscovered for days; David's recurring dream of trying to find his way through a decaying house with high ceilings and cobwebs hanging from moth-eaten drapes; his boyhood desire to become invisible whenever he had to face his father's anger.

In the dark of the new moon, he reached into his pocket and drew out the white tablet, thrust it into his mouth, and rolled it around on his tongue as he again considered postponing this part of his plan. Finally he swallowed it. Instead of relaxing and allowing his mind to trip with the acid, he tensed all his muscles and tried to force himself to concentrate on the images he had lived with for days. Acid usually drew everything into you, but a bad trip drew you further into yourself. After what seemed like an interminable wait, the locker began to morph into a long, dark bilge tunnel, a passageway leading him toward madness; he watched himself, a tiny fly searching for the end but each time finding only another darkened opening. Inside his mind he climbed to the fog-shrouded flight deck, let go of his safety rope, and tried to lose himself in the opaque dampness, hoping this time the lifeline would not hold him.

A freighter's horn groaned in the dusk. It was time: David pulled himself out through the hole in the storage locker. A thrill pulsed from his stomach to his forehead as he clenched his fists and headed across the athletic field and down the pavement toward the one-storey dispensary. For a long moment he stood on the curb and looked across the dusty street where the brig stood in semi-darkness. His stomach tightening, he walked through the door of the dispensary and stood at the end of a short line of men before the small table where a corpsman sat checking people in. Then no one blocked his view, and he looked into the upturned face. The man's eyes widened and his head tilted back.

"Can I help you?"

"I don't feel so good," David answered as he threw the ID card onto the table.

"Wait over there."

David sat on the short bench against the wall. He was not invisible after all—the corpsman spoke to him and he heard his own voice answer; he felt his own hand holding the ID card. They didn't seem very busy today, and people walked up and down the hallways with a relaxed gait. David watched the floor, grinding his teeth and trying to recall the images of the trip the night before. Someone made a phone call and another man picked up his pace; David knew the moment had come when he would prove whether or not he could fulfill his purpose. He felt strangely calm now that he had made the decision irrevocably to go through with his plan. Standing up, he took off down the hallway to his left, knowing vaguely where the psychiatric offices were, and turned the corner, hearing footfalls and shouting behind him. He passed exam rooms, restrooms, and water fountains, running faster as the noise behind him increased. Finally turning another corner he saw the psychiatric offices and bolted into a restroom across the hall. In a mirror above the sink he caught sight of a face nearly black with grime, hair matted to his skull, and dirty growth of beard. Peering out from the filth were his two hazel, bloodshot eyes. Men ran in after him, and he felt his arms being held by two of them guiding him outside. People around him talked at once—he couldn't tell how many. Then a man stood before him with wing bars on his uniform. Somehow, David felt dissociated from his own body as if he were not the man they restrained but someone else observing the whole scene from a distance.

"What happened?" The lieutenant spoke more to the corpsmen than to him.

"He reported sick and then took off. When we pulled his records we found he's been UA for almost five months."

"Bring him into my office."

The gray walls were lined with bookshelves and filing cabinets, and the windows were shuttered with gray Venetian blinds. Two of them put him into a large wooden armchair and stood behind him while the lieutenant sat down in front of him.

"You can go now," he said to the corpsmen. "Wait outside." The man's light brown eyes looked pinched and tired.

"What's your name, sailor?"

David rubbed his face.

"I'm a psychologist," the lieutenant said. "Tell me why you came here today."

He had to make them think he was crazy.

"I felt sick."

"You've been gone a long time. Where were you?"

"In the hills."

"What hills?"

"I don't know."

"Do you know where you are?"

"On a ship."

"What ship?'

"I don't know."

"How long have you been gone?"

"I don't know."

The lieutenant brought his hands together on the table.

"What's your name?"

David heard voices and footsteps shuffling outside the room. The broad-shouldered man who sat across the table from him was probably in his early forties and had ruddy skin that wrinkled prematurely into a craggy face and thick hair the color of mud. He didn't look like an enemy. Clenching his fists and his jaw, David told himself to remember why he was doing this, why he wanted them to think he was crazy, but at that moment all he wanted was to be able to tell this man who he was. His friends would say he had sold out or given in if he did not go through with his plan. He would betray the part of himself that loved Diane and Tim, who now must be hiding somewhere in the city—or maybe not; maybe he'd gone back after all and was serving on the *Loyola*. "No, I can't imagine ever going back there," David had said. If he told the truth he was sure he would lose Diane forever because even she wouldn't be able to understand or forgive him. Still, he felt the layers of his identity peeling away like the skin of an onion. Would he give away the core of his being, the last piece of himself—his honesty, his name? For two weeks he had asked himself who he was and what he wanted, but only now did he realize he could not give up the little he knew to be himself. If he gave it up—if he lied to this man—he would not be himself anymore and would float away, truly invisible with no rope to guide him back. The Navy would own not only his body, but also his soul. He could feel the blood rushing to his face. No; he would own himself, no matter what the consequences.

"David Shields, Seaman."

"Suppose you tell me what you've been doing for the last five months?"

Then the words rushed out, spilling over themselves like waves; David heard himself speaking, unraveling the past, telling this man whom he did not know everything he'd done since he took the bus back to Treasure Island—lived in a storage locker, gone out at night to get water, stolen mattresses from the supply dump. When the officer asked him what he did before coming back to the base, David told him he couldn't remember much since he spent most of his time stoned. He lived in the hills, he said, and slept in some crash pads, but he didn't even know where they were.

"When was the last time you ate?"

"Couple of weeks," David answered.

Finally the doctor stood, pushed back his chair, and called the corpsmen in as he straightened the papers on the table in front of him. David heard him give the order to take him across the road. When David tried to stand his legs nearly gave way, so the corpsmen held him up. Outside, dark night had settled over the island. As he walked through the entranceway of the brig he felt like someone else, a character in a movie he was watching. When the door to the cell banged shut behind him with a heavy, final, metallic sound that echoed along the corridor, he knew there was no going back; he would have to face whatever they decided. Looking at the far wall above the cot he drew air deep into his lungs and exhaled. He had finally killed David Shields, first clarinetist, basketball star, honor student.

Footsteps above. The sentry in his olive-drab Marine uniform paced along the parapet. David focused on the words on the page: "All night the ship pierced her course, and at morning, too." When he heard the footsteps echoing away he looked up through the rectangular screen at the lighted bulb suspended in the darkness above high metal rafters like the ceiling of a hangar deck. Sentries let the men sit on mats during the day but not on their cots, and they had to stay awake from reveille to taps. They called the men by their identification numbers instead of their names; numbers stitched onto patches on their uniforms began to take on personality. The color of the man's patch indicated his level of cooperation: white for those who didn't give the sentries any guff, brown for the recalcitrants, orange for the malcontents. David refused to march in the yard, earning for himself an orange badge and rescission of exercise privileges. So he did push-ups in his nine by seven cell four times a day. Shrinks came to talk to him from time to time; he gave them vague answers and told them he couldn't remember anything about where he'd been or what he'd done between the time he left the Navy and the time he returned to TI.

Before he left the Haight he told Diane and Rennie not to try to see or call him because if they did, he'd be sure to lose his nerve. Most importantly, they shouldn't write to him or expect to hear from him. People in the legal office read all incoming and outgoing mail, and he wasn't going to take a chance on the house being raided. He sent a letter to Diane at Switchboard using the name they'd agreed on, Penny Freiberg, cautioning her in language no censor could understand to make sure there were no drugs in the house—*remember what I told you*—and letting her know she should not try to see him. Now he was truly alone, unable to reach any friend, but it hadn't taken very long to figure out how to endure the solitude: abandon all expectation or hope of ever getting out of here.

He raised his eyes from the page. White pinpoints of light sparkled at the edges of his field of vision, grew larger and moved to the center of his sight. He closed his eyes for a moment, opened them, blinked, and saw only the solid bricks again. But was the wall solid? If 250 mikes of acid could change the world before his eyes, then how sure could he be about anything he saw? He rose slowly from the mat, walked three steps to the brick wall, and put his palms against it, feeling the little canals of mortar. What was the mason thinking when he smoothed it, set another brick, and scraped off the excess? Did he imagine the men who would live there, cut off from the world, for whatever reason he could never know? Probably not if he was focused on his work. If he was lucky, he looked up now and then and saw the dark water of the bay, the blue sky, and a few wisps of cloud. He'd probably been a civilian construction worker who didn't know why he was doing this, but doing it just the same because it was his job and he had a family to support. With only a little effort, David felt he could become part of that wall, forever part of those cold, damp blocks. He stood a moment, turned, took three steps, and sat down on the mat.

Leaning against the wall, he grasped his hands behind his head. If people were the center of the universe, then what they dreamed must be more important than what was real; the world inside the cranium was more solid than the brick walls, the corridor, and the outer walls of the compound itself. So the chief task of the mind must be to describe itself, where it came from, where it is, where it wants to go. They can cage limbs and hands, but not minds, which are more real than these bricks. Freedom was not a possession but a condition of thought. On the outside, people built cages for themselves out of their schedules, possessions, desires, and willingness to let others tell them what their minds were like. In fact, no barrier separated him from the wind off the bay, the hills of Mount Tamilpais, the people in Berkeley and San Francisco; on the contrary, confinement allowed the mind more space: that was the meaning of the vision in the mirror when he dropped acid in the house on Oak Street. Now David knew he had been looking at his soul even as he watched the reflection of his face. He was not alone after all. Here he was a shaved brig rat, but even if he never left this cell, he would never be completely alone, and he would never be confined because his soul was a door into the world, not something separated from his body or detached from the earth. He was not cut off; he was in it and part of it, wherever he was. He did not need to be with Diane in order to love her; like the recollection of music, she filled his mind even when she was not with him, because in a sense she *was* with him. Time stood still, and there was no life but this—his lungs filling with this close air. As in the mountains, no matter where he was, he could not be lost or alone.

David's body jumped at a loud bang. The bolt shot open. He saw a face at the hole, the ugliest he'd ever seen, like a bulldog's with jowls hanging like flaps, lower jaw protruding, and eyes bulging and fierce. The sentry was a young man, and yet even old age would not make him uglier. A loud laugh came from David's throat.

"Prisoner three-four-seven," the man bellowed, "this is a bunch a shit, ain't it?"

The window shot closed. David sat cross-legged on the mat, imagining the face—the huge, fiery eyes, bulbous nose, enormous jaws. He laughed quietly so no one would hear him, his upper body shaking with soundless mirth, longer than he could ever remember laughing in his life.

"What are you doing here, David?"

Lying on the cot he stared upward through the screen at the red light that burned from evening until morning.

"What are you doing here, David?" It was his father's laconic voice, but the tone wasn't angry.

David sat up. He was alone in the cell, but he knew he had heard his father speaking. David almost asked him how he managed to get through all the locked doors. His right hand reached out to touch his father's arm but groped empty space.

"No, you can't see me. I don't exist anymore."

"Then how can you talk to me?"

"Because I'm part of you and live inside you."

David gritted his teeth and swallowed hard to keep the tears from welling in his eyes.

"Was it painful?" he asked.

"No. I don't even remember. I was gone before I knew."

"Why weren't we friends?"

When there was no answer David swallowed again and cleared his throat.

"You pushed me away."

"I didn't want to," his father said. "It was something I couldn't understand."

"I was just a kid," David whispered hoarsely.

"You don't need to understand everything that happened; it doesn't even matter now. Just understand yourself."

"How can I, if I don't understand what was going on between me and you, between you and Mom?"

There was no answer. With the back of his hand David rubbed his eyes to hold the tears back. He lay down again on the cot, remembering how as a kid he'd cried himself to sleep. When he asked Bill Jr. questions about their parents, his brother—the one he loved most in those days who taught him to ride a bike, row a boat, drive a car, and shoot a gun—gave him some vague answer. He'd tried to put Bill in their father's place, but it hadn't worked, especially after his brother had his own sons. Those boys were growing up now. What were they thinking now? What was Bill telling them about where their uncle was?

Lying awake and staring at the ceiling, David exhaled and relaxed all his muscles, pushing the tension away and allowing peace to flow into his body. He loved Diane, and she loved him, and even if he never saw her again, which he was sure he would not, their souls had joined, even though they didn't fully realize it at the time. He had not said good-bye to her or to Rennie because, he told them, he would see them again, soon. Never before had he loved a woman, and probably he never would again, but he loved Diane and was certain she loved him; therefore, he knew he could bear the rest of his life, even if he had to be apart from her.

Then David felt his own death within his body and the reality of death more completely than he ever had: you lose your individuality but you become part of everything else. At the same time he felt as if he were floating slightly above the cot, and he could feel his blood circulating within him, not pulsing like the throb of an artery, but buzzing like a cat purring or a cicada chirring in the late Midwestern summer. The blood vibrated through him until he was a mass of energy, his whole body trembling. His love for Diane was part of the sensation, but now his feelings were indistinguishable from everything else. The earth was telling him that his life was infinite, and as he felt the energy grow stronger within him he wanted to laugh, to yell to the ugly guard that he was free, that he was no longer Prisoner 347, or David Shields, and that the guard could be free too, if he could find the space in his mind that freed the soul to join with the one great energy. Yet he could not yell or even laugh; the sound struggled in his throat because his body was no longer solid but ethereal, the way he felt on acid. The vibration felt like a woman's orgasm, but this lasted much longer, and when it finally stopped, a door opened within himself, and he passed through it into one unhesitating, immense tide that buoyed him into the vastness of the universe.

On the morning of December 21st, marching between two Marine sentries from the brig across the flat, dusty expanse of Treasure Island, David asked himself what they thought he was going to do—break and run to the end of a military base? The brown legal building looked like an enormous dark cube with many windows sitting at an angle to the street. They marched across the grass to the covered concrete parking lot, up the steps to the back entrance, and into a room on the first floor.

The Judge Adjutant General sat at the end of the table in his well-fitting tan uniform with three gold bars and star on the black background of his shoulder patch. He looked only mildly interested, his gray-green eyes partly closed, his lined face serious and inscrutable. Beyond him the walls were gray, and there were high windows shuttered with cream-colored blinds on two sides of the room. Looking out of place in that sterile room, an old-fashioned wooden clock hung on the wall behind the JAG's table, its pendulum clicking with each swing.

The psychologist who questioned him in the dispensary testified that although David was not crazy when he returned to the base on Treasure Island, only someone who was mentally unbalanced would do what David had done, and the Navy did not have the resources to help him. In his letter in the file, the psychologist recommended an immediate administrative discharge, and the consulting psychiatrist agreed. The appointed Navy lawyer spoke for a long time: David deserted because he felt the Navy had not lived up to its own promises; prior to deserting he served well, having been named honor man and earning the highest score on the qualifying exam in electronics. He read three letters from Brownlee, Hammond, and Henderson testifying to David's hard work. The Navy prosecutor in his turn cited the dates on which David left and returned, raising his chin every time he read a fact, trying to make eye contact with the JAG who was looking down. He'd read through the voluminous file and had more cases to hear that day. This wasn't the JAG's first court martial for a deserter, and it wouldn't be his last.

Earlier the sea had been flat, but now it was beginning to roll, and David stood with legs spread and hands gripping the lifeline of the fantail looking at the slanted rays of sunlight pouring from low clouds onto the vast gray water. It reminded him of his old dream about running through an empty ship with a great hole in the bow, searching for a way to cast himself overboard. He didn't have that dream anymore; for weeks now his unconscious mind conjured up a jumbled story in which he ran for no reason through mist so thick he didn't know where he was. Eventually he'd find a rail or bulkhead and reach out only to wake up the instant before he could touch anything.

All morning they'd been launching. When the planes took off, the ship vibrated as if it would burst apart and the hangar deck filled with the deafening roar of jet engines at full throttle; then the whole ship lurched forward as JATO snapped the plane out over the bow. From the electronics shop in the island they could sometimes see the carrier in the distance off starboard launching and recovering at the same time, but they couldn't do that on this ship. David worked with OE Division in the tower, but around 14:00, the old warrant officer came in and asked him to take a message down to the Chief in the aviation electronics shop on the hangar deck. The other guys started razzing him about getting out of work, but without answering David pocketed the note and headed down the ladder.

It was May 1969, and David still had more than a year to go. His brig sentence was five months, same time he'd been gone, and the time he spent in the brig before the court martial didn't count. It was a light sentence, the Navy lawyer told him, because he'd turned himself in and the judge believed his story about getting involved with a group of druggies and forgetting where he was. They could have given him four years.

The judge granted him an administrative discharge after he finished his sentence, but in a letter David requested to be allowed to finish his hitch, telling the judge that spending time in isolation had taught him to think clearly, and he wanted to fulfill what he'd given his word to do. They assigned him to this carrier, the *Hazard Perry*, docked at Hunter's Point. David felt a certain avuncular indulgence for the young guys he worked with who made jokes about being members of the "Tonkin Gulf Yacht Club." Nixon got elected last fall promising to end the war, but they were all still here in this whole horrific, irrational mess that was still going on fifteen years after it started. On the ship he still hung out with some of the malcontents, but he didn't join in any more when they groused about how much they hated the Navy. Saying nothing made the time go by faster. At Subic he headed out of town into the countryside and up a steep, eroded path to look down over the red tile roofs among the lower slopes. He watched the mist rising from the forested mountains and the sun shining on the clear water of the bay and tried to recall how it felt when this was all new, but he couldn't make himself forget what happened in between or recall his emotions clearly when he stood there for the first time.

These guys thought it was cool that David wore the same hash mark on his sleeve that the old-timers had—diagonal red slanted stripe from his elbow to his wrist—and yet the white stripe on his shoulder indicated his rank was the same as theirs—seaman, E2. He'd still be E1, he told them, if the old warrant officer hadn't put the chit in for him. When the officer asked why he didn't apply for the promotions he deserved, David responded he would not ask the Navy for anything. The old guy tried to be nice to him and prodded David to talk about himself. He had a way of inspiring men to want to work well for him, but David still said little. Instead he worked on automatic pilot, performing whatever task they told him to. When you didn't fight them it was like they didn't exist anymore. His reflexes were theirs, but not his mind; they could never own him again, and day after day he crawled closer to freedom.

One morning at Hunter's Point a few weeks after he was out of the brig, a lieutenant JG stepped up to him.

"You know, Shields," the officer said casually, "the Navy always needs people to help us investigate some of the organizations and networks around here. You might consider that." David shook his head, and the officer turned and walked away. About a week later David was reporting for some detail, and the same officer stepped from around a corner and faced him. David saluted.

"We can use bright people in the NIS," the man said.

"No, sir," David responded. "That's not for me."

"You wouldn't have to serve on a ship again."

David shook his head. "No, Sir, I wouldn't be any good at that type of work," he answered, trying to sound disinterested although a sick feeling rose in his stomach. The officer frowned, put his hands on his hips, grunted, and turned away, shaking his head. David never saw him after that encounter.

At first he thought he was sure to go crazy and desert again if he dwelt much on Diane or his friends. He resisted the temptation to go back to visit the old house, but when he finally did last summer, nobody he knew still lived there and the current residents didn't know anything about them. Even Andrea had moved out of the house on Del Mar. He'd sent Diane a second letter addressed to Switchboard explaining his change of heart and telling her he was going to finish his hitch; he still didn't want her to visit or write to him because he was afraid of losing his resolve and going over the hill again; she should live her own life. He loved her, so he would let her go. Anyway, none of them would be able to understand why he'd decided in the end to finish his hitch even though he had the chance to leave, and he'd never be able to explain it to them.

He took long walks in the city the way he had before he'd gone over the hill and tried to remember who he'd been in those days, why he'd felt so confused. People said it was easy to look back and know what you should have done, but he still couldn't say with any certainty what that was. He couldn't even say what he intended to do when all this was over.

He delivered the message to the PO in charge but hadn't been able to help them out much in the aviation workshop; the old warrant officer was only trying to encourage him, but David felt useless and foolish in there. Aviation techs were checking planes out, so there would be another launch in a few hours, and he shouldn't be hanging around here. There'd been an incident a few months ago when a plane came in too low, hit the round down, and broke apart. Though they'd rolled the divider closed between the bays and had the fire out in minutes, the wreckage from that plane had been strewn in the passageways leading to the fantail.

David headed across the deck where some red shirts pulled loaded skids from the bomb elevators and pushed them alongside other skids waiting near the bulkhead. They usually didn't store this many bombs in the hangar bays; the squadron must have had some kind of setback or change of plan.

The ship rose on a swell. He glanced around Hangar Bay Three, a vast steel cavern stretching almost a hundred yards with girders like a giant grid spanning the length and breadth of the ceiling. The lights cast an eerie yellow glow onto the black floor. On the opposite wall the Navy insignia hung next to a ladder, the refueling tank, and roll-up door to Elevator Two. Elevator One stood forward like a giant black hole. NO SMOKING was painted in red on the far wall. An A4 stood ready for the tow motor to push it onto the elevator. He watched a man open the hatch on a Skyhawk next to it, leap into the pilot's seat, pull the canopy down, and start messing with some controls.

The first plane was coming in; it slammed onto the deck, sending vibrations throughout the ship. Minutes later the second one landed. You had to be good, David pondered, damn good to land those things right. Thinking he'd better get back up to the workshop before he got some kind of reprimand, David headed across the deck between an A-4 and a Marine helicopter. He was almost to the hatch when he jumped at a boom like a pressurized canister exploding inside a barrel. Loud noises didn't usually bother him at all, he'd become so used to them. Glancing forward he saw a balloon of orange and pink flame burst from somewhere and spread halfway down Hangar Bay One. He couldn't tell where it came from, but the smoke obscured the opening to Elevator One and the A-4 parked in front of it.

They were all going to be in for it this time. Men dragged hoses from the locker at Conflag Three. Damage Control had some of the best-trained guys in the Navy; even David had been instructed in the use of fire equipment, especially when the yard birds came in to do welding on the ship in dry dock. The trick would be to keep it from spreading to the planes and the refueling station near starboard bulkhead. Fire could burn through any metal if it got hot enough. There were enough liquid oxygen canisters, barrels of flammable paint, and tanks of aviation fuel on board to incinerate the entire ship. Red shirts and boatswain's mates were running toward the skids where two-hundred-fifty and five-hundred-pound bombs could explode and blast through the bulkhead or engulf the hangar bay in flames. Lots of men died two years ago when some ship caught fire in the Gulf, carrying older bombs that cooked off in half the time these new ones did. Men in Hangar Bay Two started rolling the divider shut as the klaxon sounded above the roar and the ensign's voice blared from the IMC that there was a fire in frame 44 and all men were ordered to GQ—this is no drill, he repeated. At that moment another fireball exploded sideways and black smoke poured into the vast cavern of the deck and upward toward the ceiling.

David's GQ on this ship was the ECM dome, the same as on the *Loyola*, and he knew the penalty for disobeying orders; he also knew the men rolling those bombs out of reach of the fire would need help. In the time it took to listen to the order he decided they could court martial him again if they wanted. He ran toward a skid where a young guy was trying to snap the handle into the slot. You activated the brakes by weight; releasing the spring took the weight off the back and let you get the thing going. The bombs were strapped on and weren't going anywhere.

The kid didn't seem to know what to do, so David shouted, "Get a run toward the lifeline when the ship dips to starboard."

From his days in G Division David knew how to play the waves. When the ship rolled, it was like pushing hundreds of pounds uphill, but when the wave peaked and the ship rolled the other way, you could lose control of the skid until you lowered the handle to set the brakes again and either slowed or stopped the skid altogether. To get moving, you had only to turn the skid the way the ship was lurching, lift the handle, and time your forward momentum with the waves. The kid didn't need any convincing and threw himself onto the handle; working together, they rolled it the twenty yards or so to the side. A dozen or more red shirts were pushing skids against the lifeline.

"They'll explode against the hull!" the kid shouted.

"They aren't fused," David cried. "They won't explode. I've seen them fall down elevator shafts and not go off. Get them over the side." Someone cut the lifeline with a hacksaw and the men shoved the skids over.

Black smoke poured from the forward part of the ship and rose, curling along the ceiling and darkening the lights. In their yellow suits and wearing OBAs, the Damage Control men held the hose; the man in front pointed the nozzle at the plane's engine, now engulfed in black smoke, while the second man trained a water hose on the guy in front. Water washed across the floor of the deck while the men farther forward sprayed foam onto the blaze. The klaxons blared, audible over the roaring of the fire that sounded like an engine. As David ran back again and again to push more skids from the deck, he could see the DC guys were beginning to contain the flames in the forward bay, but smoke was still pouring from forward and filling the whole area.

Running toward the middle of the deck, David thought he saw movement in the cockpit of the Skyhawk, but he wasn't sure. He looked again and saw only black smoke. Maybe the man who'd climbed into the pilot's seat hadn't been able to get the canopy open for some reason. The fire crews working feverishly to hose down the planes wouldn't have been able to see him. Flames reached toward the A-4 and the refuel tank in front of it, and now smoke enveloped the Skyhawk. David knew heat could cause the ejection seat to go off, in which case if there was a man inside he would be slammed against the canopy; on the other hand, if the canopy opened, he would be catapulted against the steel beams supporting the bottom of the flight deck. Black ash and white hot magnesium now rained down from the flames that reached almost to the ceiling, and acrid black smoke concealed everything forward of the divider between the first and second hangar bays. It would take David minutes to run into the head and soak down his clothes, by which time the fire might have spread to the Skyhawk.

Tying his handkerchief over his face he took off across the deck toward the plane. Although he ran as fast as he could, it seemed to take forever, as in a nightmare where he tried to run on paralyzed legs. Nothing made sense now except that he would not let another man die a violent death if he could help it. Gulping air beneath the black cloud that billowed upward, he ran toward the Skyhawk. Heat repulsed him like a wall, his skin felt like burning parchment, and the acrid smoke suffocated him. Suddenly he could see the side of the plane. His hands searched the hard, smooth surface in front of the wing. In the swirling blackness his fingers gripped the rescue handle, and he pulled.

TEN

Diane dropped bean seeds like tiny white kidneys about two inches from each other into the soft soil. Sunlight glimmered on the plowed earth. She straightened her shoulders to relieve the ache in her back, walked across the garden to the old hydrant, and pulled the heavy hose to the edge of the row. Aiming the nozzle at her beans, she irrigated them generously, threw the hose down, raked soil over the little white shapes, and watered the row again. Sighing, she dropped the wooden rake worn smooth as a baby's face, trod back to the spigot, and turned the dripping handle. Never leave the spigot turned on, Neil told her. Water was precious. A yellow-breasted chat clucked loudly from an overgrown grape arbor at the end of the garden. Diane could smell rotting leaves in the compost heap.

The nickel-plated hydrant rose like a serpent from the dirt beside a small barn with a sagging roof where Neil parked his '62 Rambler, another member of the group named Garratt left his old blue Mustang and a broken-down Harley, and Neil's wife Rachel set up her potting wheel. They stashed the garden tools there along with used tires, old rakes, half-rotten window frames, and odd boards abandoned by former tenants. Behind the barn, thistles, ragweed, and dandelion thrust through the crumbling concrete foundation of what had been a milking shed. With an old power mower he somehow coaxed into starting, Neil mowed the grass about a half mile to a row of southwestern pines that formed the edge of the back yard where Rachel had built her kiln. Across the driveway, cottonwoods half-hid the two-story white clapboard house where the group lived, and across a sagging wire fence, waist-high grass trembled in the wind. The field reached far to a stand of locusts, and beyond that, more than thirty miles away, the foothills of the Rockies drew a blue line against the horizon.

Diane knelt again and began pulling broadleaf and grass stems from around the tomato plants and threw them into piles. When she got to the end she gathered up the little mounds and carried them to the field edge where she dumped them. Shading her eyes from the noon sun, she pulled off her bandana, rubbed the sweat from her forehead with it, and swept the dirt from the knees of her jeans. The group she lived with always grew their own vegetables, and Neil expected everybody who lived in the house to help.

One morning last December Diane left the Haight, took a bus downtown, changed to the northbound line, and rode all the way to Fairfax where she climbed the steep slope of Baldy through the woods to the ridge trail. Low clouds shrouded the peaks, and fog obscured the valleys. Above Phoenix Lake she looked out over the gray water of the North Bay, staring for long time at the brown rectangle of Treasure Island beside the green mound of Yerba Buena as wind dried her tears.

She could quote David's letters from memory, having read them so often to herself, searching for every nuance he might be trying to send her; still, she took the papers from her hip pocket, unfolded the lined white pages, and let her eyes scan the writing. He'd addressed them to Switchboard so the Navy censors wouldn't find out the Oak Street address and used the name Penelope Freiburg because everyone knew Switchboard was under police surveillance.

> Don't try to see me. I'm not allowed visitors anyway. My court martial hasn't been scheduled yet, but the Navy lawyer tells me I may get an administrative discharge. My brother offered to hire a civilian lawyer but I won't let him. He wrote to me that the FBI came to his house to find out if he knew where I was. Remember what I told you.

The last sentence meant she was supposed to make sure there was no contraband in the house in case somehow the police found out where she lived. No sweat there: Terry wasn't letting people sleep over any more; he'd finally bought a ticket for Kathmandu and given the landlord notice. Rennie was living at Andrea's and going back to SF State in January. Daryl came back once or twice, but then he disappeared and they never saw him again. David also warned Diane before he left that all incoming and outgoing brig mail got censored, so he wouldn't be able to describe exactly what was happening. When she first read the letters in the living room in the house on Oak Street, she felt her stomach tighten. Now, on the side of the mountain, she felt an eerie light-headedness.

Diane placed that letter underneath and read the next one, sent after his court martial.

> Don't send any letters or try to see me. My sentence is five months. They were going to give me an administrative discharge, but I asked them to reinstate me, and they did. I can't tell you everything. I'm going to finish my hitch, which is another two years or so after I get out of here. If I see you again I will lose my nerve. Don't wait for me. I love you.

Something caught in her throat, and she wiped the tears with the back of her hand. She felt disappointment and fear but also anger at the whole mess this war made of people's lives. What was he leaving out? She tried to read behind every word, to understand why he was doing it. David wouldn't lie to her; there must be something he was trying to tell her. Or had they made a liar out of him in that place where everyone deceived? There he was, only a few miles away, and he wouldn't let her see him even one more time.

Diane folded the letters, shoved them back into her pocket, and rubbed her face with her arm. She walked south along the trail toward Mount Tam, not knowing how far she would walk before she turned back, if she turned back at all. She kicked a stone from the path into the long grass.

A truck driver on Interstate 80 took her to Nevada where she spent the first night at a rest stop shivering in a torn sleeping bag, irritated at herself for not bringing more clothes. The next morning she got a lift with an older fellow who asked her to go to Vegas with him; when she said no he let her out at an intersection where he thought she'd be able to get a lift. In Utah a man in his late twenties driving a van stopped for her—he was clean-cut and wore a cowboy hat. They tried to camp in a picnic area near the highway, but a sheriff told them they couldn't stay there, so they drove into the desert, parked along the roadside, and made out in the back on some blankets. The next day the guy went out of his way to take her all the way to the Grassmans' house on Linden in Fort Collins. The last she saw of him was the Colorado license plate on the back of the van.

She knocked gently on the screen door, gritting her teeth and shivering in the cold. After a few moments she heard footsteps. The door swung back and Martin's face appeared, first worried, then delighted.

"Diane! What brings you here?" He stepped out onto the porch and hugged her.

"A van," she said.

"C'mon, you know what I mean. How'd you get here?"

"Hitchhiked."

"Now that was crazy," he said. "Why didn't you let us know?"

"Wanted to surprise you."

"And what if we hadn't been home?"

"Thought I'd take a chance."

"You like that, don't you—taking chances and surprising people? Come on in." He reached for her knapsack. "Nothing else?"

"Nothing."

"Well, it all looks the same," she said, stepping into the living room and recognizing the picture of the wedding in Glen Helen and the teacups from Hong Kong. Martin had gained a few pounds since last spring. An eager, opaque expression, dense and alert, replaced the worried look she'd noticed in his eyes the last time she saw him.

"It's so good to see you." He hugged her again.

"Where's Elaine?" Diane asked.

"Working. She has a new job at a homeless shelter."

"She like it?"

"Loves it."

"Cody and Tess?"

"At the baby sitter's," he said. "While I try to get some work done."

"Oh shit, I'm interrupting you."

"Nonsense," he said. "It isn't every day *you* fly in. Sit down. I'm going to call Elaine. Maybe she can get off early."

They talked about her trip to Colorado, San Francisco, his teaching. He loved methods, but not research. Now he had only his thesis to finish—he hoped—by August.

"Then what?"

"Remains to be seen," he answered, turning his eyes toward the front where the Honduran curtains were drawn across a picture window.

"You used to want to start your own school," she pursued. "So you could do things your way."

"Yes," he said. "I don't know now."

"Why not?"

The door opened with a sound like a sigh and Elaine walked into the room, exclaiming in a high-pitched tone as she threw her shoulder bag onto a chair and stepped toward Diane with her arms outstretched.

"Here you are out of the blue," Elaine said, hugging her.

Elaine made corn pudding and a stew with eggplant and tomatoes, and they sat at the kitchen table where a paper lantern shed a halo of light on the round metal table. Elaine and Diane talked about what they'd been doing since last spring; Martin sat at looking out the window over the small back yard surrounded by ragged hedges.

"Why don't you stay here with us?" Elaine suggested. "I could use help with the kids. You can get a part-time job somewhere."

"I don't know how long I'm going to be here," Diane answered, although she'd already decided to find a place to live in Fort Collins.

She stayed two months at the crash pad on Remington, a two-story Victorian with a wide front porch, while she worked a temporary job on campus. She met Neil, a graduate student, who rented a farmhouse outside town and ran it as a commune with his wife Rachel; they had a room open and he told her she could come and live there. She'd be able to walk to town, but a lot of the time she could ride with somebody who was driving in. The Remington house was closer to work, but it was crowded, and the police were always watching. Later she found a full-time job in a vegetable processing plant on Hilliard Street. The work was monotonous—mostly cutting the ends off beets and Brussels sprouts—but it paid well, and by the time she qualified for in-state status she'd have enough money to go full-time to CSU and finish her degree. When she worked the graveyard shift she'd crash at the house on Remington before she hiked back to the farm in the morning. She liked walking out of town as the sun came up past the single-story wooden houses with old cars in the driveways and little bare yards fenced with sheep wire.

※ ※ ※   ※ ※ ※   ※ ※ ※

Diane tossed the last of the weeds onto the pile near the barn and noticed a car coming down the road. She expected it to continue on past, but instead it slowed and turned into the driveway, and she recognized Martin's sand-colored VW. She could taste the dust the tires raised as the car pulled to a stop and the door opened. Diane strode to the edge of the gravel.

"Hi," he called out, slamming the door.

"What brings you out here?" She hadn't seen him for nearly two weeks. "You're growing a beard."

"Wanted to see your place," he said, running his palm along his jaw and walking toward her as the wind gusted in the pine branches. His white polo shirt was unbuttoned at the neck.

"It's only the garden and the house," she said, bending to untie her sneakers and empty the dirt.

"Your classes going okay?" she began.

"I like the students," he answered, scanning the foothills in the distance.

"That's the old Martin," she said. "Or part of him."

"What do you mean? I'm the same as I always was."

"No, you're not."

"What's different? Besides my beard, I mean."

"Your eyes."

"What about them?"

"They belong to a hunter."

"And what did they use to look like before?"

"Like you knew what you wanted."

"And now I don't?"

"No," she said. "You don't."

"And you?" he asked.

"It doesn't matter right now," she said. "I just want to go on here."

She trembled inwardly as he stepped toward her and put his hand on her shoulder.

"Let's see the house," he suggested.

They walked through the back door onto the scuffed kitchen tile and smelled onions and stale grease.

"Do people really do their chores?" Martin asked, scanning handwritten notes pinned on the corkboard.

"Neil gets after them if they don't," she answered, opening the old refrigerator. "But Rachel does most of the cleaning—far more than anyone else. We have Coke, iced tea, and beer if you want a drink."

"Not right now. Let's see the rest of the house."

She washed her hands at the sink and dried them on a frayed dish towel that hung from the handle of the old oven. They walked into the living room with a sagging green couch, rocker, and faded brown easy chair where a large, short-haired, orange and white cat groomed its tail intently. There were holes in the blue-gray carpet near the front door. A motorcycle maintenance magazine lay on a coffee table next to a glass ashtray full of cigarette butts.

"This is where Neil argues politics."

"With who?"

"Anybody who'll listen."

"Including you?" he asked.

"I don't think it matters who gets elected. The whole system has to change before they'll end the war."

"You're cynical."

She shrugged.

"How many people live here?" Martin asked, running his hand along the cat's head and back.

"Six right now. Three men, three women."

"Sounds cozy."

"Neil and Rachel are married. Two are living together. The biker's alone. Garrett."

"And you?"

"Free and staying that way."

Martin turned toward her.

"What's upstairs?" he asked.

"Bedrooms, of course."

The bare wooden stairs creaked under their feet.

"And here's my space," she said, turning a loose, old-fashioned ceramic knob.

A mattress lay on the floor and an old wooden dresser stood in the corner, an easel next to it along the west wall holding a bare canvas. A new black guitar case lay on its side on the floor.

"Very Boho," he said.

"I travel light."

"You sure do. Anybody else here?" he asked.

"No," she answered, pulling off her bandana and running her fingers through her hair.

"When will they be back?"

"Maybe hours. You picked the right day."

"Right day for what?" he asked.

"Right day to tell me whatever it was you came here to tell me." She straightened her shoulders and thrust her hands into her back pockets.

"How do you know I have something to tell you?"

"C'mon, Martin. Your eyes give you away."

"I've left Elaine," he answered, facing her and putting his hands on his hips.

"I know," she shrugged.

"How?"

"The minute I saw you last year I knew it was coming. I just didn't know when, and I wasn't sure why." She picked up a pair of jeans from the floor and tossed them onto a stool.

"I never know what you're going to say."

"How's she taking it?"

"Pretty well. She knew it was coming, too."

"I'd better go see her." Diane turned away from him but felt his hands on her shoulders.

"She wants to see you," he said.

"Where you living?"

"I have an apartment on McAlister."

She let him kiss her for a long time. He unbuttoned her blouse and unfastened her bra before she pulled her jeans down. Stepping out of them, she took his hand and led him to the mattress.

"Do you take precautions?" he asked, lying on his side, his head propped up on his right hand. Martin was shorter than David and not so muscular.

"I have an IUD, if that's what you mean," she answered.

"Am I the first since San Francisco?"

"First one that mattered."

"Quite a compliment."

"Don't flatter yourself."

She could say what she wanted. He was in love with her. She had always admired him and now she could have him if she wanted—but it was too late. She really wanted David, who was lost to her.

※ ※ ※   ※ ※ ※   ※ ※ ※

They listened to the wind in the tree branches.

"How many have there been?" she asked, lying on her back.

"How do you know there've been others?"

"C'mon."

"Two."

"Who were they?"

"Grad student and a Psych prof."

Diane laughed. "Your student?"

"We didn't get involved until the class was over."

"Now?"

"She's with somebody else."

"Were they married?"

"The prof was. Is."

"Does her husband know?"

"Not then. Maybe now."

"Did Elaine know?"

"I think she knew about the grad student."

"I'll bet she knew about them both. She's sharper than you give her credit for. Why didn't they work out?"

"What do you mean, sharper than I give her credit for? I know she's sharp," he said. "I didn't want them to work out."

Diane rolled over to face him, bent her elbow, and propped her head on her left hand.

"What is it you're looking for?"

"I don't know," he said, raising his hands and then clasping them beneath his head. "I wanted to find out what all those beautiful bodies were like, find out if . . ."

"If what?"

"If I even want to stay married."

"You can't do better than Elaine."

"I know that."

"So from me you want to find out whether you really want to stay with her."

"No," he insisted. "Nothing like that."

"What then?"

"I want to know you as you are, not like my protégé. When I saw you last year . . ."

"I know," she said.

"But you ran away. . ."

"I didn't 'run away'," she said, irritated. "I just left."

". . . and I thought you'd never come back, so I tried to forget about you. Then you did come back, but it looked like you were avoiding me, so I left you alone. Until today."

"Don't give me that shit. You know you've been planning this." She sat up.

"All right," he said. "Yes, I have."

"It's the script thing," he continued after a pause. "I don't know if I've written a drama for myself and I'm destined to play it, like it or not."

"You felt trapped."

"Yes," he said, unclasping his hands and sitting up. "Or maybe it's something else. Everything changed when the kids came along."

"Why don't you help Elaine with them? Then she'd have more time for you."

"It's not that. I do spend a lot of time with them."

"You wanted kids."

"I love kids," he answered, "and I love Cody and Tess. When I'm away from them I can't wait to see them again but . . . sometimes I feel like they're part of the trap. I didn't know my feelings would change toward Elaine."

"How *do* you feel about her?"

"Almost like someone else wrote the script for me. If I could be twenty-two again, I'd do it all differently. I want to find out what I've missed."

"You had no choice?"

"Of course I did, but I feel like I squandered my youth. I got married and decided on a career too young. I thought we'd be partners and blaze trails.

Instead we're like every other married couple."

"Every other married couple my ass. How many people get to do what you've been able to do?"

"Whose side are you on, anyway?"

"I love her too, you know," Diane said, raising herself and sitting cross-legged. "You'd be a fool to leave a woman like Elaine."

"I know, I know. I've been told that before."

"By who?"

"Friends. I even told my psychiatrist that."

"Why don't you talk it all out with Elaine instead of some shrink who's making money off you? They don't know shit."

"We talked it out. I just want some time to myself," he said. "I didn't want those others. You make me feel like there's more."

She rolled her eyes, and he lay back again and stared at the ceiling.

"Did Elaine know you were coming here today?"

"No," he said quickly. "Don't tell her yet."

"Why not?"

"I just need time to find out . . ."

"Find out if you want me or her? I don't want you two-timing me while you figure out if you really want her. And I'm not sleeping with you if you don't tell her about me."

She uncrossed her legs and started to get up.

"Don't go yet," he said, his right hand on her arm. "We have a lot to talk about. How do you like living here?"

"It's okay," she answered. "Rachel and Neil keep it together. When they decide they want to live by themselves, everything will fall apart."

"What about you?"

"What about me?"

"You never did tell me very much about San Francisco," he said.

"Yes I did. I told you all there was."

"You didn't tell me much about the guy from Ohio."

"Well, he's gone now," she answered.

"Gone where?"

"Back to the Navy. He told me not to wait for him."

"Then you shouldn't. Sounds like he doesn't intend to come back. You're lucky he told you the truth."

Martin lay back and stared at the cream-colored ceiling.

"You won't see him again, if he said that."

She stood up and grabbed a towel.

"How old are you?" he asked, rolling onto his side.

"Twenty-one last month. Rachel made me a birthday cake. First one I've had since I was thirteen," she said.

"That's a great age. Don't settle down. Be an artist. You'll never have another chance to be young."

She rolled her eyes again, taking up her jeans. "Now where have I heard *that* before?"

He rose from the bed and went into the bathroom. When he came back she was buttoning her shirt. He zipped his trousers with a turn of his long wrist, followed her downstairs, and walked outside onto the porch. The chromium on the VW gleamed.

"I want to see you again," he said, squeezing her elbow.

"Then you know what you have to do."

He walked to his car, opened the door, slid onto the seat, and turned the key. As the engine caught and he closed the door, Neil's old Rambler turned into the driveway and stopped, and Rachel got out. Martin backed the VW around and drove away. A curtain of dust rose behind his car.

"Friend of yours?" Rachel asked as she climbed the steps. Her thin face was freckled the same color as her hair.

"Old friend from Antioch who lives in Fort Collins now," Diane answered, stepping off the porch and heading toward the garden.

❋ ❋ ❋   ❋ ❋ ❋   ❋ ❋ ❋

The road ran miles past alfalfa fields and pasture and into the rocky country of the Poudre Canyon. Near the flats Martin turned down a narrow lane crowded on both sides by Norway spruce and hemlock.

"Here," Diane said suddenly as they drove around a bend and saw Garrett's blue Mustang and a few other cars and motorcycles beside the road. A wooden post held a rusting mailbox with no name on it. Martin pulled the VW up behind one of the cycles and set the parking brake. He got out and looked across the gully at the orange tile roof and metal stovepipe barely visible among pine branches in the fading light. They could hear the river booming far below. Diane strode quickly down a path into the gully and up the other side.

"Wait, Diane," Martin called out, hurrying after her. "Who owns this place?" he asked, taking her arm.

"Somebody Garratt knows," Diane answered, pulling away from his grasp and walking toward the cabin.

People sitting on an old couch in front of the windows looked suspiciously at Martin, who was dressed in creased black pants and a red and white polo shirt. Diane wasn't looking very hip that day, either, in new striped bell-bottoms held up with a sash and a new blue and gold satin blouse she'd bought in a shop in Old Town. Every one of them had very long hair; most wore Indian bands and beads, the men mostly shirtless, the women in long shifts.

"Hey, over here," someone called, and she saw Garratt with people sitting in a circle on the floor. Diane stepped around four squatters in the middle of the room.

"Reade has the shit over there," he said, pointing to a skinny man in torn jeans and no shirt who leaned against a table laden with food. Long green beads hung against his hairless chest. "Join us."

"Is this his cabin? Martin's a little uptight."

"No, but Reade knows the guy who owns it," Garratt answered, his mouth widening in a huge grin. "No sweat. I been here before."

"Can we walk outside?" she asked, glancing through the back windows that looked out over the canyon.

"Yeah, just be careful of snakes," Garratt warned, smiling. "You look like a swan."

"Your hair is turning into snakes," a girl said beside him, reaching for his stringy hair.

"Who owns this place?" Martin asked Reade.

"This is God's house," Reade answered, smiling and peering at him through thick lenses in wire-rimmed frames. "And we are God's people. Help yourself to loaves and fishes. The communion wine's coming around." As he toked a joint he jerked his right thumb backward to indicate bowls of crackers, olives, dates, and bricks of cheese. People passed a jug of Chianti around and drank from the spout.

"And here's the sacrament," Reade continued, handing Martin a small straw basket with oval purple tablets in it. Diane took the basket and retrieved two ovoids.

"How many?"

"Two-five-o."

"You sure?" she asked.

The man shrugged, grinned, and extended his arms. "Look at them."

"They're zonked out of their gourds," she said.

Reade kept grinning. "It's a party, man."

"He doesn't know," Martin whispered to Diane, taking her arm.

"Know what?'

"The owner."

"So?"

"They're trespassing," Martin whispered.

"Garratt says Reade knows him and Garratt's been here before," she answered. "Let's go outside. You're freaking people out."

The cabin, made of brown asbestos tile, perched on the edge of a cliff far above the water rushing furiously where the canyon narrowed. Lodgepole pines rose high from the steep gorge. Branches of fir and hemlock nearly hid the front from view. Reade followed them outside.

"Is he cool?"

"He's okay," Diane whispered. "Novice."

"I hope he knows what he's doing," Reade said, stepping back inside.

"You look a little too straight for them," Diane explained. "They're afraid you're going to get them busted."

"I'm not worried about *him*," Martin told her. "I'm worried about trespassing."

"You want to split?" she asked impatiently.

"I could lose my license."

"Go if you want, then. I'll get a ride home."

"I'm not leaving you here."

"Don't be so hung up. Go if you don't like it. I'll be okay."

"I said I'm not leaving you here."

"And you said you wanted to try it. Break it in two if you don't want to drop the whole thing." She opened her palm to reveal the two tablets. He took one hesitantly.

"Listen to that," she said, gesturing toward the cliff. "The voice of the river."

They sat on a large, round stone. The cold penetrated their clothes.

"We're in Eden," she said, raising her hand to her mouth and swallowing one pill.

He looked at the purple ovoid lying in his palm, broke it, and swallowed half. Diane grinned, taking the remaining half and shoving it into her pocket.

"Now relax and don't fight it. The first time is the most important." She spread her arms.

The river boomed, and hemlock limbs sighed in the wind. Martin's brow was creased.

"You're too tense," she said. "I can feel it."

Wind played in the tree limbs. Diane thought Martin's head began to look flattened and extended. His trip was beginning, too; his eyes shone and he stared at the trunk of a tall oak.

"What do you see?" she asked.

"It reaches all the way to heaven," he said.

"I thought you didn't believe in heaven."

"I think I was wrong."

As they walked further down the path along the canyon, the trees began to take on the vaulted look of a cathedral ceiling, and the song of a dusky sparrow sounded like a flute.

"I think my life will always be bound with yours," he said, putting his arms around her waist.

The trees rose hundreds of feet into the darkening sky while the river boomed like a tympanum. She could feel the force of the planet hurtling through space. Walking away from Martin, she stepped toward the rim of the canyon. A rock let go under her sandal and plunged over the edge, swallowed in the tidal wave the river had become. The bottomless canyon yawned far below.

Weeks later a warbler awakened her from a dream in which she was swimming beyond a buoy in a lake of dark water. Throwing back the covers she rolled out of bed, but as she pulled on her jeans, nausea choked her. It was the fourth day she'd awakened feeling this way. The first time she thought it must have been the hash she and Martin smoked the night before; the next morning she attributed it to hunger, since she hadn't eaten for twenty-four hours.

But hash didn't make you sick four days in a row. She stumbled into the bathroom and threw up into the toilet.

After work Diane walked to Martin's apartment, inserted the key, and opened the door. She waited, sitting cross-legged on the floor, practicing deep-breathing exercises and half listening to one of her own Grass Roots albums. When she heard the wooden steps squeaking with Martin's weight, she inhaled deeply and watched the door open. His forehead was wet with sweat and his hair fell around the collar of his white shirt partly pulled from his pants.

"Hi. Didn't know you'd be here." He pulled his key from the lock.

"I got off work early," she said, lifting the arm of the stereo and setting it on the cradle.

"I'm supposed to pick up Cody and Tess today," he said.

"I forgot."

"Want to go?"

"No."

"Can you wait while I pick them up?"

"Yeah."

She sat up and raised her shoulders.

"What would happen if you got one of your girlfriends pregnant?"

"I'd be *really* disappointed. Why? You aren't pregnant, are you?"

"No," she said quickly. "Why disappointed?"

"I can't deal with any more right now. I'm almost done with this damn thesis."

"So what's the problem if you're almost done?"

"I just don't want to be tied down again," he said, rubbing the back of his neck. "Why are you asking about my girlfriends? You're the only one."

"Sure?"

"Diane, what's wrong?" He faced her now, pulling at his tie.

"Nothing," she said shrugging. "Just thought I'd ask."

"You've been smoking so much of that stuff you don't know what you're saying." He headed for the bedroom, his sport coat and tie in his hand. When he came back he was wearing jeans.

"I'll be back in a half hour," he said. "Want to go Old Town for a pizza?"

"Okay," she answered without looking at him. She waited until the sound of his footsteps faded, grabbed her Indian bag, headed out the door, and walked quickly down McAlister to the main road and out the dusty highway that led to the farmhouse.

By the time she got there the sun was below the tops of the trees, the sky dark blue. Diane walked around to the back of the house. Above the chirring of katydids she heard voices inside and saw the light come on in the kitchen. The talking grew louder, and she could hear Neil's clear, deep voice above the others. He and Rachel were talking to Garratt and his new girlfriend. Diane could make out the words "war" and "Humphrey."

Diane didn't care who won; none of them really wanted to stop the war. In the still place behind her conscious thought she saw David inside one of the dark lower decks of a ship screwing detonators onto the ends of bombs as he had described to her once. She remembered the carriers sailing out of the bay, but the only notion she had about what they looked like inside was what she saw in movies about World War II, and while she knew those images couldn't be right, she had nothing else to go on. David might be out there somewhere in the Pacific while people over here shouted and demonstrated against the war and still it dragged on. Diane couldn't remember a time when the lead news story every night had been about anything other than Vietnam. It was never going to end.

"Rachel, I think I'm going to leave this week," Diane told her in the kitchen of the old farmhouse.

Rachel filled the kettle and turned on the gas.

"Do you want to tell me why you've been so sick lately?"

"You know why," Diane said.

Rachel knitted her brows as she lifted two green ceramic mugs from the cupboard and dropped a bag of herb tea into each.

"Have a seat, why don't you?"

Diane pulled out a kitchen chair and straddled it. They could hear Neil talking to someone outside.

"Is it Martin's?"

"Of course."

"What happened?"

"The IUD just stopped working," Diane answered. "I don't know why."

"Have you seen a doctor?"

"Yep."

The kettle whistled. Rachel poured the boiling water into the two mugs and carried them and the sugar bowl to the table where she pulled out a chair.

"Will you keep it or give it up?"

"Give it up."

"Have you thought about this?"

"Sure I have. Long and hard."

"But why not marry the guy? You told me you liked him. He looks good to me." She raised the bag from her mug, laid it on a saucer, and stirred a teaspoonful of sugar into her tea.

"I used to like him. I tried to make myself love him."

"Does he love you?" Rachel asked, resting her chin on her hand.

"Says he does, but I'm not sure."

"Why?"

"He's going through this the middle-aged thing. He's thirty and wants to be free for a while. I asked what would happen if I got pregnant, and he said he'd be disappointed because he doesn't want to be tied down again. He's already got two kids."

"Maybe he'd feel different if you told him the truth."

"I'm not sure I want to get married."

Rachel raised her mug to her lips.

"Don't you think he has a right to know?" she asked, setting the mug down.

"I've thought all that through. I don't think he's ready to hear," Diane said, swallowing some of the bitter tea.

"So where do you think you'll go?"

"My parents.' It's a good place to think. Nothing ever happens in Columbus so I'll be able to focus for a change. Maybe finish my degree at OSU instead of CSU. All the big state universities are alike."

"Have you told them?"

Diane shook her head.

"For some reason I'm not sorry it happened," she said after a pause.

She touched her forehead with the tips of her long fingers and sobbed once behind her hand. Rachel stood and put her arms around Diane.

"No, no, it's okay," Diane said, sitting up.

"Have you heard from . . . ?"

"No. Not since before I left San Francisco. He doesn't know where I am, and I don't even know if he's still alive. He told me not to try to contact him or he'd lose his nerve."

Diane packed her clothes and canvases into boxes and mailed them to Columbus the same day she gave notice at her job. On August 26th Rachel drove her to Highway 75. Diane got out of the car, pulled her knapsack over her shoulders, waved once to Rachel, and walked up the ramp. Sharp-bladed grass and ragweed grew among the tar and gravel at the edge of the pavement. Turning in the high wind to face the oncoming cars and trucks, Diane extended her arm and stuck out her thumb.

ELEVEN

The Ohio State University *Lantern*

Tuesday, April 21, 1970

PROTEST MARCH

> There will be a rally and march at noon today on the Oval to
> the Ohio Union to protest the war profiteering industries and
> military recruiters. This march is sponsored by the Student
> Mobilization Committee, the Columbus Moratorium
> Committee and the Third World Solidarity Committee.

Students near Diane spoke with muffled voices as they meandered among long
tables set up on the shiny wooden floor in the back ballroom of the student
union. One or two people sat behind each of the tables loaded with pamphlets
and draped with the names of companies. A large white banner reading
PROSPECTUS '70 hung above the glass doors that looked out over the back
lawn and across College Street to the wooded park they called the Little Oval.
The trees were in leaf, the day warm, and the mood in the room languid. Diane

turned back to reading the lists of jobs the companies recruited for.

She had walked over after her morning studio class hoping to find some kind of job after she graduated this term. She needed to support her son Marty, who would be a year old in May, but Diane didn't see anything for people with degrees in art, not even in public relations. Right now ADC just covered her expenses and upkeep on an old maroon Fiat with over 100,000 miles on it. She lived free in a two-room cabin on the edge of her parents' property. They wanted to pay her tuition, but Diane couldn't stand being in debt to them.

"Here they come," a man standing near her said to no one in particular.

Six men wearing black robes and red bandanas lugged something down College Road and across the grass. As they neared the Union, Diane saw that they carried a coffin draped in black. A group following them shouted in unison, "Big firms get rich! GIs die!" They forced their way through the glass doors and stood chanting before the tables. Some of them threw pamphlets onto the floor and turned over cardboard displays.

A bald, paunchy man in a dark suit walked to the front of the room and tried to talk to the demonstrators, but Diane couldn't hear what he was saying above the noise. Another, taller man in a gray suit approached the demonstrators and tried to persuade them to leave. After about ten minutes, campus police in their black pants, white shirts, and helmets entered through the back door of the ballroom, marched in line to the front, and confronted the six men carrying the box.

"What's going on?" someone asked.

"They're arresting the demonstrators," another student answered.

"They can't do that."

"Why not?"

"They didn't do anything wrong."

"Everyone in this room must leave or be subject to arrest," a policeman announced through a bullhorn.

The crowd streamed toward the back doors. Something hit her on the head as Diane tried to get through the bottleneck. She ran down the corridor towards a side entrance where a group was pushing its way through the metal emergency doors. Outside people talked excitedly.

"There weren't even any big businesses here to picket. And the military wasn't here."

"They didn't have to call the cops. It was peaceful till they came."

Diane walked around the side of the building where police pushed the six men into squad cars that pulled away up College Street. She headed across the lawn called the Oval toward the new art building that looked like a giant box made of red brick held up in front by concrete stilts.

Inside, she took her paints out of her locker and carried them to the long studio with its gray concrete floor. On the way down she looked through the dark window of one of the studios used by a painting instructor who'd taken her to see *The Night Thoreau Spent in Jail* last weekend. She dipped the brush into brown paint and began filling in the white space with short strokes that might be Impressionist leaves. When the brush was dry she dipped it into the green paint and with long strokes allowed spherical and conical shapes to grow. Her hand moved up and down over the canvas like a bird flying into wind.

🌾 🌾 🌾   🌾 🌾 🌾   🌾 🌾 🌾

On May 10, 1969, Diane awoke and remembered where she was—her parents' cabin. She lay in the comfortable stupor of half-sleep and listened to the wood frogs and spring peepers singing loudly from the pond behind the house. A katydid clinging to the back screen shrilled loudly in the dark night. Then she realized what woke her—the first contraction.

The round face of the electric alarm clock showed five after one. She reached over to the night stand and turned on the lamp, got up, and paced around the small room, peering out the window at the darkness and watching her oval face mirrored in the window glass—high cheekbones, eyes half-closed, uncombed wavy hair reaching to her shoulders.

She was supposed to call the nurse midwife as soon as she was sure she was going into labor, and Ulana wanted to know as soon as it started, but

Diane felt like being alone, at least for now. Stubborn, her mother called her when she was a girl, and stubborn she still was. Every day for the last seven months she sometimes felt extraordinary peace, sometimes panic, sometimes a new sensation she couldn't describe. During the last two months the baby jumped when any door slammed or car started up. She knew this child already. No one else would ever understand it the way she did, ever feel the excitement she did when it kicked. One way or another, if you loved a man he found a way to leave you, or you got rid of him. With this child things would be different. Over many months she'd made the decision to keep it, no matter what other people might say.

Diane watched the clock's long hand sweep around the circle, the short hand work its way down the arc of the morning. She rested between contractions, several times falling asleep only to be awakened by the pain that rose gradually, increasing in intensity as it crested and she entered into a kind of ecstasy as the sharpness gripped the insides of her bones and spread up her spine. She pulled her breath in through her nose and expelled it through her mouth as the nurse told her to do.

At twelve minutes after four she felt the urge to push—she would be free if she could push hard and long enough. Suddenly an intense contraction made her scream involuntarily, as if the sound came from somewhere outside her. At first she felt afraid, but she reminded herself most births were perfectly normal, most women did okay. Her own mother hadn't had any trouble with either of her children. When the pain eased off she lay back against the pillow, breathing hard and sweating.

Her hand reached toward the table beside the bed, and her fingers gripped the telephone receiver.

"How many of them are striking?" a guy asked.

"About a hundred and fifty, they say," a woman answered who wore large gold loop earrings.

Four students sat under the shade of the red brick archway of Hayes Hall, the old art building. They all wore jeans splattered with paint. One of the girls had blotches of blue paint in her pale brown hair. Diane raised an aluminum can to her lips and drank the dark cola that stung her nose.

"That's not many for a place with 50,000 students."

"It is for a small school like Social Work," Diane suggested.

"What do they want?"

"Fifty-fifty representation and voting rights on all policies," the woman said. "The faculty wants to give them seven seats. *Seven.* What can seven people do?"

"A hell of a lot, if they try," the guy answered.

"This administration'll never give them fifty percent," the girl with the brown hair said.

"What do students know about running a department?"

"What does the administration know about the student experience?" the other woman said. "It should be their job to know that, and none of them knows shit about what we do."

"I tell you what it would be like if students ran this place," the guy said.

"What?"

"Chaos."

"Jesus, that's what we have now," the girl with the brown hair said.

Diane headed up the stairs to the fifth floor of Denney Hall on Seventeenth Avenue. At the top of the stairs she climbed a ladder reaching to the low ceiling and pushed a discolored panel just above her head. She forced the panel all the way up and climbed into a small rectangular room that housed the elevator and air conditioning equipment. She propped the door open with a stick, walked to the edge of the flat roof, and looked down on the maple and sycamore trees behind the building.

She took off her shirt and jeans and laid them out on the roof, then her underwear and sandals, and lay on her clothes in the warm sun of April. The tar and gravel on the roof surface reflected heat like a sauna. Her right elbow lying across her face, she contemplated the forked yellow patterns behind her eyelids.

What would she do after she graduated? Her decision to keep Marty set her on a course she couldn't change. She didn't regret keeping him, but now she had to face raising him alone with no profession or skill. All her life she'd taken too much for granted.

Days earlier, Diane got a letter from Martin in Fort Collins asking her why she never wrote to him. It had been over a year; he was divorced; Elaine remarried; he finished his Master's and had a year's research appointment. What was she doing? Diane kept the letter to herself and formulated answers but never wrote them down.

How much time passed she didn't know when she woke up on the roof to shouts and whistles. She raised her head to see two workmen calling to her from the roof of Derby Hall across the street. Waving back at them, she got up and pulled on her clothes. When she walked back to the shed she found the door blown shut and locked from the inside, but a horizontal window facing the street stood part way open. Her arm wasn't long enough to reach through the window to the door handle, so she pushed the glass as far open as it would go, bent over, and thrust her leg through. Flattening her stomach as much as she could, she wedged herself into the opening that still wasn't wide enough, but she wiggled through and stood at last inside the shed. She quickly lowered herself through the opening at the top of the ladder, pulled the ceiling panel behind her, climbed down the rungs, and leaped to the floor of the hallway.

Heading for the amphitheater, Diane stepped onto the grass beside Mirror Lake where the jet of water rose high in the air, curved, and plunged to the surface. Rhododendron bushes bloomed purple and red in front of a grove of white and southwestern pine on the hillside between the lake and library. People sat on the grass or benches, and some squatted on a cobblestone walkway. A man in baggy corduroy trousers stood at a microphone on the opposite hillside naming the species killed by industrial pollution. When he stopped, the listeners applauded and a tall, bearded, and balding man stood up to read a poem. She had to miss some of the speeches because Marty made her late that morning by crying and hanging on to her when she took him to the baby-sitter's.

On the slope behind the platform beside the water was a circular hedge where she once saw a couple having sex, concealed on every side except from above. The gardeners should have known what college students would do with a circular hedge. She tried to concentrate on the speakers but couldn't get out of her mind what she saw on her way up Neil Avenue this morning: two young men walking toward her, waving their hands, their eyes intense in concentration. Abruptly they stopped, turned toward each other, and gestured rapidly, touching their foreheads, eyes, and ears, moving their fingers together and apart, thumping their chests with their palms and fists. She thought deaf people were silent, but she heard involuntary grunting and the shushing sound clothes make on waving arms. These men used their whole bodies to talk to each other like actors in a play. Then they turned and walked beside each other again. She stood aside to let them pass but watched their backs moving and their shirts constricting with the movement of their muscles as they continued down the street. In their excitement they hadn't noticed her.

The speeches and poetry readings went on past nine but Diane had to leave for an economics class held in a lecture hall with a pudgy professor who looked older than he was with his pink, shaved face. He drew lines on the board and labeled them "supply" and "demand," as if that was all there was to it, and said the reason the economy in Britain was bad was that it was socialist. One day he told the students the way to help migrant farm workers was not to boycott grapes, but to eat as many as they could without spending twenty-four hours on the john. Diane raised her hand and started to tell him the problem was that immigrant labor wasn't being paid no matter how hard they worked. The professor cut her off, saying he didn't take questions during lecture and to ask her teaching assistant. She complained to the TA—a young, bearded man with long, shaggy hair who had a picture of Karl Marx above his desk on the wall. He told her he'd be happy to answer her questions; after that he asked her to go out with him.

She headed across the Oval, late for the econ class, sighing because she was twenty-three and still taking requirements.

"What in hell do they want?"

"Afro Am and the other Black student organizations want amnesty for the demonstrators that took over the Administration Building back in March."

"Why should they get amnesty? They broke windows and set off the fire alarms. If we did that we'd be shot."

"Well, shit, look at what they've been through . . ."

"Oh come on. Why don't they just go through student government?"

"Because it's a piece of crap and doesn't do anything. They tried to meet with the president back in March."

"To do what?"

"Present a list of demands."

"If I did that they'd throw me out."

"They waited a hundred years . . ."

"What have they done to *earn* any rights?"

"Rights belong to the people."

"So? If they don't like it here they can leave."

"The disruption rule is a continuation of the University's repressive pseudo-parental code," the short, rotund, bearded political science professor said through a bullhorn. Diane estimated there were about two hundred students sitting or standing in a semicircle, listening or half-listening to him under the trees on the grassy Oval about three acres in size. The library towered like a gray stone monolith at the west end surrounded by trees and shrubs. Most students walked past the speaker and his audience. A few yards away, four guys in shorts tossed a Frisbee.

The Ohio State University *Lantern*

Friday, April 24, 1970

> We demand amnesty for all the students named in the injunction served on March 13. We demand disruption charges be dropped and amnesty for five students arrested April 21 from all University disciplinary action.

> We demand that no sanctions be taken against University students and workers who participate in activities which are critical of University policy.

> We demand the repeal of all University rules and regulations which have a 'chilling' effect on free speech.

> We agree with the demands of Afro-Am and the Black Studies Department that the University recruit enough Black people to constitute 23% of the student body and that a proportionate number of slots should remain open to Indians, poor whites, Chicanos, and Puerto Ricans.

> We demand that the University open extensions in 3 Black communities that will be operated under the jurisdiction of the Black Studies Committee.

> We demand that students in each department have 50% voting representation on all faculty committees relating to curriculum, recruiting, and allocation of financial and other types of resources.

> We endorse the demands made by Black students on March 13.

> We demand the university sever all ties with war research and the military.

We demand an immediate termination of the ROTC program on campus.

We demand the immediate dismissal of administrators who have violated the rights of students.

The Ad Hoc Committee for Student Rights to President Novice G. Fawcett

The Ohio State University *Lantern*

Wednesday, April 29, 1970

We will respond to the Student Assembly's resolution by giving it the sincere consideration it deserves. Within a week or ten days, we will prepare a comprehensive report which will specifically communicate where we stand at this time as well as plans for the future.

Obviously, there is a great need to strengthen our channels of communication . . .

Vice President Mount to the Student Assembly

Wednesday, April 29, was warm and bright. That morning on her way to class, Diane had seen black students picketing the administration building with signs that read "ON STRIKE, SHUT IT DOWN," "OSU CENTENNIEL: 100 YEARS OF RACISM," and "WE WANT BLACK POWER NOW." When she walked outside after her studio class at 5:00, small groups of students gathered before the doors of several buildings. Diane crossed the street and started across the grass, but stopped to listen to students making speeches. She walked around to the back of the crowd.

"Apathetic students are finally getting together and showing their power on this campus," a small young woman said from the concrete porch. "For weeks and actually for years I have said that the time is not yet right. I didn't believe a violent confrontation was the way to achieve these demands and I still don't. The way to do it is to set up a long-term program of action. We must come out here day after day."

"Who are they?" Diane asked.

"Ad Hoc Committee for Student Rights, Women's Lib, and Afro-Am," a guy said. "The ones that met with Mount a few days ago."

"What have women got to complain about? They already run everything," another guy said, smirking.

"Shut up, asshole," the first man said.

"The gateway to the campus is closed," one of the black men on the porch shouted through a bullhorn. "We need to keep the demonstration on our own campus. This concerns students and the administration. The vice president has issued a statement saying that he will finally work with other groups besides the student assembly. We are asking people to disperse and come back tomorrow at 10:00 am when talks will resume."

"Campus is closed. We closed the campus," a student shouted as he ran across the grass toward the crowd. "SHUT IT DOWN. THE POLICE ARE ALREADY HERE." He was wearing jeans and no shirt; the elastic band of his white shorts was visible above his belt. He was panting, and sweat ran down the sides of his face.

"Closed where?" someone else shouted.

"Eleventh and Neil. People sat down in the street. The Highway Patrol tried to open the gates and when people pushed back they hauled them off in their cop cars." The student's eyes were wide; at the same time a shudder trembled through his lanky frame. Other students began to chant and raise their fists. Diane felt a thrill rise in her throat.

"SHUT IT DOWN," screamed a woman with bushy eyebrows that formed one continuous line over her eyes.

Diane heard breaking glass. Someone had thrown a rock through a front window of the administration building. Students began chipping the bricks out of a walkway and hurling them through windows; others carried chairs from another building and smashed them on the pavement. The ones in the front surged forward onto the porch. The steadily growing crowd now covered almost the entire northwest side of the Oval, which was close to three acres in size.

"They've got tear gas," a man shouted, running into the crowd from the direction of the lake.

"Where?"

"Eleventh and Neil. Columbus police and the Highway Patrol. They're busting people. They're coming this way. "

People ran from the building as police marched in from the front gate of the campus. White smoke rose from behind trees. Groups of students ran in different directions, some turning to shout at the police who paced directly toward them. Diane headed across the grass and into Hopkins where she took her books out of her knapsack and shoved them into her locker, pulled her knapsack back on, and ran out the back door toward Seventeenth just as a line of city police cars rolled down the street and stopped. The doors opened and helmeted men in body armor swarmed out and hurled tear gas canisters. The crowd scattered. The Columbus police had a reputation for brutality, people said; the previous winter there'd been furor about a black boy being shot to death for stealing soda pop somewhere downtown.

Diane turned and ran down an alley, across the grass, between two buildings, and onto the park behind the student union. She headed toward Twelfth; if she could get across High Street she might be able to get to her car a few blocks away. Students covered the lawns and parking lots.

"MOTHERFUCKER," someone shouted at a man who hung from his waist out the window of a tall brick dormitory and raised his middle finger at the demonstrators.

"Did you just learn a new word?" the guy in the window shouted back.

"MOTH-ER-FUCK-ER," came from the guy on the ground.

"ASS-HOLE HIP-PIE."

"MOTH-ER-FUCK-ER."

City police and Highway Patrolmen in riot gear marched from between two dormitories and circled a large group of students who were not throwing rocks or taunting anyone; most of them in their T-shirts and jeans did not look like demonstrators to Diane. Both sides faced each other in silence, students milling around in the street and parking lot, police circling them in formation, cutting off their access to the group on the Oval. Behind the union the lawn was deserted, except for a line of police, whether city cops or Highway Patrol, Diane couldn't tell. She turned away from the group and walked alone all the way down College Road, past the row of white-shirted police officers. Each one held a rifle; in the eerie silence, she thought any one of them in a moment could shoot her or any other student. As she reached the Oval, what she thought might happen did: lobbing gray canisters about the size of soup cans, the police moved in on the demonstrators. In the barrage of tear gas, the students dispersed like BBs hitting the wall.

Diane headed for the east end of the Oval, hoping to find a side alley she could use to get to her car. It was nearly six. Just when she thought they'd been routed, crowds of students surged across the Oval chanting "Out now! Out now!" and "Pigs off campus!" As they neared the main gate to the university at Fifteenth and High, the police launched more tear gas, but instead of running away, this time the students rushed toward them. The police surged at them swinging their clubs and throwing more gray canisters. Running toward the street Diane felt her throat close. Her body seemed to be suspended above the ground. She doubled over, strangling, her legs immobilized, her throat paralyzed as if she'd fallen from a great height, hitting water with the flat of her stomach and then sinking into the depths. She felt that she would drown before she could rise to the surface again.

"Stand still," a woman said. "Hold your head back," and Diane felt water pouring into her eyes. Diane breathed and staggered forward.

"Hold a towel over your face," the woman said.

"Thanks," Diane said, wiping the water from her neck, but the woman ran with her plastic yellow bucket toward the street before the oncoming police.

A patrol car drove up over the curb of South Oval Drive and cruised across the grass. A helmeted cop leaned out the open window, shook his fist, and shouted at a student, "You dirty hippie." The object of his dislike, shirtless and wearing striped bell-bottom denims and no shoes, picked up a canister from which the gray gas still flowed, and, flinging it overhand, shouted, "All we want are student rights." The gray projectile sailed in a perfect arc back toward the police car, which took off toward the pavement again.

"Let's go to High Street," someone shouted.

"Fuck High Street," another man answered. "Let's stay on our own campus."

"OUT NOW! OUT NOW!"

"PIGS OFF CAMPUS."

"MOTHERFUCKER."

"ASSHOLE."

"FASCIST PIGS."

High Street, which bordered the campus, was now empty of traffic other than police cars. Sticks, flat white boards from smashed police barricades, pieces of broken glass, and rocks lay on the pavement; water gushing from opened fire hydrants flooded the curbs. Diane ran up Fifteenth away from the campus and followed three women through the door of a rooming house. People congregated at the back of the building in an air-conditioned cafeteria with a tile floor and long tables with straight chairs.

"There's gas in the front," someone shouted. Police had pursued the demonstrators up the street and thrown canisters randomly into the residences and fraternity houses. Now Diane was stuck waiting with all these people, and there was no telling for how long. Everyone was talking about whether the police or the demonstrators provoked the violence. Even straight-looking kids were mad at the police.

"We're supposed to have the right to peaceable assembly in this lousy country."

"Those fascists never heard of the right to peaceable assembly."

"Nothing was happening till the cops got here."

"If the police want the straight kids pissed off at the demonstrators, they picked the wrong way to do it."

"Goddamn pigs."

For about forty-five minutes the closed door kept the gas out, but when it began seeping into the room, a woman who seemed to be in charge opened the back windows. Suddenly full of purpose, men climbed out first and helped the women jump down to the alley at the rear of the building. Everybody headed into the Unitarian church next door where a tall man in a navy-blue vest and tie ushered people inside. No tear gas canisters had been thrown through the rectangular windows or the fluted, stained-glass steeple that swept upward from the flat roof. As people packed into the basement, Diane walked down several dark hallways looking for a pay phone. When she found one way in the back she lifted the black receiver and dialed her mother's number.

"Can you pick up Marty at the baby-sitter's? I don't know when I'll get home."

"What happened?"

"There was a demonstration, the police came, and it turned into a riot."

"Do you want Richard to come and pick you up?"

"He'll never get through. Traffic's cordoned off. It's like a war zone. I can't even get to my car. I'm at the Unitarian church on Fifteenth. I'll be okay here if you can just pick up Marty."

"I'll get Marty. You just be careful. As soon as you can, get away from there and come home."

"I will," Diane answered. "I just don't know when. Look, I have to get off; there's a line here waiting to use the phone." She hung up the receiver, wondering how long it would take for the gas to clear and the police to lift their curfew.

※ ※ ※   ※ ※ ※   ※ ※ ※

She was awakened by people stirring, so she pulled herself up, dizzy and stiff from having spent the night slumped against a wall. Students lay on rugs or blankets, their heads propped up on rucksacks or books. Others slept on vinyl couches with no blankets. A man wearing a clerical collar walked among them offering coffee in Styrofoam cups to some who were awake. Through large windows facing the back, Diane could see the bright green leaves of maple saplings. A few people stood by the door talking quietly about the previous day—who had been at fault, whether the university officials really needed to call the police, whether the student demands were justified.

Diane drank black coffee and threw the Styrofoam cup into a trash bin. In the restroom she washed her face and threaded her hair into a braid. From the pay phone she called Ulana and asked her to take Marty to the sitter's before work. Then she opened a sliding glass door at the back of the building and headed down the alley strewn with broken concrete and glass.

She paced off two blocks along High Street, still cordoned off. Glass, bricks, and wooden boards lay on the pavement. Red brick row houses lined Thirteenth Avenue where two years ago she'd gone to a coffeehouse called the Venus and smoked weed and listened to music upstairs in a room illuminated by blue light. The coffeehouses were gone, the space rented out to tenants. Trendy boutiques and pizza shops replaced hip stores and cafés. Two or three miles down that street you came to the statehouse where the governor was probably huddled with his henchmen trying to figure out what to do. Cow town, people called it, the buckle on the Bible belt, one of the most segregated cities in the North, on a line between Cleveland with its ethnic neighborhoods and Cincinnati with its music and riverboats.

Diane didn't have time to stop by her locker to get her books, so she went straight to the econ class where she could daydream for an hour. By 10:00 when that lecture was over, the Oval was filled with demonstrators shouting at the police and highway patrolmen who lined the street. Speakers stood on a platform leading chants and encouraging students to boycott classes. A young man pressed a leaflet into her hand.

"We're calling on the vice president to meet with student leaders to discuss our demands," he said. "We're boycotting classes today to convince the administration to get the Highway Patrol and the city police off the campus. Join us, and let your voice be heard."

"The governor already put the National Guard on standby," someone else said. "We have to keep them off our campus."

It wasn't clear who the leaders were, but no one was breaking glass or starting any skirmishes with police. Diane leaned against a tree and read the printed page. Afro-Am was demanding amnesty for demonstrators and calling for scholarships for black students, a Black Studies program, and cessation of all military research on the campus. She saw more black students—mostly men sporting Afros—than she'd ever seen before at Ohio State. Not all the demonstrators had long hair and beards; lots of straight-looking kids were here, too.

At that moment a squad of police in black and white uniforms ran from behind the administration building toward the students on the Oval. Demonstrators blocking the front door scrambled down the concrete steps, and people ran in all directions. At the trees they turned, large groups of them chanting "pigs off campus" and facing the police in their gas masks and flak jackets advancing on the crowd, waving truncheons, and launching tear gas canisters. Clouds of white and gray smoke drifted along the grass.

※ ※ ※　　※ ※ ※　　※ ※ ※

It was after noon on Monday, May 4. The day was already warm, but the grass was cool in the shade where Diane read some pages from Kirkegaard— even though she hadn't been to a class all day. Groups of demonstrators picketed buildings, and there were speakers on the Oval. Police guarded the entrances to buildings, keeping demonstrators from hassling people who tried to go to class, but she saw no violence, and no one seemed tense. The *Lantern* carried the announcement that over the weekend the vice presidents met with the various student groups and approved money to launch the new Black Studies department and named a director to recruit black students. It also carried the story that Nixon had authorized the bombing of targets in Cambodia that were suspected communist sanctuaries.

Last Thursday when she finally got home, Marty ran toward her, giggling and laughing. Richard and Ulana loved having him stay overnight. As they ate supper together, Richard said the president shouldn't have called in the police so fast; if they'd left the students alone they'd have dispersed and there wouldn't have been nearly so much rock-throwing. Ulana wanted Diane to stay home on Monday but she drove to campus anyway, parked way across campus on a side street near the river, and walked almost a half mile, thinking the police wouldn't block the streets that far away.

As she sat on the grass, a heavy-set man wearing Army camouflage fatigues strode past her shouting in a loud voice "Are you getting a nice sun tan? The National Guard just killed four students at Kent State." A mass of curly brown hair boiled from his head, and his eyes bulged angrily from large red cheeks. No one seemed to be paying attention to him, but as she tried to read, Diane became vaguely aware of students marching again in large numbers. She closed the book and stood up.

"Where are they going?" she asked one of the marchers.

"French Field House. There's a ROTC review."

"To protest the Cambodian invasion."

"And show support for the students at Kent State."

"PIGS OFF CAMPUS."

"RIGHT ON."

Diane walked to Hopkins and painted into the late afternoon when she decided she'd better head for home before anything happened. Stowing her canvas, she left the building and started across the Oval that was now crowded with demonstrators and police. Walking down the wide pavement in the center, a man strode toward her in full-dress ROTC uniform—brown jacket with gold bars on the shoulders, red and blue ribbons above his left breast pocket, gold braid over his left upper arm. He took long, measured strides, holding himself upright, his jaw set. Behind him rose the gray tower of the library. Although demonstrators shouted and milled around on all sides, no one heckled him.

When he was nearly even with Diane she looked into his face shadowed by the cap and said, "You are very brave." They both kept walking.

The president closed the campus on May 6. At home Diane found it hard to concentrate on anything, so she played with Marty, who was elated that his mother was with him every day.

He squealed and ran after a ball she rolled toward him. She clenched her teeth to fight the impulse to reach for a cigarette, wondering how long it would take to get over the cravings. Marty scooped up the ball and ran toward her on his stubby, uncertain legs, blowing and grinning. He fell and the ball rolled away, but he pushed himself up, still laughing, grabbed the ball, and ran toward her again. He was dressed in a T-shirt and red and white coveralls Ulana bought for him. The pants, clean that morning, were now dirty and grass-stained. He looked like his father with his mass of curly brown hair and big dark eyes. He shoved the prize into her lap and stood giggling; she rolled it away again, and he chased it. Although he was laughing now, he could be willful and stubborn.

Just after the birth last May, she admitted to herself she didn't really love him even while she held him—red, pudgy, and slobbering—close to her. He demanded almost all her time. A baby was a mouth for feeding and screaming and an asshole for shitting. She felt trapped. Sometime later when she picked him up to nurse him, she felt she had really begun to love him, not because he was helpless or because she was the only one who cared about him other than her own parents, but because he was hers. She still felt tied down, but she couldn't have given Marty up. He was part of her life now, though raising a child was harder than she ever imagined. What would she do without Ulana's help? But she saw her mother's knowing smirk whenever Marty shouted "No!" at Diane. She still couldn't talk to Ulana.

Watching her son running, she remembered that she had played in this yard when she was a kid, and the cabin had been her refuge when she was a teen-ager. Now her own child played on the sparse grass that managed to survive in the shade, and she lived in the cabin with him. She regretted that she'd caused Ulana and Richard so much grief when she was a teenager; their arguments had almost always been about her.

Marty was kicking the ball among some trees at the edge of the yard, so Diane took out a sketchbook and started shading in some detail on a study for a painting. She'd done some of her best work since she'd come back to Columbus; everybody said so, even her mother and father. Her idea came from the picture they printed in the newspapers and showed over and over again on television—a black and white photo of a girl at Kent State screaming and kneeling with her arms raised over the body of a student lying dead in a pool of blood on the pavement. What a weird place for that to happen—the only campus in Ohio that was more of a party school than Ohio State, and where the students were straighter, too. Nobody expected *them* to burn their ROTC building down. Diane wanted to represent the girl's open mouth like the ghostly figure's mouth in *The Scream* where the landscape became impressionistic swirls of color, but she also wanted to paint the girl's body to look like a *pieta* where the surrounding figures hovered, seemingly unconcerned, as the onlookers did in that photo. She wanted to paint the horror after something momentous that happened in seconds, something no one could ever change, justify, or explain away. She wanted to capture the wordless despair.

Marty ran giggling toward her again from under the trees and tripped over a root. When he didn't get up but started howling, Diane put the drawing down and walked toward him.

"It's only a little scrape," she chided, but he flung his arms around her neck and continued to cry as she stroked his back.

She kept meaning to answer Martin's letter but always put it off. Diane acknowledged to herself that she didn't know how she felt about him anymore: she no longer resented his attitude as she had when she left Fort Collins, and she had liked and respected him years ago. No relationship had turned into anything since Fort Collins. Martin was after all her son's father. Maybe she should give him a chance. She had loved both Will and David, and both had sent her away. At least she knew what happened to Will; she didn't know anything about what happened to David.

Marty stopped crying and ran back toward the trees. She picked up her drawing and started penciling in more lines.

"They try to tell you we aren't real students, we're people from 'outside'," the slender young black man on the platform shouted through the microphone. He wore a light-colored shirt with the sleeves rolled up to his elbows. Sunglasses obscured his eyes beneath the halo of his close-cropped Afro.

"Well, I'm here to tell you we *are* students, and that it's *students* who are frustrated."

A cheer rose from the crowd. Many wore their plastic ID cards—required to get onto campus or into a building—on cords around their necks. Diane sat on the grass.

It was Thursday, May 21. The previous Monday classes started up again with divisions of National Guard troops stationed on all sides of the campus and at the entrances to every building. Olive-green trucks rolled up and down the campus streets carrying helmeted men gripping rifles with fixed bayonets. Two more students had been killed last week at Jackson State in Mississippi when the police opened fire on a crowd, although the press didn't make as much of that shooting since the students were black.

A British professor stood up and spoke through a microphone, "When a man leaves his own country and comes to another one, it's because he believes in the principles for which that country stands."

"Oh, man, look around you," a woman shouted.

"Let him talk," someone else demanded, but the professor's voice was drowned by heckling.

The rotund political science professor got up and lectured the crowd that thousands of people running around and shouting "Right on" didn't make a strike.

"Unfortunately," one of the black men said through the microphone, "violence is the only thing reactionary leaders understand. We do not want violence, but we will not be left out of negotiations. People ask us why not go through student government. The answer is that we will not wait for student government."

The crowd exploded with cheering.

Just before 5:00, Diane headed south along High Street where large numbers of students gathered. The letters of the Agora movie theater rose on its vertical marquee just north of the state liquor store. On the other side, the Ohio National Bank sign formed a T reaching over the pavement. Telephone poles like the masts of sailing ships lined the street as far as she could see. Thousands of students in jeans and shorts milled around in the street near the intersection of Eleventh and High where the One Way sign pointed west. Another group of students formed where the One Way sign at Tenth pointed east. Most of them looked like kids she saw in classes every day. City police, sheriff's deputies, Highway Patrolmen, and riot squads in black pants and white shirts, their faces entirely hidden by gas masks, blocked the street at the intersection. They held rifles and tear gas launchers, and truncheons hung from their belts.

TWELVE

Still dizzy from the whiskey his friends bought him the night before, David stepped down from the Haight Street bus at Masonic and faced the corner café with its new name. He headed up the street, looking into one window after another and trying to remember the shops as they had been three years ago. A man slouched in a doorway threw his cigarette onto the pavement. David turned at Ashbury and headed toward Oak, feeling a thrill of anticipation as he walked along the edge of the Panhandle toward the house he lived in for only a few months, the only home where he'd ever really felt happy or known love.

Or was it another emotion he confused with love? When he tried to imagine a life with Diane, he couldn't. Would they have lived in the Haight? Berkeley? What would he have done? A little electronics maybe, but he hadn't earned any kind of certificate. He certainly wasn't going back to college: he was twenty-four, too old for that stuff anymore. What kind of life had she made for herself? Where was Rennie now?

Some kind of canvas drape covered the front bay window, and the porch still needed paint. If he knocked and asked someone to see the inside they'd probably suspect him of being a thief; besides, it probably didn't look anything like it used to.

David followed Oak Street, crossed Stanyan, and walked across the grass to a level place below the hill. A barefooted man in black pants and no shirt, pale skin, and gnarled hair asked him for change. David pulled a bill from his pocket and folded it into the man's creased hand. A rock band ground out its beat while people sprawled in the sunlight. It was September, the best weather of the year in this city, and Saturday. He flung down his backpack and sat on the ground underneath the old Monterey cypress where more than three years ago he played his recorder and savored his freedom. From now on his decisions would be his own. He closed his eyes.

Right after muster that morning, David trudged to the barracks at Alameda, stripped off his uniform, and rolled it up. He changed to a red flannel shirt and jeans, stuffed his discharge papers into his knapsack, pulled it over his shoulders, and headed out the door and down the pavement to the edge of the lagoon. A pelican folded its wings and dove straight into the gray-green water that smelled of algae and salt. Bobbing to the surface, it shook its head and long empty bill. Gulls circled, shrieking. The sun glanced on the huge gray cargo ships moored at the end of the pier with the *Hazard Perry*. It would sail again for the Gulf, but he would not be on it. He was actually getting out early—he would have been assigned another tour of duty on that ship, but his time would have been up when it was still on line, so the Navy discharged him.

David pulled his Vietnam service medal from his pocket and hurled it overhand. He reached for the Medal of Honor. He'd been right: there had been a man trapped inside the Skyhawk because of a jammed release. They'd both been treated for smoke inhalation and third-degree burns in the ship's infirmary. Damage Control had kept the fire inside Hangar Bay One, though there was extensive damage to the bulkhead. One man died of asphyxiation and one had been burned to death in the original explosion. They still weren't entirely sure how the fire got started, but they thought an electrical spark from a bad wire caused it, and the flames spread to a locker full of oxygen canisters. David crumpled the ribbon, sent the medal flying, and watched it arc high over the smooth, dark surface of the lagoon, its blue cloth unfolding like the tail of a kite before it sank into the gray water. The last medal was for the pistol team in

Long Beach. He had after all liked the ship's commander as well as most of the men he'd served with. He turned it over twice and tossed it into the lagoon.

After the medal hit the water and disappeared, he turned and strode across Ocean Drive and past the rectangular, cream-colored buildings, stopping at the end of one where a wicker fence surrounded two dumpsters. Lifting the lid on one of them, he stuffed his rolled-up uniform into it and let the lid slam shut. Someone called his name as he walked out of the enclosure. Two guys from his division who had taken him drinking the night before saluted and called out "Don't burn too much rubber, Son of a Bitch." He waved back and headed down the pavement. Those guys would be setting out for the Gulf again in a matter of weeks. He strode past the gate, and the Navy passed out of his life.

Traffic lumbered loudly beside him as he paced off the mile or so to Webster and caught the downtown bus.

※ ※ ※   ※ ※ ※   ※ ※ ※

Voices woke David from a fitful dream. As his head cleared he watched the people walking across the grass and aspen leaves rippling in the slight breeze.

"David."

He looked up. Diane stood in front of him.

"I thought it was you."

She was wearing jeans and a pink cowboy shirt with fake pearl buttons on the pockets. Her long hair was held at the sides with barrettes. Although she'd gained a few pounds, she was still slender and looked even better than he remembered. He stood, and she put her arms around him.

"I don't believe it," she said, stepping back. "Are you out now?"

"As of today."

"No shit? Totally out?"

"The Navy's no more to me now than the wind," he said. "What are

259

you doing?"

"I was just giving a drawing lesson at the Cultural Arts Center." She tipped her head toward her left shoulder.

"You live here?"

"Since June. Before that I was in Columbus for two years. Remember I showed you my grandmother's house in Berkeley once?"

"I remember it."

"I have the first floor," she said, pulling back a strand of hair that had blown across her face.

"You live there by yourself?"

She drew a deep breath. "My son lives with me."

"Your son," he repeated.

"Yeah. One year and three months."

"You're married?"

"No. His father lives in Oakland." She threw her head back and straightened her shoulders.

David crushed the small hope that rose in his throat in the last few seconds.

"I got the letters you sent to Switchboard," she said. "You told me not to write." She placed her hands on her hips. "Then you said you weren't coming back, so I left San Francisco and went to Colorado. Remember I told you about a guy I thought was attracted to me when I stayed with him and his wife in Fort Collins? He'd been my mentor on a co-op."

"Yes."

"He's my son's father."

David shoved his hands into his pockets to stop himself from showing any feeling. He should have known she would find someone. He was the one who told her to live her own life, and she was not one to wait passively for things to happen.

"After I got your second letter I decided to go back there. The house on Oak was breaking up. Things were getting hairy around here." She raised her chin toward the hill where the band played.

"It was a rough time for you."

"Not as rough for me as for you," she said quickly. "Anyway, he'd been looking for an excuse to break up with his wife, and when he did, we got involved."

"But you said you were living in Columbus."

"I had my son there. I'd left his father by that time; he didn't even know about his son until last May. It's a long story. Tell me about you."

"Nothing to tell. I can't show you my medals because I threw them all into the lagoon at Alameda. Wish I could throw the memories away."

He looked at his hands. This was what it was like to see someone you once loved—embarrassing, and a little sad.

"Come with me," she said.

"Where?"

"Up to Mount Tam. Unless you have something to do."

He hesitated, but considering he had nothing to do, replied, "Okay."

"My car's on Fulton."

Striding across the lawn, she said, "At least I quit smoking."

In a meadow above Phoenix Lake, they sat in the grass and looked out over the bay. David leaned against his backpack.

"Nobody we know stayed very long after you left," Diane told him. "You remember Daryl moved out because of that shit at McClure's Beach. I haven't seen or heard from him since. And good riddance."

"He saved my life."

"If it hadn't been for him you'd never have seen those goons," she insisted. "Terry finally took his ass to Kathmandu."

"Is he still there?" David asked.

"I wouldn't know."

"Rennie?"

"Went back to SF State. Wrote to me a couple of times when I was in Colorado. Sounded like she was getting along okay. Asked if I'd heard from you. Said she might go to Arcata or Oregon after she finished. I always meant to, but I never wrote back, so we lost touch."

"Where's your son now?" David asked.

"With his dad. He wrote to me last May asking why I left without telling him and never got in touch. I wrote and told him about Marty. Boy, was he bent out of shape. Called me heartless and callous. But he calmed down and came out here right after I did, saying he was going to have a relationship with his son, even though his other two kids are still in Fort Collins with their mother. He got a job running a school for delinquent boys in Oakland. It's not what he wanted to do, but it pays. I told him he wasn't moving into my house yet. He had to start all over again with me."

"And did he?"

"We see each other," she said. "I couldn't tell him to get lost; he has a right to see his son." She gazed at the wooded hills of Marin and across to the east bay.

"God, David," she said, shaking her head, "you don't know how many times I tried to get onto that island in spite of what you wrote. I didn't know from your letter whether you really wanted me to come but you couldn't say so or whether you really meant it. Once I even took the bus to Union and waited for the 108, but when it came I didn't get on. I decided to do what you told me."

"You did the right thing. If I'd seen you I could never have—"

"They were going to give you a discharge," she said, turning toward him. "Why didn't you take it?"

"Because they'd have had me forever. It would all have been a lie. Do you understand?"

"No." She shook her head and looked down.

"I don't respect the Navy or what it's doing over there. I hated the uniform I wore every day. But even so, I had to finish what I'd agreed to. If I hadn't, then everything I did from then on, no matter where I was, I'd have been their creature." He drew a long breath. "If I'd let you come to see me, I'd have been thinking all the time about deserting again."

Diane straightened her shoulders and tipped her head back. She stared at the bay for a long time before she spoke.

"I felt cut loose," she said. "So I hitchhiked to Fort Collins and lived on this sort of commune outside town. It was a good place to be, but I wasn't happy. I had this factory job I hated where I spent all day cutting the ends off beets. And one day Martin drove out there and told me he'd separated from Elaine and wanted to be with me."

"And that's how you hooked up with him."

"He'd already decided to leave her, so I wasn't the one who broke them up." Her eyes met his. "Nothing else was happening for me."

She shrugged her shoulders. "Of course, I didn't count on getting pregnant. The IUD just stopped working."

"Why didn't you marry him then?"

"I asked him what he would do if one of his girlfriends got pregnant. He said he'd be disappointed; he wanted to be free for awhile."

"So you didn't tell him."

"Not then. I walked back to the farmhouse where I lived and told the only friend I had left in the world." She sat up. "I told her I was leaving, and she drove me to the highway ramp. I hitchhiked all the way back to Columbus, where I figured on having the baby and giving it up for adoption. I thought I'd just finish my degree at Ohio State where nothing ever happens." She rolled her eyes. "Except all hell broke loose."

"But you didn't give him up."

"I couldn't. My mother wanted me to, but now she's glad I didn't because she adores him." Diane lifted her head. "Things got insane in Columbus, but when they settled down it was just the same old place. Like some kind of miracle the renters moved out of the first floor in my grandmother's house, and my dad didn't want to keep paying an agency to look after it, so my dad and I worked out a deal. I don't pay any rent, and we split the money for the other two apartments."

She grinned at him. "I'm a landlord now," she laughed, throwing her head back.

"You're doing just what your grandmother did," David said, leaning back and propping himself up on straightened arms. "And you're a teacher."

"The thing at the Art Center's just temporary. I have some paintings with a dealer but haven't sold any yet. I'd really like to get a job with the city teaching at a community center, but nobody's hiring right now."

"Sounds like you have a plan," he offered.

"Marty's father says he knows what he wants now."

"And does he?"

"Only time tells."

"You don't sound like you love him."

"Marty loves him." She grinned. "You should see him run to his dad when he comes over."

She rubbed her face with her hands, and he ran his palm across her shoulders.

"Why don't you stay here for awhile?" she asked, sitting up and shaking her hair back.

"No."

"Why not? Because I have a son?"

"No. It isn't you."

"What then?" she asked. "What ties do you have?" She pulled up a stem of clover and picked the flower apart.

"None," he answered. "But when I saw a man about to burn to death I knew what to do."

"What happened?"

"My last tour of duty," he said. "There was a fire on one of the decks. I pulled the release handle on a plane because I thought there was a guy inside. It was the only time in my life I ever knew exactly what I had to do."

She was searching his face.

"Our moment has passed," he said. "Or rather, we never really had a chance."

"We can give ourselves a chance."

"The time wasn't right and now everything's changed."

"Where will you go?"

"East."

"To your family?"

"No. I don't know exactly where yet, but I want to live there for a while. Maybe in a way I want to find out where I really came from."

"God, this sucks, David. We find each other and you turn around and run away again." Her eyes were shining.

"I crawled into a tunnel when I signed those papers joining the Navy and I've crept along in the dark for almost five years," he said. "Now the light's so bright I can't see ten feet in front of me. You have a life here. You've got talent and energy, and I know you have strength. Far more than I will ever have."

"If I'm so strong, why am I about to cry?"

"After a while you won't cry anymore. Not for me anyway. You'll turn to the next thing. You're a person things happen to."

He stood.

"You're not going yet." She got to her feet.

"Yes. I'm going to walk down to the road."

"At least let me drive you to San Francisco."

"I'll get a lift from Fairfax to the highway. I hitched out here and I'm going back that way. Besides, I want to remember you in the place where you really belong."

He kissed the palm of her right hand, shouldered his backpack, and started down the hill and across a meadow. At the edge of the trees he turned to look at her again, thinking that if she started toward him he would go back to her and never leave. She was standing where they had been, her legs apart, watching him, the wind blowing her hair. The mountain rose behind her as if she held it lightly on her shoulders.

He waved and started down the pathway into the woods.